THE PEKING DIAMONDS

Also by Peter Read

Diamond Mine (The Book Guild)

Gemmological Instruments (Butterworths)
Beginner's Guide to Gemmology (Heinemann)
Gems—Questions and Answers (Heinemann)
Dictionary of Gemmology (Butterworths)
Gemmology (Butterworth-Heinemann)

PETER READ

The *Peking Diamonds*

GEMBOOKS
1995

First published 1995 by
Gembooks
16 Green Park
Manor Road
Bournemouth
Dorset

ISBN 0-9525315-0-X

Typeset in New Century 10/12pt by Scriptmate Editions
Manufacture coordinated in UK by Book-in-Hand Ltd
20 Shepherds Hill, London N6 5AH

To my years at De Beers, without which this novel would not have been possible, and to my wife Joan for her constructive criticisms and suggestions

PREFACE

The events revealed in the pages of this book took place in Europe and the Far East as the first cracks were appearing in the foundations of the communist world. In the vast landmass of the Union of Soviet Socialist Republics, time was beginning to run out as Five Year Plan succeeded Five Year Plan. The living standard of all but the ruling elite reflected the underlying problems of the country's inefficient and bureaucratic management of industry, farming and food distribution, and envious eyes were beginning to compare the communist system with the market-led economy of the West.

In the People's Republic of China, life under the communist rule of the centralist government in Peking was even harder. Chinese workers and peasants, however, had never experienced more than a subsistence-level standard of living, and could not easily compare their lot with that enjoyed in the West. The 7-week student-led 'Beijing Spring', inspired by the Gorbachev reforms in the USSR, had more to do with free speech and the craving for democracy than living standards. In 1981 when the story unfolds, this and the uprising and killings in Tian'anmen Square that occurred during the 40th Anniversary of the foundation of the Chinese People's Republic, were still in the future.

Eight years before Tian'anmen Square, and eleven years before the break-up of the USSR, a few farsighted department heads in sections of the Soviet Government saw the economic abyss opening at their feet. At great risk to themselves, some of these men began making secret plans to reduce the looming threat of starvation brought about by the country's dwindling reserves of foreign currency and credit. This is the story of one such plan—a plan which threatened to wreck the delicate balance of the world's largest diamond marketing monopoly.

CHAPTER 1

PEKING (Beijing)

Monday 5 January, 1981

Lin Chung hunched his shoulders against the cold and pedalled his brand new Phoenix bicycle past the huge portrait of Mao Tse-tung in Chang'an Avenue. He shot a sidelong glance at its proclamation 'LONG LIVE THE UNITY OF THE PEOPLES OF THE WORLD' just visible through the freezing grey haze of the bleak January morning. It was a sentiment politely ignored by hundreds of other cyclists streaming across Tian'anmen Square.

Winter in Peking is an unpleasant combination of high pollution, a dry atmosphere and sub-zero temperatures. Biting winds carry fine brown dust into the city from the Gobi desert, and when the winds are not blowing, the air is liberally laced with soot from the coal fires burning in thousands of cramped single-storey *pingfang* homes.

Lin Chung had taken delivery of his Shanghai-manufactured bicycle only that weekend, and was enjoying his first experience of freedom from the dangerously overcrowded buses. There were over three million registered bicycles in Peking, and Chung had waited an interminable year for the allocation of a special purchase certificate which allowed him to buy this most prized of the models available in China.

Chung counted himself lucky to have escaped the excesses of the ten disastrous years of the Cultural Revolution. During this time of unrest and upheaval he had managed to cling to his job as laboratory assistant in the Synthetic Crystals Research Department of Beijing University, a position which in common with other secure government jobs was collectively referred to as 'the iron rice bowl'.

In the terrible years immediately preceding the death of Chairman Mao, the self-appointed Red Guards in the University, following the Maoist dictum 'destroy the old, create the new', had brought the life of the city to a near standstill. School children, waving the little red book of Mao's thoughts, disciplined their parents and informed on them, while managers, officials and even senior party members were banished to lowly farm jobs in the surrounding country to 're-learn the basic values of the revolution'. Thousands of accused 'revisionists' and 'reactionaries' simply disappeared, never to be seen again. In the stunned lull that followed Mao's death, it was estimated that four-hundred thousand people had died during this ten years of cultural schizophrenia.

Through it all, Chung and millions like him survived by keeping a low profile. With the downfall of the 'Gang of Four' three weeks after Mao's death, living conditions slowly improved. Released from the scourge of the Cultural Revolution, the Chinese peasants and other low-paid workers were quick to take advantage of the profit-incentive reforms introduced by Chairman Deng Xiaoping. The Western expression 'make hay while the sun shines' reflected the Chinese workers' outlook over the highs and lows of these long hard years. In common with many of his friends Chung now enjoyed the materialistic delights of a refrigerator and a colour TV.

Last year he had even acquired a Western pen pal! With China's improving international relations, a cultural exchange group from the UK had toured China the previous summer. While in Peking they were invited to a reception at Beijing University. During the visit, Chung, in an uncharacteristic moment of recklessness and in the hope of improving his limited command of the English language, introduced himself to one of the lady members of the group. Using a grubby secondhand dictionary which he had discovered in the University library, Chung wrote a monthly letter to his new British friend, and eagerly awaited her replies. Little did he realise at the time that this seemingly harmless correspondence was soon to involve him in an international incident.

Chung braked hard and spat out a missile of phlegm as an unlit blue and white bus charged in his direction blaring its horn. Reluctantly he gave way, and swung out of the vehicle's path, missing it by inches. He made a right turn out of Chang'an Avenue and then pedalled south, heading towards Chongwen District and the grey edifice of the Beijing University complex.

In the side streets the wind had slackened, but now carried flurries of fine snow particles which were already beginning to dust the pavements white. At this point in his daily trek to work he would have fought his way out of a crowded bus, and be hurrying on foot over the last mile of his journey. Today he eased back on the pedals enjoying the freedom and independence of his own transport as he coasted past the grey stone frontage of the University.

At the far end of the building he wheeled left into a side street and pedalled the last fifty yards to the University's science annex. He dismounted and carefully guided his machine across the pavement and down the worn stone steps which led to the Synthetic Crystals Research Department. The ancient wrinkled doorkeeper sitting huddled against the cold inside the entrance hall looked up from his copy of *The People's Daily*.

'So you've got your brand new Phoenix bicycle at last!' the old man exclaimed.

Chung nodded proudly. 'With your permission my old friend, I'll padlock it safely inside the cloakroom.'

The doorkeeper folded his newspaper. 'Next thing, you'll be buying a car—you young people have life far too easy these days.'

Chung laughed. He was thirty-two years old, although his unlined oval face, lively brown eyes and cheerful disposition made him appear much younger. 'I'm not that young, my ancient friend, and the bicycle has given me a second reason for celebrating tonight—it's my child's fifth birthday and my wife has arranged a party.'

'Remind me, is your child a boy or a girl?'

'A boy, his name's Duan.'

'A boy, eh, that's just as well—a girl would have lowered your roof by three feet!'

With China's population breaching the billion mark, the government had introduced tax incentives for one-child couples, and a series of fines for bigger families, a control which increased the already high female infanticide rate. Chung and his wife had been shocked to read in *The People's Daily* that four out of five girl babies were being killed in some provinces.

Chung wheeled his bicycle past the doorkeeper and into the cloakroom. At this time of the year, he relished his job. Back home it was difficult to keep even his small flat much above freezing point, but in the Synthetic Crystals laboratory he could remove his bulky outer coat and luxuriate in temperatures reaching the mid 60s. The rest of the building was icy cold, but here in the laboratory the electric heaters in two rows of bench-mounted crystal-growing equipment helped generate the warmth of early summer.

The manufacture of experimental synthetic crystals for the department's research program made it necessary for the units to be kept running at a controlled temperature day and night for up to eight months at a time. Chung's job was to record the temperature of each apparatus at hourly intervals, and to keep their reactor vessels supplied with the appropriate raw materials. It was also his responsibility to check the appearance of the growing crystals through the heat-filtered inspection windows in the sides of the various installations, and to keep Ho Zheng, the head laboratory technician, informed of any significant changes.

By midmorning, he was just completing a series of temperature checks on a large cylindrical autoclave used to produce synthetic quartz crystals, when a faint noise drew him back to one of the flux-melt installations. He bent down in front of its metal casing for several seconds trying to locate the source of the noise. The heat radiated from the outside surface of the equipment forced him to shield his face as he squinted through the small four-inch square inspection window. Inside the unit a rectangular platinum crucible glowed a dull red. He could see its molten contents in the angled metal mirror suspended just above the crucible. As his eyes adjusted themselves to the glare he was suddenly aware of several shapes breaking through the crust which lay on the surface of the crucible's molten contents. He straightened up in surprise and hesitated for a moment, uncertain of the vaguely familiar forms he had just glimpsed. Then, turning on his heel, he hurried across to the head technician's office at the end of the laboratory.

'Come quickly, Mr Zheng,' he exclaimed, his voice cracking in excitement, 'the crystals in Project 7 are already breaking through the surface of the melt—they look like perfect octahedrons!'

Ho Zheng sighed, and while his assistant fidgeted impatiently in the doorway he grabbed a stained white laboratory coat and pulled it on over his shabby threadbare suit. 'Calm down, Chung, it takes months to grow those crystals—they won't change much in the next few minutes.'

* * *

By late afternoon, the flux-melt installation that had attracted Chung's attention was sufficiently cool for Ho Zheng to open it up. Gripping a pair of insulated long-handled tongs, he delicately extracted the dozen crystals which had formed in the solidified crust at the top of the crucible. Zheng placed the crystals on the bench and gently prised the brittle coating of flux residues from their colourless glistening surfaces.

Chung's eyes opened wide in amazement. 'Mr Zheng—these are perfect transparent eight-sided crystals. Just like those uncut octahedral diamonds in the University museum—the ones that came from Russia's Yakutia mines.'

Zheng nodded thoughtfully. 'This is the first time I've seen synthetic spinel crystals of such perfect shape. It seems that the catalyst we introduced into the flux to improve the growth rate has also improved the shape of the spinels. Perhaps in the same way that nitrogen impurity atoms in diamond seem to produce more symmetrically shaped crystals.' He paused, turning the spinels over in his hand. 'Listen carefully, Chung. I want you to prepare a detailed report of the furnace temperature profile and the flux constituents on Project 7. Start work on it immediately—I'll get someone else to look after the other projects.'

* * *

The following morning, Zheng was granted an interview with Professor Sang Liang, Director of Synthetic Crystals Research.

He tapped nervously on the director's door, then opened it and entered Liang's office.

The professor looked up from the papers on his desk and waved Zheng to a chair. He and his chief laboratory technician had spent two years together in exile cleaning out pig pens and cow sheds on a remote farm in northern China.

He smiled kindly at Zheng. 'Now, what's all this excitement about?'

Zheng placed the twelve octahedral crystals on his director's desk.

'I removed these yesterday from the furnace of Project 7.'

Liang leant forward and picked up one of the crystals. He pulled a hand lens from the pocket of his jacket and spent several minutes in silent inspection of the stone's surfaces. 'Remarkable,' he whispered, 'there are even trigon etch marks on the faces.' He made a similar inspection of the remaining eleven stones and finally looked up at Zheng. 'I hope you've recorded all the growth parameters.'

'Of course, sir, here's the complete report.' He placed a blue folder on his director's desk. 'Would you like me to run a second experiment under the same conditions?'

Professor Liang paused in thought. 'We may need further samples in a hurry, so I want you to duplicate it on all the flux-melt units not in current use.' He beckoned his colleague closer, and dropped his voice. 'Strictly between ourselves Zheng, I've heard a rumour that there's to be an initiative put before the next formal assembly of our politburo. It seems that our masters are preparing the ground for a Sino-Soviet reconciliation. One of the sweetners being offered is an exchange of hitherto classified research information.' He tapped the blue folder lying on his desk. 'The results of Project 7 could well form a part of this exchange.'

CHAPTER 2

MOSCOW
Friday 27 February, 1981

The ten-foot red stars perched on top of the Kremlin towers glowed brightly against the darkening late afternoon sky. Beneath them, the frozen parade-ground of Red Square glistened like white sugar icing in the frosty air, and a snow-laden east wind quickened the pace of the tourists as they stumbled back to their centrally heated hotels.

Temperatures during the day had fallen steadily, and the digital thermometer in the famous GUM store was registering minus 40 degrees C, a condition which caused globules of ice to form in the nostrils and discouraged the few remaining sightseers from lingering in the failing light.

The gilt hands of the clock above the main entrance to the Kremlin registered five o'clock, and with precision timing, a squad of four soldiers wearing grey winter-issue greatcoats and armed with Kalashnikov assault rifles, goose-stepped into the square to relieve their comrades guarding the red granite edifice of the Lenin Mausoleum. Detachments of the Red Army were also stationed at intervals around the high perimeter walls of the Kremlin as a token of security during the week-long meeting of deputies at the 26th Party Congress. The Congress was convened at five-yearly intervals for the purpose of re-affirming the USSR's domestic, trade and foreign policies. This year the meeting was being held in the green-domed Conference Hall within the Kremlin's walls.

On this bleak February day in 1981, two-thousand two-hundred and fifty deputies, representing all regions of the fifteen Soviet Republics, had been listening to Brezhnev, Chairman of the Supreme Soviet, deliver a marathon six-hour speech on the content of the 11th Five Year Plan. As he regained his seat between Chernenko, First Secretary of the Praesidium, and Foreign Minister Gromyko ('Mr Nyet'), the serried ranks of deputies, some of them senior army officers resplendent in bemedalled uniforms, rose to their feet and broke into a dutifully sustained round of applause.

The next speaker to be announced had the task of proposing the first of a series of amendments, which traditionally introduced changes in Soviet policy. Deputy Nicoli Rostov had been especially chosen to propose this particular amendment because he came from the Kirgizskaya region on the USSR's southernmost border with China.

Rostov climbed the steps of the platform. He turned and bowed to Brezhnev, Chernenko and the row of ministers and senior Party officials who sat dwarfed beneath the hall's gigantic portrait of Lenin. Rostov positioned himself at the speaker's rostrum, and cleared his throat nervously. He was twenty-eight years old and this was his first Party Congress.

'Comrade Chairman, First Secretary, senior Party Members and comrade Deputies,' he began. 'I am honoured to have been chosen to propose the first Amendment at this the 26th Party Congress. As you are aware, on October 12 1954 a Friendship Agreement was signed by comrades Khrushchev and Bulganin in Peking. For the next five years our country and China marched shoulder to shoulder as communist brothers, sharing their technologies and cultural heritages. Sadly, following a visit to China by comrades Khrushchev and Gromyko in January 1959, these relationships began to deteriorate. By June 1959 we had rescinded the Sino-Soviet atomic agreement, and by the time the July 1963 Sino-Soviet talks took place here in Moscow, further deterioration had occurred, and co-operation between our two countries was virtually at an end.'

He paused and took a sip of water from the glass on the rostrum. 'In August 1978, China signed a treaty of peace and friendship with Japan, and we made our protests known to Chairman Deng Xiaoping at this further indication of the ever widening gap between us.'

He paused again, aware of the vast audience's awakening interest.

'Last year, negotiations aimed at the normalisation of relations with China were suspended because of their objections to our military support of the beleaguered government in Afghanistan. Comrades, the time has come to attempt once again a reconciliation between our two great communist countries. The People's Republic of China has already made the first tentative approaches to the Supreme Soviet, and to show their goodwill have sent us full details of their most recent technological advances.'

Rostov had now reached the high point of his presentation. He half turned towards the impassive figures of Brezhnev, Chernenko and Gromyko and held up his agenda paper.

'Comrade Chairman, First Secretary, senior Party Members and comrade Deputies, I propose that Amendment 1 on the agenda be adopted by this Congress, thus making it possible to restart the normalisation of relations with our comrades in China.'

Brezhnev stood up and began the applause. The young man had communicated the first of the leadership's intentions well, he ruminated, and nodded approvingly at Gromyko and the other Party members flanking him on the platform. Now it only required the rubber-stamp formality of a vote to change a significant section of his nation's foreign policy. Many more such amendments were due to be proposed during the final days of the Congress, each presented by a Deputy chosen for his special qualifications. Then it would be up to the numerous committees and sub-committees to flesh out the Politburo's policies and begin the process of implementing them.

* * *

Later that afternoon, the Politburo's Trade Policy Committee met in one of the small conference rooms within the Kremlin's complex of government buildings. Now that the principle of Sino-Soviet reconciliation had been formally approved by Congress, the committee's Chairman, Oleg Aristov, was free to reveal the outline of a secret plan devised by the head of the Soviet Foreign Trade Association, Russalmaz. This group was responsible for the sale of rough and polished diamonds, diamond jewellery, gold and platinum to the rest of the world.

Aristov was a short stocky man in his mid fifties, his close-cropped hair prematurely grey from the gruelling years spent in promoting his country's products in the often antagonistic world beyond the USSR's boundaries. Seated around the small conference table in the sparsely furnished room were six men and one woman, all specialists in various sections of Soviet trade with the West.

'My friends,' he began, 'I know it's getting late, and you must all be anxious to get away for the weekend break, so I'll be as brief as possible.'

He removed some handwritten notes from his executive case and arranged them carefully in front of him. 'You have probably noticed that there is no secretary present to take the minutes of this meeting. The reasons for this will soon become clear. What I'm about to tell you is strictly off the record and top secret.'

At these words, the Friday evening atmosphere of lethargy evaporated, and the committee members looked at their chairman with heightened interest.

Aristov glanced around the table and smiled. 'Yes, I thought that would stimulate you. Now, we've all been aware of the increasing difficulty over these last few years of earning enough foreign currency to finance purchases of grain and other necessities from the West.'

Galina Bykov, a tall redhead responsible for trade with the USA and Canada, interrupted. 'One of the main factors in our trade deficit has been the appalling grain harvests over the period of the last Five Year Plan—this has been mainly due to the inefficiency of the collective farms and the disinterest of the workers. Last year alone we were forced to buy 46 million tons of grain from the USA...'

Aristov raised his hand to stop what had become a familiar complaint from the members of his committee. 'Galina, we're all too painfully aware of the root causes of the problem, but what I have to make clear to you all tonight is the stark reality of the USSR's financial position. As of this year we are, in effect, a bankrupt nation, and very soon the West will stop giving us credit for foodstuffs we're unable to pay for. Next winter we may well be faced with near famine in our cities as food stocks run out.'

'You paint a bleak picture, comrade chairman,' commented Anton Chubais an elderly bearded man who represented the country's mineral exports. 'Surely the foreign exchange we receive from the sale of our gold, platinum and diamonds is sufficient in itself to ensure our people won't actually starve?'

Aristov shook his head. 'Sadly, as it stands at the moment, it's not even enough to keep abreast of our soaring import bill. Although we can, with some effort, increase the production of these so-called hard assets, there is a limit to what the rest of the world can absorb. The price of both gold and platinum would drop sharply if we attempted to oversupply the market,

'Rough diamonds, which are our principal currency earner, are restricted in their sales by the four-year contract we have with the UK Diamond Syndicate's central marketing organisation. In the new contact currently being negotiated with the CMO, they are using the weaker market in diamonds as an excuse to force our prices down even further.'

Nicoli Vesselovski, a short bespectacled young man who, as assistant to Anton Chublais, was principally concerned with the export of diamonds, raised his hand. Aristov nodded to him. 'Say your piece Nicoli.'

Vesselovski pushed his glasses back on the bridge of his nose. 'For some years we've been hearing rumours from our colleagues in Russalmaz that they're planning to break the agreement with the Syndicate and market our diamonds directly to the rest of the world. While not in the same league as ourselves, Angola has already ended its contract with the CMO, and sells through Antwerp. If we followed suit and marketed stones at the right price, as we did with the sale of our polished diamonds in Belgium, we could reduce our balance of payments deficit by grabbing a larger share of the market.'

'You're getting warm, Nicoli,' replied Aristov with a nod of approval. 'If you recall, our brief success in selling polished diamonds at slightly below the going price in Antwerp was nipped in the bud by the Syndicate—they threatened to cut back on the quota of rough diamonds purchased from us if we didn't toe the line. They were of course under pressure from their Belgian Sight Holders who were having trouble selling their own polished goods in competition with ours.' He extracted a page from his notes and continued. 'However, if we were in the position to market our rough diamonds independently, we would be free to manipulate both rough and polished prices without hinderance from the Syndicate.'

Chubais pulled at his beard and frowned. 'I see what you're getting at comrade chairman, but our entire production of rough diamonds currently represents only about a quarter of the Syndicate's sales. If we suddenly stopped selling them our stones, I'm quite sure they'd be delighted to increase production from their own South African mines to satisfy their customers' needs. After all, they still control the sale of eighty percent of all mined diamonds in the world, and although we're obviously a thorn in their flesh, they realise that the only way to keep control of the market is to purchase just enough of our stones to keep us quiet.'

Aristov nodded. 'Thank you, Anton, that's an excellent summing up. Now we approach the crux of the matter. If we're to increase our foreign currency earnings by marketing our own rough diamonds independently of the Syndicate, there's one essential step we must take first.' He looked around at the members of his committee, and tried to guess how they would react to the drastic scheme that was about to be unveiled.

'I've asked Vassily Kolov, Head of Russalmaz, to join us here this evening so he can describe to you in his own words the plan his department has put forward—a plan which fulfils the requirement of my first essential step, and one which has been unofficially approved by Breznev's foreign trade adviser.'

During the ensuing buzz of conversation, Aristov dialled a number on the internal telephone and spoke softly into the mouthpiece. A few minutes later a gaunt white-haired man entered the room.

Aristov rose and shook his hand. 'Thank you for agreeing to talk to us tonight Vassily—please take a seat. I've brought my colleagues up to date, and we're ready at last to hear your plan for the independent marketing of our diamond production.'

Vassily Kolov cleared his throat and spread his hands out on the table. 'First of all I'd like to outline our current strengths. We began mining diamonds in quantity in the Ural mountains just after the last war, and later we developed other mines in an area described as the "Siberian Platform". Because we had little previous experience in marketing rough diamonds to the West, we decided to sell the bulk of our production though the Syndicate. However, over the last twenty years we slowly developed skills at sorting and valuing the stones we sent to them by introducing what is, in effect, a duplicate sorting operation. Every five weeks, before the start of the Syndicate's own sequence of sorting which culminates in their 'Sights', we sorted and valued our diamonds into more than three thousand different categories of colour, shape, quality and weight,

'The details were carefully recorded. Then all the diamonds were mixed back together again and sent to the Syndicate's London-based central marketing organisation—the CMO. There the diamonds were re-sorted into appropriate categories by their experts. I joined our team of on-site inspectors in the CMO's London offices to compare their results with Moscow's. If there were no major discrepancies, then the transaction was approved and payment for the diamonds was received in Moscow. In this way we have not only benefited from the Syndicate's marketing expertise, but slowly developed the necessary valuation skills for marketing our own diamonds. Now, under the existing four-year contract with the Syndicate, we no longer mix our diamonds back together after sorting, but in return for a modest increase in payment supply them still separated into their various categories.'

'That's all very fine and creditable,' objected Vesselovski, 'but what about the point Chubais was making just before you came in—if we go it alone, the Syndicate is quite capable of producing enough diamonds from its own mines to continue supplying its customers. That would leave us out in the cold with no buyers at all!'

Kolov smiled coldly at the young man. 'Have patience, Nicoli, I was just about to describe the final step in this operation. The first move was to acquire the necessary sorting and valuation expertise, now we must create the favourable climate. This is the essential step that comrade Aristov has already mentioned.'

'And just how do you propose to do that,' interjected Chubais in defence of his young assistant.

'By discrediting the Syndicate in the eyes of its clients!'

Kolov raised his hand to silence the clamour of questions being thrown at him by members of the committee. 'Please bear with me for a few more minutes,' he pleaded. 'What I'm about to tell you now must not go beyond these walls. You will have heard that the move towards a reconciliation with Peking has been approved by the Party Congress. As part of this move, the Chinese government has sent us detailed information on their latest research work. In addition to this, they have supplied us with experimental specimens from one particular project. This project concerns a new method of synthesizing spinel—a method which produces crystals identical in appearance to uncut diamonds.'

Kolov paused and pulled a grey linen bag from his pocket. He released the drawstring at the mouth of the bag and emptied its contents on the table. Over two hundred colourless transparent crystals of perfect octahedral shape cascaded from the bag and landed in a heap in the centre of the table. He picked up a handful of the stones and held them out for all to see.

'These not only look like our own top grade diamonds, but they have a similar density—the main difference is their hardness. Apart from this it would be difficult to distinguish them by eye from the real thing. We mixed some of the synthetic spinels with an equal number of rough diamonds and gave them to our top diamond sorters to value. I'm pleased to report that when we questioned them after the test, none were aware that half of the stones they had handled were fakes.'

'But you still haven't told us how you intend to use these look-alike diamonds to discredit the Syndicate,' objected Galina Bykov.

'My plan is quite simple. I've made arrangements for small quantities of these spinel crystals to be mixed with some of the incoming batches of stones in the Syndicate's London office at the sorting stage. Eventually, a few of the fake diamonds will find their way into the assortments sold to the Syndicate's clients, and when the diamond polishers come to cut them, they will soon realise from their comparative softness that they're fakes.'

'Do you really think that salting a few dud stones into a five-weekly sale consisting of millions of carats will have much effect,' scoffed Vesselovski.

'Of course not. Only a minor embarrassment to the Syndicate. They'll simply replace the fake stones. But after two months we'll step up the operation and substitute massive amounts for equal weights of diamond in our main shipments. This'll be done in Thailand where our diamonds pass through the Bangkok office of ThaiExport en route to London. When these large contaminated consignments begin to filter through to the main cutting centres of the world, the chaos in the diamond polishing workshops will have the Sight Holders in an uproar, and the Syndicate's reputation will sink to an all-time low. At this point we'll launch our own marketing operation aimed directly at the disgruntled Sight Holders. With luck we should be able to increase our share of the market by at least thirty percent.'

Aristov turned to Kolov. 'I assume that neither of our two departments will be involved directly in any of these special "arrangements" of yours?'

'That's correct—once all the details have been finalised, the ground work will be taken care of by agents of the SMERSH branch of the KGB. For my part, I'll liaise with the Synthetic Crystals Research Department of Beijing University so we can have a range of crystal shapes available that closely match the diamonds they'll replace. It may also be necessary to provide facilities in our own department so that the Chinese technicians can set up a production plant here in Moscow.'

Aristov stood up. 'Thank you, Comrade Kolov, for your contribution to our meeting. I give you my guarantee that you and your department will have the full support of the Trade Policy Committee when the time is ripe for a marketing launch.'

He turned to the members of his committee. 'Tonight, you've been made aware of the severity of our country's problems, and of a plan designed to reduce them. I must stress again the importance of complete secrecy in this matter—nothing of what you have heard tonight must be divulged to anyone outside this committee. Having said that, I'll bring the meeting to a close. Thank you for your comments and your time—have a good weekend.'

When the members of the committee had said their farewells and left the room, Kolov sighed and sat down again. 'Tell me, Comrade Aristov, is your young Vesselovski always so aggressive?'

Aristov laughed and joined him at the table. 'He certainly has an abrasive style—sometimes I think it's his way of compensating for being vertically disadvantaged! He's married to one of Gromyko's nieces, so I have to endure him.'

He moved closer to Kolov and lowered his voice. 'Now that we are alone, I must warn you that until this operation is successfully completed, we both have our heads on the block. Although the foreign trade adviser has given his unofficial blessing to the plan, he has made it very clear that any failure resulting in a public scandal will be attributed to unauthorized criminal actions, and the ringleaders will be punished with the utmost severity.'

He grimaced at his white-haired colleague. 'Once again it looks as if it's 'heads' they win and 'tails' we lose!'

Kolov shrugged his shoulders. 'Our lives are effectively in the hands of the KGB's SMERSH agents—if they blunder we'll pay dearly for it, but it's a risk we've just got to take if it helps save our people from near starvation.'

'At this stage, I'm more than thankful I plugged the information leak in my department. As you well know, back in 1977 someone in the organisation was passing on our policy decisions to the Syndicate in London and to the Pretoria Mining Company in Johannesburg. Both the spy, and Gregoriev his accomplice in the Russian section of the Syndicate's London office, were eliminated by SMERSH later that year. So at least we start this present operation with a clean house.'

Aristov gathered up his notes and replaced them in his executive case. He was just about to close the lid when he paused and pulled out a small leather container. He opened it, and lifted out two glasses and a bottle. 'You'll join me in a glass of vodka?'

Kolov smiled his acceptance. 'Russian vodka remains the one reliable comfort in a cold uncertain future.'

Aristov filled the glasses, and the two men toasted their commitment to an operation destined to send shock waves throughout the diamond world.

* * *

The hands on the Kremlin tower clock stood at nine. The last few tourists had left Red Square, and in the city's empty food stores the staff were locking up for the night. In the streets, mechanical snow clearers were at work, their twin alternating scrapper arms scooping in the icy slush like gigantic ravenous insects. Atop the Kremlin towers the huge red stars continued to glow defiantly in a world where communism was slowly beginning to wane.

CHAPTER 3

LONDON
Monday 30 March, 1981

Paul Remington raised himself on one elbow and squinted at his watch.

'Oh, my God,' he muttered, rubbing his eyes, 'it's eight o'clock.'

He rolled over and shook the sleeping form beside him. A muffled groan came from under the duvet.

'Steffi, wake up—we've overslept.'

A tousled head emerged from the duvet's warm embrace. 'What day is it?'

'Monday—you'd better get moving'.

He yanked the duvet to the floor, and stood gazing in admiration at the girl's flawless white nakedness and the careless disarray of her flaming red hair. Stephanie turned over and buried her face in the pillow.

'It's just as well I'm strong willed,' he sighed and smacked her bottom. 'Wake up—it's Monday and we're late!'

Stephanie raised her head and slowly opened one eye. Then, suddenly comprehending what Paul had said she sat bolt upright. 'Monday,' she hissed. 'It's Sights week—why the hell didn't you set the alarm?'

He tossed her a robe. 'Last night we had other priorities—remember? Just get some clothes on—I'll make the coffee.'

Paul Remington and Stephanie Goddard lived together in a modern third-floor flat which overlooked the northern perimeter of Regents Park. The arrangement, while not pleasing either set of parents, was a convenient one as they were both employed in the Diamond Syndicate's London-based central marketing organisation, and during the week were able to make the twenty-minute journey to work together in Paul's car.

Paul was Head of Special Operations, a small section which

served the Syndicate's security surveillance and internal audit departments. It was an interesting position which took him to parts of the world where diamond smuggling was a way of life, and where life itself was often expendable. His qualifications for the job included skills acquired as a commissioned officer in the SAS and a dislike of the everyday routine regarded by the majority as normal living. To this he rapidly added a thorough knowledge of both the legal and illegal world of diamond trading. He was in his mid-thirties, tall and bronzed with close-cropped dark brown hair, the lean muscular body of a middleweight boxer and the reflexes of a tennis doubles player.

Stephanie Goddard, a slim redhead in her late twenties with curves where it mattered and emerald green eyes, matched Paul in height but not in temperament. Hers with its unpredictable moods served as a foil to his more easy-going style. She was employed as private secretary to Sir James Crichton, Chairman of the Diamond Syndicate, her position ranking level with department heads in a company not overly concerned with equality between the sexes. She had joined the Syndicate five years ago fresh from business college, and started in the lowly position of copy typist. Her shorthand expertise, ability to compose a convincing letter from the skimpiest of dictated notes, and a truly phenomenal typing speed soon singled her out. From then on she progressed steadily up the ladder of promotion until her ability and looks came to the notice of Sir James.

During her time in the company Stephanie had indulged in several brief and unsatisfactory affairs, but it was not until Paul joined the Syndicate that she had felt tempted at last to risk a more permanent involvement.

Back in the flat, Stephanie and Paul showered and downed hasty cups of coffee. Stephanie, now in a thoroughly bad mood, struggled into a white polo-neck sweater and dark green skirt and jacket. She left Paul to lock up the flat, and set off on foot with the intention of hailing a passing taxi. Paul retrieved his red XJ12 from the parking lot, and drove it out into Prince Albert Road. He picked up Stephanie just as she reached the entrance to London Zoo, and a few minutes later was alarming both pedestrians and fellow motorists as he drove aggressively down the Euston Road. By the dextrous use of back streets, and a few racing-gear changes, he managed to arrive at the Syndicate's building in 2 Manorhouse Street at ten to nine, barely five minutes late.

Paul dropped Stephanie off at the impressive colonnaded entrance and drove to the rear of the block. He swung down the ramp to the underground garage, parked the XJ12 in a bay marked with his initials, and walked over to the lift. For security reasons, the lift went no further than the building's ground floor reception area, and in place of the usual call button there was a security card reader, operative only during office hours. He retrieved a plastic card from his wallet and wiped it through the reader. After a few seconds, the doors opened and he stepped into the waiting lift.

Paul emerged into the marble-tiled foyer and checked in with the security officer sitting at a large desk equipped with a television monitor and several telephones. He paused in front of one of the mirrored walls to straighten his tie and remove a hair from the shoulder of his dark blue pinstripe suit. Then he walked across to another lift that gave access to the six floors containing the Syndicate's offices and diamond sorting departments.

Rob Scot, the Syndicate's information officer, was ushering a group of visiting jewellers into the lift. He acknowledged Paul with a nod.

'You're running a bit late this morning.'

Paul sighed. 'Unlike some people, clock-watching has never been my forte.'

Rob and his visitors left the lift on the first floor and moved off in the direction of the Diamond Information Office. By the time Paul reached his own office on the second floor, Stephanie was caught up in the five-weekly bustle of activity as the first group of Sight Holders arrived and were shepherded into separate Showing Rooms to inspect their boxes of diamonds.

Meanwhile, in the Diamond Information Office, Rob Scot's secretary was busy serving the visiting jewellers cups of coffee while they looked at the collections of fancy coloured and unusual diamonds on view under the glass-domed display stands. When they had finished their coffee, Rob handed out brochures on the Syndicate's marketing operations, and then invited them to move into the small lecture theatre at one end of the room.

'Before we start our tour of the sorting floors,' he began, 'I want to say a few words on the history and operation of the company, so please make yourselves comfortable.' He threw a switch, and a map of the world appeared on the screen behind him. Small white diamond symbols marked the sites of all the major diamond mines.'

'As I'm sure you're all aware,' he continued, 'the Diamond Syndicate is an organisation unique in the gemstone world. Unlike the dozens of bourses and trading companies that market coloured stones, the Syndicate is a single entity, and over the years has acquired a controlling interest in the majority of the major diamond mines in Southern Africa.'

'During the depression of the early 30s when diamond prices slumped, Edward Crichton, Sir James' father who founded the company, realised he had to achieve two vital objectives if price stability was ever to be realised in the diamond market. The first of these objectives was to obtain the exclusive marketing rights for the diamonds produced by any mine of importance outside his own group. This he did with great success over the next forty years, culminating in the more recent acquisition of the Coastal Diamond Corporation's desert mining operation at Edeldorp in Namibia.'

'His second objective was to form an association of all the major diamond mining companies and diamond producing countries of the world. This association, like the multi-national OPEC organisation which regulates oil production, would have the power to control the quantity of diamonds mined by its members. The Diamond Association he created in the 40s was at last able to stabilise prices during both good times and bad by keeping the see-saw of diamond supply and demand in balance.'

'By the time Edward Crichton retired and handed the business over to his son James, the Syndicate's central marketing organisation, better known to yourselves and the media as the CMO, had achieved control over the sale of 80 percent of the world's rough diamonds. This control has come to be regarded by some as a monopoly, particularly by certain of our American friends, but I'm sure you'll agree with me that the advantages gained in terms of price stability make "beneficent monopoly" a more accurate description.'

Rob paused while his visitors nodded and murmured their agreement.

'The actions of the CMO during the recent depression in the trade are a good example of these policies in action. In order to keep the mining companies in business, we bought and stockpiled many of the rough diamonds that the trade was unable to absorb. At the same time we cut back on the volume of sales, with the result that most diamond cutting firms have by now used up their stocks, and are processing stones as they buy them. Most of the surplus stones purchased by the CMO are still swelling the stockpile in our steel-lined basement vaults in readiness for the expected upturn in business.'

'Whatever the market condition,' he continued, 'the Syndicate, through its Diamond Association, is able to regulate both the mining and sale of rough diamonds. This ensures that a supply of diamonds, appropriate to the market's needs, are dispatched month-by-month from all over the world by the various producers. Stones are delivered by courier, private plane, armoured car and security post to this building in Manorhouse Street, where they are valued and sorted into over three thousand categories of shape, quality, colour and weight,

'Since 1960 the one exception to this procedure are the diamonds mined in the USSR. Because of the anti-apartheid political stance taken by the Supreme Soviet after the Sharpeville massacre in South Africa, the USSR did not want to be seen trading with a company associated with that country. To get round the problem, diamonds from the Soviet Republics are no longer sent direct to this office, but are routed via an intermediary company in Bangkok.'

'Sounds like an old-fashioned laundering operation,' commented one of the jewellers.'

'Well, off the record, our Russian friends do have strange ways of doing business at times,' agreed Rob. 'But to get back to the main story, the arrival in London of diamond shipments from the world's major producers is regulated so it coincides with a cycle of sorting and valuing that culminates in the Syndicate's five-weekly sale of diamonds in what are called the "Sights".'

'First of all, the hundreds of thousands of diamonds received from each supplier are checkweighed. Stones having any surface discolouration are separated out and sent to the acidising department, where they are treated in molten potassium nitrate or in a witch's brew of hydrochloric and hydrofluoric acids. This rather drastic course of action lightens the colour of the diamonds and improves their value. Because of the toxic fumes generated by these processes, the acidising department is sited on the top floor of this building,

'The next operation is to divide the stones into twelve different size ranges which are distributed to twelve groups of specialist sorters. The weight "breakup" into these size ranges is done by means of automatic sieving machines.'

Rob pointed to a chrome-plated cylinder mounted on a set of springs. 'That's what they look like. An electric motor driving an off-centre weight is bolted to the side of the cylinder and causes the whole assembly to vibrate with a circular motion. It certainly takes the pain out of an operation previously done by hand.'

'Each of the twelve groups of diamond sorters then separates the stones into the appropriate selling categories of shape, quality and colour. Then the same categories of diamond from each of the twelve groups are mixed together, and each stone in that category is precision weighed by automatic computer-controlled machines into a series of weight divisions. These range from a fraction of a carat up to fourteen carats. When this is completed, the value of each of the resulting three-thousand types is determined from our price book by the chief valuator, who incidentally is also the manager of the sorting floors.'

'What happens to the larger diamonds?' asked one of the jewellers.

'These are graded separately because of their exceptional value,' explained Rob. 'Even when the smaller diamonds are weighed on the automatic machines, the accuracy has to be better than five thousandths of a carat. I'll be showing you the automatic weighing room later this morning.'

'How many sorters do you employ?' asked a jeweller.

'Just over four hundred. The numbers have been increasing steadily since the end of World War Two, and although I'm sure you'll be impressed when you see them in action shortly, perhaps the most stunning part of the CMO's operation occurs at what is called a "layout". The entire month's intake of diamonds, sorted into three-thousand different categories, is tipped onto long tables whose top surfaces are covered with sheets of white sorting paper. For reasons of security it's not possible to show you a layout, so I can only give you an impression of it.'

He pressed a switch, and the map of the world was replaced by a view of one of the sorting floors. A gasp came from his audience as they looked at a scene depicting a row of tables covered in glistening piles of diamonds.

'The extent of these layouts has steadily increased year by year. It now consists of hundreds of heaps of stones, which somebody once graphically described as scintillating like freshly crushed ice cubes. To give you some idea of the mass of stones involved, the heaps containing the smaller weight categories often measure up to thirty inches in diameter. As you can see, in the top weight categories the stones dwindle in numbers to just a few, which emphasises the rarity of these larger gems.'

He switched off the projector. 'Of course the main purpose behind this Aladdin's cave display of rough diamonds is to give Sir James and his fellow directors the opportunity to inspect the end results of the month's sorting operations. It also affords them the chance to disagree over the grading of particular stones, and if necessary to have them moved from one pile to another. Strictly between ourselves, the attendant department managers have been known to deliberately salt the layout with one or two incorrectly graded stones to give Sir James an excuse to demonstrate his expertise.'

Rob Scot was well known for his 'off the record' and 'strictly between ourselves' stories, all of which were carefully cleared in advance with Sir James.

'What about your security arrangements,' asked one of the jewellers. 'With such a large number of people handling the diamonds, this must be quite a problem.'

Rob Scot sighed. He had hoped to avoid the sensitive subject of security. 'As you'll shortly be seeing, we take all the usual physical and electronic precautions against theft. The sorters leave their personal effects in special lockers before they enter the diamond rooms and of course we employ television surveillance. Employment contracts also require members of staff to submit to random spot searches.'

'Have you ever suffered a major theft of diamonds?' asked the same jeweller.

Rob Scot gave the man a frosty smile. 'I think you're referring to the incident some years ago when a box of ten thousand carats of diamonds went missing. Well, as you can imagine, that created quite a stir. Eventually the CID pinned the theft down to one young man who had been planted in the company by a gang. He and his companions in crime were subsequently arrested and tried. I might add that it's the policy of the CMO to dismiss instantly anyone even suspected of theft. About the only other crime that warrants dismissal is murder!'

Rob Scot paused, hoping that no-one else would pursue this line of enquiry. 'Now, if there are no more questions, I'm going to take you on a tour of the diamond sorting departments.'

* * *

The layout at the end of the March sorting cycle had gone smoothly, and had been approved by Sir James and his fellow directors during the previous week. The diamonds had then been divided up and packed into hundreds of brown cardboard boxes. Each box contained packets of diamonds carefully selected, check-weighed, and priced to meet the specific orders placed by each of the eighty privileged Sight Holders. These Sight Holders, consisting of brokers and representatives of diamond cutting firms, had already deposited their bank drafts with the Syndicate to cover their orders. They had then been given individual appointments, spread out over the five days of the Sight, to inspect and approve the contents of their boxes.

While not directly involved in the activities of the CMO's sales department during the Sights period, Stephanie was on constant call to Sir James, who made it his business to attend personally to the requirements of the top echelon of the CMO's clients. These were buyers whose purchases exceeded one million dollars per Sight, and whose membership of this affluent inner circle had been handed down from father to son since the days of Edward Crichton.

It was nine o'clock that morning before Stephanie arrived in her office adjoining Sir James' opulent study, and she had been immediately summoned by him to attend a member of this inner circle. When she entered the principal Showing Room on the third floor, Sir James was discussing the merits of a sixteen carat top-colour diamond with Hank Winton, a valued client from New York. The two men were sitting at a side table looking at the stone under the colour-balanced light of a grading lamp, and in their concentration were momentarily oblivious of her presence in the room.

Sir James passed the American his gold hand lens. 'The inclusion is very near the surface fracture. If you remove them both by cleaving the stone parallel to the opposite face, the weight loss will be minimal.'

Hank Winton took the lens and rotated the diamond expertly between thumb and forefinger. 'I guess you're right, but I still think the price can stand some trimming.'

He handed the stone back to Sir James and looked up at Stephanie.

'Well, if it isn't my favourite girl—how are you, honey?'

'I'm fine thank you, Mr Winton. How was your flight yesterday?'

'About average—either I'm getting bigger or they're cramming more seats into first class.'

Sir James put the diamond back into its packet and gazed pensively at his private secretary. His carefully groomed white hair and gold rimmed glasses reminded Stephanie of the gaunt-looking elderly specialist she had recently consulted in Harley Street, an impression enhanced by Sir James' dark grey pinstripe suit.

Sir James turned and offered the American his hand. 'I think we can squeeze a small adjustment on the price of the stone, but first let's have some coffee. After that, I'll get George in to take you through the rest of the stones.'

He looked across at Stephanie. 'You know how Mr Winton likes his coffee, and I'll have some tea this morning for a change.'

Sir James dismissed her with a nod, and turned back to the American.

'Now is there anything else I can do for you on this trip?'

'Well, since you ask, my wife is very keen to see the Royal Ballet's new Mayerling production, but when I rang the Opera House last night they were sold out.'

'That's no problem. I can let you have the two company seats they're holding for tonight's performance. I'll get Stephanie to pick up the tickets and deliver them to your hotel.'

'I sure do appreciate that.' The American leant forward and laid a confiding hand on Sir James' knee. 'Ballet's not my scene as you know, but when Martha joins me on these trips, the Playboy club is definitely out of bounds.'

* * *

Paul heard the key turn in the front door, and switched off the six-o'clock news he had been watching on the TV. Stephanie sauntered into the lounge and collapsed beside him into the yielding contours of the white leather settee.

He turned and kissed her on the nose. 'And where have you been?'

Stephanie kicked off her shoes and frowned. 'Covent Garden box office, and then to the Savoy to deliver some tickets—Sir James was doing his fawning act for Hank Winton's benefit this time. When I got to Winton's suite his wife was with him, and they insisted I stayed on for a drink. At least I didn't get propositioned by him this time. How was your day?'

'Not much better. There's a bit of a flap brewing in Security Surveillance—I've spent hours in front of their videos looking at what Ken Burridge calls "suspicious actions". Several sorters were caught scratching themselves, and another could be seen picking his nose!'

Stephanie grimaced. 'Spare me the gruesome details—I was

beginning to fancy my dinner, which reminds me, it's your turn to cook tonight.'

'This was on the mat when I got in.'

Stephanie took the airmail envelope Paul handed to her and looked at the postmark.

'Pretoria—we don't get much mail from there.'

She slit the letter open and extracted a sheet of notepaper.

'It's from Christine Reece—she and Mike are planning a seven-week holiday touring the UK and the Continent. It'll be Christine's first trip overseas.'

She gave the letter to Paul. 'They're bringing their daughter—she must be about two and a half years old now.'

'I haven't seen Mike Reece since that bomb affair at the Pretoria mine back in '78. He married Christine just after that—she must have been at least three months pregnant by then.'

Stephanie glared at him. 'I hope you're not going to bring that up when you meet them.'

'Of course not—but you must admit the affair created quite a stir at the time, particularly when her first husband, Richard Keogh, was found dead at the bottom of that mine shaft with a knife in his guts.'

Stephanie shrugged her shoulders. 'Well, they managed to survive all the unpleasantness, and now Mike's a happily married man with a young daughter—she says he's just been promoted to mine manager at the Pretoria.'

'I see they're planning to arrive at the end of June. She doesn't mention where they're staying.'

'I think Mike's got a maiden aunt somewhere in Chelsea who owns a large flat. With the unfavourable South African exchange rate they'll probably be glad to make use of her spare rooms.'

Paul got up and strolled over to the drinks cabinet. He mixed two generous vodka and tonics, added some ice from the built-in fridge and handed a glass to Stephanie. 'What are you smiling at?'

Stephanie chuckled. 'I was just remembering something in the letter Christine wrote me after her wedding to Mike.'

Paul took a sip from his glass. 'So let's have it.'

'At the end of their honeymoon in Cape Town, they travelled

back to Pretoria on the Blue Train. The train left at nine o'clock in the morning, and when they retired to their compartment that night and started to undress, Christine asked Mike to close the venetian blind. He laughed at her. 'Who on earth can see us—we're in the middle of the open veld.' A few minutes later they were indulging in a serious bout of "flagrante delecto" when the train slowed down and stopped at an unlit wayside halt. Suddenly there were dozens of grinning African faces at the window. When the train moved on Christine said she and Mike were so helpless with laughter it was ages before they were able to recapture the mood!'

Paul grinned. 'The Blue Train must be a prime source of evening entertainment at that halt.' He picked up Christine's letter again. 'I see she's asked if we can get them tickets for Wimbledon—can you wheedle some out of Sir James?'

Stephanie sampled her drink and wrinkled her nose approvingly.

'Sure, providing none of the Sight Holders get to him first. Now what about this meal—you know I can't get in the mood on an empty stomach.'

CHAPTER 4

MOSCOW

Monday 6 April, 1981

Moscow University lies some two miles south-west of the Kremlin between the Universitetski and Lomonosovski prospekts. The white stone 'wedding-cake' tiers of its central tower and its twin flanking wings look out over flower fringed lawns that reach across to the serpentine curve of the Moskva river.

Lin Chung had never in his life seen anything quite so beautiful as the university building and its surrounds. Flowers were not a Chinese priority even in Peking's Temple of Heaven Park or the Palace Museum, and in Chung's opinion, the moat which surrounded what had once been the walled city of Peking bore no comparison to the wild torrent of the Moskva.

He arrived in Moscow the previous Friday evening in the company of his superiors Ho Zheng and Professor Sang Liang. Chung had never flown before, and found himself sucking in his breath whenever he recalled the thrill of the take-off and the excitement of the long nine-hour journey in the big jet of the Civil Aviation Administration of China airline.

He and Zheng were allocated a room each in the university's residential quarters, while Professor Liang was invited to stay in the home of Professor Vladimir Balitsky, Head of the university's Crystal Synthesis laboratory. Liang and Balitsky had never met before, but were well acquainted with each other's work through the scientific papers that had appeared in various learned journals.

On Saturday morning, Balitsky and his principal assistant Dr Sergei Bulak took the Chinese contingent to see the Cathedral of the Assumption and the Tzarist palaces that lay within the Kremlin walls. Dr Bulag was directly involved in the setting up of the Chinese synthesis plant, but his presence was also necessary as he was one of the few Russians on the university staff who was fluent in Chinese. After the Kremlin, they visited the glass-roofed arcades of the GUM store, and Bulag presented Chung and Zheng with some roubles to buy gifts for their families. On Sunday they spent the whole day wandering around the eighty theme pavilions in Moscow's botanical gardens, an outing accompanied by frequent visits to the food stalls to keep up their stamina. Of particular fascination to Chung, who had only just got used to the idea of air travel, was the Space Pavilion.

One other thing that had delighted Chung was his inclusion in an invitation to see a performance by the Bolshoi ballet of 'Anna Karenina' that Sunday evening. Although he was more familiar with the revolutionary ballets of the Peking company, he thoroughly enjoyed the performance, particularly after he had downed several glasses of Russian champagne in the interval. Later that evening the Chinese visitors were dined and wined by their university hosts in a Russian speciality restaurant in Leninski Prospekt, and Chung sampled his first glass of vodka.

By daybreak next morning, Chung was still sleeping off the effects of his night out in Moscow. His fitful slumbers had been disturbed by a strange dream in which screaming placard-waving crowds confronted columns of tanks in Red Square. At one point he found himself on his beloved bicycle, desperately trying to escape a pursuing tank through a maze of barricades and amid bursting shells. He was glad when Zheng finally roused him, and his frightening visions evaporated in the light of morning.

* * *

By nine o'clock that Monday morning Professor Liang, Ho Zheng and Lin Chung were seated in Professor Balitsky's office at the rear of the university's west wing. The Professor did not speak Chinese and after welcoming them with a handshake they were now all waiting in polite silence for Dr Bulak to join them in his dual role of scientific observer and interpreter.

Mindful of his manners under the watchful eye of Zheng,

Chung gazed curiously around the office. Open-fronted bookcases that lined the walls were crammed with scientific books on all subjects relating to minerals and crystal growth. On top of the bookcases he could see plastic models of the main types of crystal system. Alongside them were several stick-and-ball structures representing complex molecules similar to the models he was familiar with in the Synthetic Crystals Department of Beijing University.

When Dr Bulak arrived he was full of apologies for his lateness. Professor Balitski impatiently waved him to a seat, and began his brief welcoming speech.

'The Supreme Soviet are most pleased at this sign of friendship and co-operation between our two countries. As Head of the Crystal Synthesis Department I am honoured that you have presented us with the fruits of your research work.' He paused while Bulak translated.

'Because you are only available to us for one week, all the apparatus and materials outlined in your list of requirements have already been installed in the laboratory adjoining my office. I have chosen this location for your work to ensure you have complete privacy, and so that you can instruct Dr Bulak in the details of the synthesis process without interruption.'

Professor Liang turned to Dr Bulak. 'Please thank Professor Balitsky for his hospitality, which we hope to return one day when he visits Peking. Also apologise for our inability to converse directly with him in his own language, although, if put under extreme pressure, my Chief Assistant Zheng will admit that he knows a smattering of Russian.'

Zheng looked down at his feet in embarrassment, but was saved from demonstrating his linguistic skills by the arrival of a young Russian girl student carrying a tray of cups and thermos jugs.

Balitsky smiled at his Chinese guests as the girl handed round the cups and poured out green tea from the thermos jugs.

'You see my friends, I have remembered your national drink—I have also arranged for you to be kept supplied with tea and any other refreshments you may require during your time here.'

Chung gratefully gulped down the tea. His over-indulgence of the previous evening had left him with a surprising thirst. 'Their vodka is not at all like our Mau Tai,' he whispered to Zheng at his side.

Zheng glared at him. 'Mixing champagne, wine and vodka was not a good idea. I must remind you Chung that you are here to work, not to make a fool of yourself,' he hissed.

When the contents of the thermos jugs had been consumed, Professor Balitsky rose to his feet and turned to Dr Bulak. 'I think the time has come to show our friends their place of work. Please tell them that I have instructed you to provide all the assistance they need to get the synthesis plant into production in the shortest possible time.'

He waited while Bulak translated, and then turned to Professor Liang. 'Dr Bulak will take you through to the laboratory and show you the facilities. I would appreciate it if you joined me here in my office at the end of each day so that we can discuss progress.'

* * *

It took the rest of that day for Zheng and Chung to familiarise themselves with the Russian-built synthesis equipment. They were surprised to find the laboratory had been equipped with six flux-melt crystal growing units complete with their expensive platinum crucibles and temperature-controlled heaters. The facilities in the laboratory were certainly adequate enough; it was well lit, with spacious and sturdy work benches lining three of its walls. Plenty of electric power points were provided and a powerful ventilation system was connected to extractor hoods positioned over the synthesis units.

When Chung and Zheng inspected the contents of the chemical storage bins that were fitted under the benches, they were also surprised to find a much larger quantity of the lead fluoride flux in which the crystals were to be grown than they expected. The high purity alumina and magnesia chemicals which formed the constituent materials for producing the synthetic spinel crystals were also present in equally large quantities.

At lunch time, the same girl student brought them trays of

sandwiches and more thermos jugs of tea. During the break, Dr Bulak was called away to a meeting, and Zheng took the opportunity to speak his mind to Professor Liang.

'I find all this very strange,' he complained. 'It's certainly going to take us much longer than a week to get six units up and running.'

Chung was equally puzzled. 'I agree with Mr Zheng—and there are enough chemicals here to produce kilos of crystals. I thought this was simply going to be a duplicate of our own small production unit.'

Professor Liang took his spectacles off and polished the lenses thoughtfully. 'This has come as a surprise to me also,' he admitted. 'However, I'm reluctant to ask our hosts why they need to scale up the original production to this extent. There is no jewellery or industrial application I'm aware of that uses colourless spinel crystals of this quality. Furnace installations already exist in Russia, and elsewhere, for large scale production of much cheaper spinel crystals.'

'Yes, that's true,' agreed Zheng. 'But the Verneuil method you refer to produces the type of rounded crystal called a "boule" in the West—it would seem that our Russian friends have a need for a method such as ours which produces high quality octahedral-shaped crystals.'

Liang sighed and shrugged his shoulders. 'Well, whatever their reason, I have been ordered by our Politburo to give them every assistance with the setting up of this project. I've also been ordered to ensure at all costs that this spearhead in the establishment of good relations between our two countries succeeds. If that means we have to work fifteen hours a day to get all the units up and working, then I'm afraid we'll just have to do it.'

'I'd like to know what the rush is all about,' grumbled Chung. 'Why can't we take an extra week and finish the work comfortably?'

Liang shook his head. 'The Russian request for our help was quite specific—they want to produce their first batch of crystals in two month's time. There's no way I can ask for an extension of even a week. What I will do, however, is ask Dr Bulak to loan us two of his laboratory assistants. In any case, it's advisable that more than one person in his department knows how to run the equipment.'

When Dr Bulak returned to the laboratory later that afternoon, Liang asked him to arrange an immediate meeting with Professor Balitsky. When they met in the professor's office, Liang turned to Bulak.

'Please tell the professor that I am most impressed with the laboratory facilities and the equipment he has made available to me. However, please also tell him that I had not been informed that my team was expected to prepare six working units during the few days at our disposal.' He waited while Bulak translated.

Professor Balitsky glanced anxiously at both the men. 'Please inform Liang that it was made clear to the president of his university that we urgently need to produce a quantity of the spinel crystals by the beginning of June. The number of units I have provided is relative to this quantity.'

'In which case,' responded Liang, 'I must respectfully request the use of two of your laboratory technicians to assist in the work. Otherwise I cannot guarantee its completion before we leave on the 11th.'

Balitsky nodded curtly to Bulak. 'Provide Professor Liang with whatever help he needs, but on no account give him any reason for the urgency. I'll hold you personally responsible if those six units are not working by the end of the week.'

* * *

By Friday afternoon, a weary Chung and Zheng, and their two Russian assistants, had all six of the synthesis plants tested and up to operating temperature. They had then switched off the power to the heaters, and when the temperature of each unit had fallen to a safe level they introduced into the still hot platinum crucibles the charges of powdered lead fluoride which were to act as the flux medium for the growing crystals.

When the units were up to working temperature again, and the flux had become molten, Zheng and Chung, closely watched by the Russians, mixed together carefully weighed amounts of the powdered alumina and magnesia chemicals and introduced them into the glowing flux in each unit. Finally they added precisely weighed amounts of the special catalyst that would speed up the crystal growth process and control the shape of the product. As the alumina and magnesia chemicals melted, and began slowly combining with each other, the automatic furnace controls that would gradually lower the temperature in the tanks by fractions of a degree each day were switched on. Over the next two months, perfectly shaped octahedral spinel crystals would slowly form within the molten flux in the same way that salt crystals grow in a tumbler of hot saturated saline solution when it starts to cool down.

Late that afternoon, Professor Balitsky joined the Chinese team and the two Russian technicians in the laboratory to toast the successful startup of the project. Dr Bulak was on the telephone in the outer office, and when Zheng and Chung, their cheeks aglow with vodka, walked through and raised their glasses to him he quickly turned his back on them and lowered his voice.

'The Chinese technician who knows a little Russian has just come in so I'll switch to English.' He waved to Zheng and Chung and continued his conversation. 'Yes, I appreciate your problems, but I can assure you the crystals will be available in time for the June sale of diamonds in London. Now I must go. I'll make a full report at the next Russalmaz meeting.'

* * *

For the farewell party that evening, Professor Balitsky reserved a room in one of the few Chinese restaurants in Moscow. He was relieved that his Department's obligation to keep the new project in step with the Russalmaz timetable had so far been successful. For the first time that week he felt he could relax and enjoy the company of his Russian staff and the three Chinese visitors.

In one of the intervals between courses, Ho Zheng was coaxed to speak a few words of his limited Russian vocabulary, his laboured high-pitched Chinese dialect causing much amusement to the two Russian laboratory assistants.

In the middle of the merriment, Professor Balitsky caught Dr Bulak's eye and stood up. He raised his glass of peppery Mau Tai liquor in a toast.

'My Chinese friends and brother communists, I give you a toast to our two great countries.'

To Balitsky's surprise, and before Dr Bulak could translate, Ho Zheng was on his feet, and with flushed cheeks gave his two compatriots a rapid-fire Chinese translation of the toast to which they both applauded.

Professor Liang stood up and smiled his thanks to Balitsky and Bulak. Together with his companions, he raised his glass and drained it. The rest of the evening passed in a haze of goodwill and back slapping, fuelled by further toasts in Mau Tai.

* * *

Next morning, a more subdued trio of Chinese was delivered by their hosts to the airport and assisted through customs and immigration. After further farewells and exchanges of friendship, Professor Liang, followed by Ho Zheng and a near-tearful Lin Chung made their way out to the waiting aircraft.

As the CAAC jet started its lumbering takeoff down the runway, Chung gripped the armrests of his seat and closed his eyes tightly. After the aircraft had lifted into the air and began its steep climb to cruising altitude, Zheng nudged him and pointed out of the cabin window. Chung opened his eyes warily and gasped as he saw the City of Moscow spread out below, the golden domes of the palaces and churches in the Kremlin glistening in the morning sunlight.

Suddenly he felt sad. His wonderful adventure had come to an end at last, and he knew in his heart he would never see such a lovely sight again. Zheng sensed his depression, and when the air stewardess came by he asked her to bring them two glasses. When she returned with them, he removed a flask from his pocket and poured a measure of colourless liquid into each tumbler.

He handed one to Chung. 'This should cheer you up.'

Chung sipped the liquid cautiously, and then his eyes lit up. 'It's vodka!' he cried and smacked his lips in appreciation.

'I saw you'd acquired a taste for it, so I bought you a souvenir bottle in the GUM store, and hid it in my case.'

Some hours later when they had crossed out of USSR air space and were flying over the northern vastness of the People's Republic of China, Chung thought it time he unburdened himself of a small nagging worry.

'Zheng, do you remember when we wandered into Professor Balitsky's office yesterday afternoon.'

'When we tried to toast Dr Bulak's health?'

'That's right—he was on the phone talking to someone in Russian. Well, when he saw us, he turned his back and lowered his voice. I didn't bother to listen until I realised he'd stopped using Russian and was talking in English. Perhaps he thought with your small knowledge of Russian you might have been be able to understand what he was saying.'

'And of course he didn't know you were a student of English. Well, out with it Chung—what did he say?'

Chung frowned and shook his head. 'He seemed to be talking to someone in the Russian gemstone export department. I heard him say the crystals would be ready in time for the June sale of diamonds in London. Do you think I should tell Professor Liang?'

'Not if you don't want to. It doesn't sound very important to me—I'd forget it if I were you.'

Chung nodded, but his nagging doubts remained. The first time he had seen the synthetic spinel crystals in the Beijing laboratory they reminded him of Russian diamonds. Perhaps he should tell someone. Then an accumulation of long hours and unaccustomed excitements overcame him, his eyelids drooped and he fell fast asleep.

CHAPTER 5

LONDON

Wednesday 24 June, 1981

Almost inevitably, with the first week of Wimbledon under way, London was being lashed by rain storms. The pavements outside the Diamond Syndicate's building in Manorhouse Street were awash, and miniature tornadoes of swirling rain turned the umbrellas of the arriving staff inside out as they fought their way into the shelter of the entrance foyer.

Throughout the building lights had been turned on to combat the gloom of the dark cloud-filled sky, but even the concealed ceiling lights in Sir James Crichton's luxurious third floor office failed to dispel the sombre atmosphere which seemed to pervade the room.

Sir James was sitting at his antique mahogany desk, his lean face looking more drawn than usual. A lock of his normally well groomed white hair had fallen forward across his forehead and his eyes had narrowed to gimlet slits behind his spectacles as he glared across the desk at the head of Security Surveillance.

'I want to be quite clear about this, Kenneth. You say you have proof on video tape that three members of staff in the 2 to 4 carat sorting room have been stealing diamonds?'

Ken Burridge shot a nervous glance at Jim Finchley, the Syndicate's chief valuator sitting beside him. He licked his thin bloodless lips and wilted under Sir James' steely gaze.

'That's what it amounts to, sir. I've examined the tapes most carefully, and there seems to be no doubt that there are several occasions when diamonds appear to have been manipulated by the three men in question.'

Sir James scowled at him. 'What the blazes do you mean by manipulated?'

Jim Finchley leaned across Ken Burridge and placed a video cassette on the desk in front of Sir James.

'This contains an edited selection of these so-called manipulations. If you allow me to play this on your machine, you'll be able to see the problem more clearly than either of us can describe it.'

Sir James nodded his head in grudging acquiescence, and swivelled his chair round to face the TV/video machine mounted alongside his drinks cabinet.

'Let's get on with it then. I've got an executive meeting in an hour.'

Ken Burridge took the cassette and slotted it in the player. He picked up the remote control unit and switched on the TV. The screen was momentarily filled with flying white spots of interference, then these faded and were replaced by a picture of one of the sorting rooms.

The security cameras in the diamond departments were concealed behind ceiling-mounted domes cast from gold-tinted one-way glass. They were set to scan slowly backwards and forwards over sections of the long diamond sorting benches, each camera's range of vision overlapping the next. The cameras were fitted with remote control zoom lenses, and could be stopped at any part of their scan and zoomed in to check the work of an individual sorter. The scene captured by each camera was fed to individual video recorders housed in the Security Surveillance's monitoring room. These machines were switched on permanently during the working day.

While Sir James and his two managers watched the TV screen, the picture showed one of the sorters picking up a rough diamond and inspecting it under his hand lens. As the camera slowly moved away from him along the bench, the hand holding the diamond could be seen moving backwards towards the edge of the bench. Then the image was lost as the camera reached the next sorter.'

'That was the first sign of trouble,' explained Ken Burridge. 'When it was pointed out to me, I asked for a camera to be left permanently focused on the man. The next clip you see was edited from several hours of tape recorded over one week.'

The picture on the screen changed to a close up view of the

same man. For several minutes he could be seen inspecting a diamond under his lens, and rotating it between thumb and forefinger. On the bench in front of him was pinned a large sheet of white sorting paper, its surface divided into a grid of squares. Then they saw him lean forward and place the stone in a pile of similar quality diamonds in one of the squares. He selected another stone from a transparent plastic tray of rough diamond crystals sitting in a metal box at his side, and repeated the process. This time, however, he appeared to palm the stone as he went through the motions of placing it in another pile. Then he sneezed, and the hand, still half closed, disappeared into his trouser pocket and re-emerged holding a handkerchief.

Ken switched off the video. 'We recorded several variations of this—in one of them he loosened his tie and seemed to insert the stone between his shirt collar and neck. On another occasion he simply bent down and pushed a finger into his shoe as if scratching his ankle.'

Sir James removed his glasses wearily and inspected his carefully manicured fingers. After a moment he looked up at Ken Burridge. 'What about the other two sorters?'

'I spent the entire weekend checking over last week's video recordings. All but two of the remaining sorters in that particular department are clean. However, the two that did call for closer inspection were using identical techniques to the one you just saw. It was as though all three of them had practised the moves together.'

Sir James paused for a moment deep in thought and then turned to Jim Finchley.

'Here's what you do. Have them taken into the TV monitoring room one at a time and shown the relevant sections of the recording. Then have them collect their belongings from the security lockers, and fire them—I want them off the premises this morning.'

Jim nodded. 'What about the police?'

'Kenneth can liaise with the CID. I want warrants issued, and their homes searched. Are any of them married?'

Ken Burridge took a notebook from his pocket and consulted

it. 'One of them has a wife and two kids, plus a mortgage with the company.'

'He should have thought of that before committing this shabby crime—but give me time to consider the implications. At all costs we must avoid any bad publicity. This must be a damage limitation exercise. We'll prosecute only as a last resort.'

Sir James got up from behind his desk and walked over to the TV.

'I'll keep the video cassette for the moment. Affairs like this play merry hell with morale among the sorters, so keep it as quiet as you can.'

He dismissed them and picked up the internal phone. 'Stephanie—I want Paul Remington in my office right away.'

A few minutes later Paul knocked on Sir James' door and walked in.

Sir James motioned him to a chair. 'We've got problems Paul. Diamonds have gone missing from one of the sorting rooms.'

'In what numbers, sir?'

'As far as I know, not that many. It seems like petty stealing—just the occasional stone.' He pointed the remote control unit at the TV and replayed the recording. When it had finished he looked questioningly at Paul.

'Well, what do you think?'

'For a start, the three of them are certainly in collusion. They probably realise that small random thefts of this kind can't be detected on the internal audit computer. With tens of thousands of carats passing through each department daily, the loss of a few carats would easily be accounted for in the bulk weighing tolerance—the difference in weight between unsorted goods in and sorted goods out. I assume that Internal Audit haven't seen any unexplained negative blip in the bulk totals?'

'Nothing other than the normal plus and minus drifts due to weighing.'

'Do you want me to do any vetting?'

'Yes, run the usual checks on these three. Bank balances, new houses, expensive cars, friends in the diamond polishing trade—that sort of thing. If it's simply a case of three rotten apples, I don't want you wasting more time on them than absolutely necessary. If you do find anything odd, let me know immediately. Now I must move—I've got an Exco meeting in five minutes.'

He paused at the door and looked back at Paul. 'One more thing, do try and get Stephanie into the office a little earlier in the mornings.'

* * *

Paul called in at the personnel department on his way back to his office.

The manager, Roy Wakefield, was in the inner office dictating to his secretary.

'I've just come from Sir James,' Paul confided in hushed tones—that was always a good opening gambit in the CMO. 'Can I have a word in private?'

Roy Wakefield's face displayed emotions ranging from irritation through alarm to curiosity.

'I can spare a few minutes if it's important, but keep it short—I'm due at the Exco meeting.'

Roy liked it known he was on the executive committee. He dismissed his secretary and closed the door behind her.

'Now what's the problem?'

'I want the files on Peter Scofield, Roger Black and David Crosley.'

'What the hell for—you know staff files are confidential.'

'Not these ones Roy, all three men have just been awarded instant dismissal by Sir James.'

Roy's complexion was palid at the best of times, but now it managed to turn a shade paler. 'Oh, my god, they haven't got any of the girls into trouble?' One of the crosses he had to bear was the occasional pregnancy among his young female trainees.

Paul laughed. 'No, it's something rather different this time. I expect Sir James may let you into the secret at Exco—and Roy, I'd like those files on my desk by lunchtime.'

When Paul reached his office on the second floor, his secretary handed him a note. 'Miss Goddard rang a few minutes ago and left this message.'

Paul took the paper from her and glanced at the scrawled note.

'Thanks, Debbie, it's to remind me about Mike Reece's visit—he and his wife are arriving at London Airport from Johannesburg Friday morning. It looks as though I'll have to meet them—Steffi is in trouble with her time-keeping. Sir James reckons I keep her in bed too long in the mornings.'

Debbie giggled, turned pink and started typing to cover her confusion.

Steven Heming, Paul's assistant handed him a cup of coffee.

'You really shouldn't tease the girl like that,' he admonished. 'I think she's got a crush on you.'

'Come into the inner sanctum, Steve, and shut the door behind you—we've got a job of work to do.'

Steven Heming was a stocky fair-haired man in his late twenties. Paul had chosen him from several applicants who replied to his carefully worded advertisement in the *Sunday Times*—'Assistant Manager required for a small Investigation Department in a Major International Group's Security Division. Must be under 30, fit and willing to travel.'

Steven, a Judo black belt, was certainly fit as he had proved at the end of his formal interview. His prospective boss shook him by the hand, and then attempted to throw him. A second later Paul found himself lying face down on the floor with Steven holding him in an armlock. Nursing a bruised shoulder he had immediately engaged the younger man.

After leaving school, Steven spent two years backpacking around the world, earning his keep with temporary jobs. On his return to the UK he joined the Metropolitan Police, and served a probationary two years on the beat. Then he transferred to the CID, and four years later sat his sergeant's promotion exam. Finally, after a further year in the CID, he became a detective sergeant. It was two years since he left the police and joined Paul Remington. During that period they had made a formidable team, tracking down several diamond 'leakages' in the long supply lines between the Syndicate's headquarters in London, and sources such as Zaire, Sierra Leone, and Angola. Steven's connections in the CID had been an added asset to Paul, and, coupled with his own contacts with former colleagues in the SAS, had proved invaluable in their frequent tangles with the diamond underworld.

Steven hitched himself onto the edge of Paul's desk. 'That summons from Sir James sounded urgent—has someone nicked his Daimler?'

'It's nearly as bad—Security Surveillance have caught three male sorters helping themselves to the diamonds.'

Steven gave a low whistle. 'That really is bad news.'

'Personnel are sending down the men's files. I want you to go through them and check out their backgrounds.'

'What are we looking for specifically?'

'Anything that ties the three of them together—their MO on the video tape makes it look as if they're in collusion. See if they have any expensive hobbies or tastes.' Paul rummaged through his desk drawer and tossed a Daily Mail press pass to Steven. 'When you've done all that, turn up on their doorsteps as a reporter and get their reactions to the dismissals—talk to their girlfriends. One of them is married with a company mortgage, so get his wife's reaction. Incidentally, Sir James is anxious to keep this out of the media, so you can drop the hint that your paper may be interested in buying their stories providing they don't talk to any other reporters.'

Steven looked at his watch. 'If Roy Wakefield is at the Exco meeting, I think I'll pay a visit to personnel. He's bound to make heavy weather of passing those files over, so I'll try a little of the old charm on his secretary.'

'Fine, but don't let him catch you at it. We've made enough enemies in the company between us. I'll meet up with you later, but first I'm going down to Security's TV monitoring room—there's something I saw in those video recordings that's bothering me, and I can't put my finger on it.'

The spacious and dimly lit Security Surveillance room at the rear of the ground floor was filled with twenty-four TV monitors, two for each of the sorting rooms. The tedious task of watching the screens was shared between the Syndicate's staff of ten uniformed security officers. These were rotated on a shift basis, four of them always being on duty in the room during the period when diamonds were out in the sorting rooms.

To provide further backup, twenty-four long-play video recorders were stacked in metal racks at one side of the room and captured the pictures from the TV cameras in each sorting room. The video machines were each capable of holding up to five days of recording, and in the event of a problem occurring it was possible to wind back at high-speed to any incident by simply punching the required date and time information into the system's computer keyboard.

Paul took out his plastic security pass and wiped it through the card reader at the side of the monitoring room door. The card reader acknowledged his authority to enter the room with a high-pitch bleep. He pushed open the door and passed through a small airlock which served to isolate the room's air-conditioned atmosphere from the rest of the building.

The temperature in the monitoring room was maintained at five degrees below the level of comfort. This helped dissipate the heat from the formidable array of electronic equipment, and kept the security personnel awake during their four-hour stints of vigilance in front of the screens. To prevent the build-up of harmful static electricity, the air in the room was also maintained at seventy percent relative humidity.

Paul shivered involuntarily as the cool atmosphere enveloped him. Four security officers were sitting at a long desk fitted with the switches and joy-stick controls necessary to manipulate the twenty four remote TV cameras in the twelve diamond sorting rooms. Each man was responsible for watching an array of six screens, and each array covered three sorting rooms. One of the officers turned and greeted Paul.

'I thought it wouldn't be long before you paid us a visit!'

Paul pulled up a chair and sat down alongside the man.

'Sorry to disturb your shift, Harry. Just thought I'd come in and cool off for a bit. I've been put in the picture by Sir James about the spot of trouble.'

'You've seen the edited tape?'

'Yes, but I'd like to see a bit more from the original.'

Harry swivelled his chair round to face Paul.

'What section in particular?'

'The sequence where the sorter sneezes.'

'That would be Roger Black in the 2 to 4 carat room last Wednesday.'

He checked his log book. 'Hang on, the complete tape is still on the standby machine behind you. I'll just punch in the time and date details and you can watch as much of it as you fancy.'

Paul moved his chair back and settled himself in front of the standby monitor screen. Harry switched the machine on, and Paul heard the tape accelerate and run for several seconds before stopping again. Harry handed him the remote control unit.

'It works just like your own domestic machine. Run, forward and reverse search, slow motion and still frame.'

Paul pressed the run button and watched the screen as the sorter, Roger Black, inspected a diamond with his hand lens. Then the man reached out and appeared to place the stone on a pile of previously sorted diamonds in one of the ruled-off squares on the sheet of white sorting paper. The man drew his hand back, sneezed and with the same hand reached into his trouser pocket. He pulled out his handkerchief, wiped his nose and returned the handkerchief to his pocket.

Paul stopped the machine. That was the section he had seen in Sir James' office. The man had held the diamond between thumb and forefinger, and as he made to drop the stone, he had clearly retracted his forefinger and moved the stone back into the palm of his hand.

It was the next few seconds that had puzzled Paul when he first viewed the tape. He pressed the start button again and watched as the sorter leant forward, reached across to the same square and with his palm facing downwards, smoothed out the pile of diamonds.

'I'm quite sure he palmed the diamond in the first shot,' Paul muttered to himself, 'but there's something else here.'

He re-ran the tape again, and when it reached the point where the sorter reached out and smoothed down the pile of diamonds, Paul saw a pin-point flash of light from between the man's thumb and forefinger. He re-ran the section again and hit the freeze button. Paul stared at the screen for a few seconds and then turned and beckoned Harry to join him.

'Take a look at this.'

He pointed to the sorter's hand. There, lodged between the man's thumb and forefinger was a diamond. Paul inched the picture on frame-by-frame, and slowly the fingers parted and the diamond disappeared.

'What do you make of that? First he palms a diamond, and puts it in his trouser pocket. Then he seems to bring the stone out again and put it back!'

CHAPTER 6

MOSCOW

Thursday 25 June, 1981

Vassily Kolov stood at his office window on the fifth floor of the Russalmaz building on Prospekt Marksa. The busy thoroughfare beneath him formed part of a semi-circle of roads penning the Kremlin, Red Square and St Basil's Cathedral to the curve of the Moskva river.

On the far side of the road he could see a group of people gathering outside one of the shops. He wondered idly what they were queuing for. Perhaps they didn't even know themselves. As soon as the rumour got around that a delivery was expected, a queue of hopeful shoppers formed in minutes. The haphazard and badly organised supply system in the USSR, coupled with chronic shortages, made random queuing a way of life for the Moscow housewife.

A knock on the office door brought Kolov out of his reverie.

'Please come in, comrades.'

The door opened and Oleg Aristov, Chairman of the Trade Policy Committee entered, followed by the portly bald-headed figure of Colonel Leo Vessovski, Head of the KGB.

Kolov signalled to the men to sit down. 'Thank you both for responding so promptly to my phone call.'

Leo Vessovski grunted. 'You made it sound as if the Kremlin itself was about to be attacked!'

Kolov ignored the colonel's sarcasm. 'Comrade Colonel, I particularly wanted you to be present at this meeting. Oleg Aristov and I may need the services of your SMERSH agents sooner than we anticipated.'

Aristov leaned forward anxiously, his short stocky figure and grey close-cropped hair contrasting with the portly stature and gross baldness of the colonel.

'What's gone wrong Vassily?'

Kolov shook his head wearily. 'I had a telephone call late last night from our man in the Diamond Syndicate's Russian Department. The three sorters have been dismissed.'

'How on earth did they get on to them so soon,' exclaimed Aristov in alarm. 'They could have only just made their move.'

'It seems we forgot to allow for human nature in our plan—the word is they stole some diamonds and were caught in the act by the Syndicate's television scanners.'

Colonel Vessovski scowled at the two men in disgust. 'This is what happens when you civilians are allowed to hatch a plot. You should have let me handle the three of them—they would have been too scared then to even think of deviating from their instructions.'

'It's all very well being wise after the event, Leo,' objected Kolov. 'You should have voiced your criticisms at the beginning when you were co-opted into our scheme.'

Aristov held up his hands in an effort to calm his companions.

'Let's not overreact to this setback. We'll simply have to abandon the second part of phase one, and go straight into phase two. With the three sorters out of the running, it's now up to the Thailand team to put on the pressure. Hopefully you've got your men in place, Leo?'

'Yes, they're staff members of our embassy in Bangkok.'

'Well, that's fine—all you've got to do is give them the go-ahead when Vassily's department sends the next diamond shipment through in July.'

Leo Vessovski nodded. 'That's no problem, but tell me, Vassily, what's the reasoning behind using my people in Bangkok? Wouldn't it be much simpler to do the job here in the privacy of your Russalmaz offices?'

'If anything goes wrong, I want to be at arm's length from the source of the trouble.'

'So it's your own necks you're protecting—well that figures, but I think you two have overlooked something.'

Kolov raised his eyebrows in surprise. 'Is this yet another criticism?'

'What about the three dismissed sorters?' sneered Vessovski.

'You've conveniently written them off, but they're still a real threat to your plans.'

'How do you make that out?' asked Aristov.

Colonel Vessovski sighed. 'Let me instruct you in the Syndicate's security organisation. First of all, there is an overall Security Surveillance Group. Under them is the basic overt security corps comprising ten guards and the normal paraphernalia of equipment. Then there is Internal Audit which keeps a check on the movement of diamonds within the building. Serving both these sections is a small department called Special Services, whose brief is to resolve problems concerning the theft or smuggling of the Syndicate's rough diamonds both inside the building, and en route from the mines.'

'I know for a fact that if anyone is dismissed for petty thieving, the next thing to happen is a thorough investigation of that person by Special Services. Such an investigation includes bank accounts, mode of living, expensive holidays, travel patterns, and so on. Special Services is run by two young men. If I pay them the compliment of saying they are on a level with my own SMERSH agents, I'm sure you will understand my fears for the continuing secrecy of your plans.'

'You make a valid point, Leo,' admitted Aristov. 'What steps should we take to prevent our link to the three men being uncovered?'

Colonel Leo Vessovski smiled for the first time since he entered the room. It was a smile that held no warmth.

'My two London agents informed me of the dismissal of the three sorters earlier today—they have assured me it will soon cease to be a problem.'

CHAPTER 7

LONDON

Friday 26 June, 1981

The SAA flight from Johannesburg landed at London Airport thirty minutes earlier than scheduled, thanks to a strong tail wind over the first leg of its journey. By the time Paul Remington found a space in the short-stay car park and reached the arrivals hall at Terminal 1, the first passengers were already beginning to come through.

Fifteen minutes later, and fast becoming convinced he had missed his visitors, Paul finally spotted Mike and Christine Reece among the surging melée of passengers and luggage trolleys. He raised both arms and waved to them.

'Great to see you again.' He grabbed Mike's hand, and then inspected the tall ash-blonde girl at his side. 'So this is your lovely wife. We've met before of course, but sadly only during office hours—Christine showed me over the Pretoria Mine when I was last in South Africa.'

Christine blushed, her South African suntan momentarily turning a deeper shade of brown, an effect which emphasised the high cheekbones of her oval face and her cornflower blue eyes.

'Take no notice of him, Chrissy,' laughed Mike, raking his fingers through his dark curly hair. 'You'll find he's quite house-trained when you get to know him better.'

Paul sighed. 'Thanks for destroying my image pal.'

Christine leaned forward and kissed him lightly on the cheek. 'Don't worry, I've heard quite a lot about you recently, and about Stephanie.'

Paul felt a tug at his trousers, and looked down at a miniature replica of Christine. 'And what's your name little girl?'

'I'm ne'ly thwee', lisped the little blonde girl. She looked up trustingly at Paul, and offered him her hand.

Paul bent down. 'I had no idea you were so grown up,' he confided.

Christine laughed. 'You really are a lady-killer—our daughter's name is Melanie by the way.'

Paul led the three of them out of the airport building to his car. They managed to cram all the suitcases and bags into the XJ12's boot, and were soon heading down the M4 towards the centre of London. When they reached the Chiswick flyover, the car telephone buzzed. Paul picked up the handset.

'Paul, this is Steve. Where are you?' Steven's voice sounded agitated.

'I'm about twenty minutes from dropping Mike and family off at Cheyne Walk, Chelsea—what's the problem?'

'There's a bit of a flap on here. Sir James has called a meeting—he wants us both there, but I've managed to stall him till ten o'clock. Can you make it by then?'

Paul looked at his watch. 'Sure—if I'm a few minutes late, you can start by telling him about the strange antics I saw on the security video.'

He replaced the handset. 'Sorry about that, folks. It seems that Sir James is having one of his tantrums. After I've delivered you to Cheyne Walk, I'm afraid I'll have to leave you. Please make my apologies to your Aunt Muriel for not stopping to see her.'

Mike grinned at Christine. 'It's all go with these yuppies.' He turned back to Paul. 'Don't forget—Muriel's throwing a dinner party for us all tonight in her Chelsea apartment.' He handed Paul a slip of paper. 'Here's her phone number in case you're running late at the CMO.'

* * *

When Paul arrived in his office, Steven Heming was waiting for him.

'What's the panic all about, Steve?'

'Am I glad to see you. We're not due upstairs for a few minutes, so I'll fill you in.'

It was clear to Paul that something had badly rattled his young assistant. 'No problem—it's better we talk here.'

Steven took a deep breath. 'I visited Roger Black's flat in Eaton Mews, Belgravia first thing this morning. His wife came to the door in her dressing gown. I asked to see Roger, and she said he had got up early and gone out. It was then that we both became aware of the muffled sound of a car engine running in the adjoining garage.'

'Oh, my god,' groaned Paul.

'That was my reaction. Roger had locked the garage door from the inside, so I had to break it open. We found him slumped in the back seat, dead.'

'You called the police?'

'You bet. It was lucky I hadn't gone into my reporter spiel with Black's wife, so I told them I was just an office friend. As soon as I got back here I phoned Sir James with the news.'

'You didn't mention the reporter ploy to him?'

'No, I simply said I'd gone there to ask a few questions.'

'Good. There's no point in Sir James knowing more than the basics.'

Steven looked at his watch. 'We'd better get moving.'

When they entered Sir James' office, Jim Finchley, Roy Wakefield and Ken Burridge were already there. Stephanie was sitting at one side of the desk, her notepad at the ready.

Sir James acknowledged Paul and Steven's presence with a baleful glare, and continued his questioning of Ken Burridge.

'The police were quite satisfied it was suicide?'

'In view of the circumstances surrounding Black's dismissal, there's no reason for them to think otherwise.'

Sir James thought about this for a moment and then turned to Steven Heming.

'Was this your first visit to the Black household?'

'That's right Sir James.'

'It was you who telephoned the police when Black's body was discovered?' 'Yes—I used the phone in their house.'

Sir James paused for a moment. 'That means you'll be a witness at the inquest.'

'I expect so—the police have my name and address.'

'In which event I must rely on your discretion—if you can avoid mentioning the CMO, I'd be grateful. By the way, what exactly was the reason for your visit to Black's home?'

Steven glanced at Paul, and received an affirmative nod.

'I hoped to learn a little more about his background. For instance, did he go out socially with Scofield and Crosley.'

Sir James sat back and placed the tips of his fingers together. The seconds ticked by in silence.

He looked hard at Steven. 'Will you give me your word you have not contacted him in any way prior to your visit this morning.'

'Yes, sir, I give you my word.'

Sir James then turned to Paul. 'And what about you?'

'I've made no direct contact, Sir James. My investigation into the affair of the alleged stolen diamonds has got no further than the paperchase stage—a study of the men's files and a few discreet enquiries.'

'What enquiries?'

'With Steven's help, I've uncovered several interesting facts concerning all three of the men in question.'

Sir James sighed. 'You'd better tell us about it.'

'The three sorters were part of a jewellery study group that made a five-day visit to Moscow at the beginning of May. Immediately after they returned home, fifteen-thousand pounds was paid in cash into each of their bank accounts. Late last night I received a phone call from Inspector Glover of the CID—his men have found a quantity of rough diamonds hidden in each of the men's homes.'

Jim Finchley turned to Paul. 'Have you found out what the study group's itinerary was in Moscow?'

'That was easy—the travel organisation put a copy in the post to me.' Paul extracted a leaflet from his pocket. 'On day two, the group visited the Moscow offices of Russalmaz.'

Ken Burridge shook his head in amazement. 'What on earth are the Ruskies up to now. I can't see the point of them bribing our people to steal a few diamonds—in all probability including some of their own stones.'

Sir James shrugged his shoulders. 'Whatever their reason,

the plot, if that's what it was, has failed with the dismissal of the three sorters.'

Paul coughed nervously, it was becoming clear that no one in the room wanted to be the first to bring up the negative publicity that would soon be generated by Roger Black's suicide.

'With Black's death, I'm afraid it's no longer going to be possible to keep the diamond thefts out of the papers, Sir James.'

'That's of little importance now.'

Sir James turned to face Roy Wakefield. 'I want you to arrange a monthly payment to Roger Black's widow of his full-term retirement pension, starting immediately. We can't be held accountable for this unfortunate affair, but I've no wish for his wife and children to suffer from the man's weakness of character.'

'I'll have the necessary forms ready for you to sign this afternoon.' Roy glanced anxiously across at Sir James. 'May I make a suggestion in connection with the pension?'

'Of course, man—out with it.'

'I don't think it would be prudent to make public our payment of Black's pension—it might be misconstrued as "conscience" money by the gutter press'.

Sir James scowled and examined his nails. 'I suppose you're right—with our South African connections it's hardly likely that the moronic illiterates who call themselves reporters will give us an unbiased coverage. In any case they're bound to make a meal out of the present situation. Now if everyone is satisfied we've discussed all aspects of this unpleasant business, I'll call the meeting to a close.'

'Excuse me, Sir James,' interrupted Ken Burridge. 'There's one further item you should know about.' He looked quizzically at Paul who shrugged his shoulders in grudging agreement.

'On Friday, Paul drew my attention to an unusual feature on the original of the edited tape that Ken and Jim showed you two days ago. In one of the sequences, Roger Black can be seen palming a diamond. Then he puts the stone in his pocket while extracting a handkerchief.'

'Yes—what of it.'

'Well, after he wipes his nose and returns the handkerchief to his pocket something odd happens. He reaches out again with the same hand to smooth down the pile of diamonds. At this point you can see what appears to be the very same diamond lodged between two of his fingers. A second later he appears to drop the stone back on the pile.'

'I don't pretend to understand that,' snapped Sir James. 'The only fact that makes sense now is the discovery of the stolen diamonds in the homes of the three men. That is quite enough evidence for the police, and for me. Good day gentlemen, this meeting is over.'

At that moment the door burst open and Rob Scot rushed in waving an early edition of the *Evening Standard*. He held it up for all to see. Across the front page a banner headline read 'THREE DEAD IN DIAMOND MYSTERY'. Below this the leading sentence was set in bold type. 'Of three men dismissed for stealing by the Diamond Syndicate, one is found dead by suspected suicide, and two are killed in road and underground train accidents.'

* * *

When Paul and Stephanie returned to their flat early that evening, Paul poured them both a double vodka and tonic.

'That was one hell of a day,' exclaimed Stephanie, kicking off her shoes and putting her legs up on the settee. 'I can just about accept Roger Black's suicide, but for the other two to die an hour later takes a bit of stomaching.'

She tucked her feet back to make room for Paul. 'Falling under a tube train might also have been suicide, but Peter Scofield was a young unmarried man with no responsibilities—he could have rebuilt his life again, particularly as Sir James was not going to press charges.'

Paul sipped his drink thoughtfully. 'I agree. That and the hit and run driver who killed David Crosley, makes it look suspiciously like a double murder. Someone wanted all three of them out of the way before they could be questioned about the diamond thefts—Roger Black's suicide was probably a convenient bonus!'

'Well, whatever we think, it's in the hands of the police now.

One thing is certain, the whole business will be played down as much as possible. Sir James carries a lot of clout where it matters. Even the government is mindful of the five-hundred million pounds of invisible import-exports the Syndicate generates here each year.'

Stephanie stretched her long slim legs across Paul's lap. 'Now for more cheerful news—after you left for the airport this morning there was a letter in the post for me.'

Paul leaned over and kissed her. 'Not a passionate missive from one of your old boyfriends I hope?'

Stephanie ignored him. 'I didn't want to worry you about it at the time, but back in March I discovered a small lump under my right arm. It wasn't any bigger than a pea, but I had it checked by a specialist in Harley Street. He said it was probably a water-filled void, but advised me to visit the Royal Marsden Hospital for a check-up.'

Paul looked at her in alarm. 'But that's the cancer treatment centre.'

'That's right. I must admit his advice rather scared me, and for the next three months I put off going—well the lump wasn't getting any bigger. Last week I plucked up courage and made an appointment. On Monday I took the afternoon off and went along. They stuck a needle in, removed some liquid and took a tissue sample for further tests. The Royal Marsden is a truly wonderful place—with my small problem I felt quite a fraud among all those brave people under treatment. While I was there I went the whole hog and had a cervical smear and an MOT check on the boobs. The letter I received this morning reports that all the tests are negative.'

'Thank god for that—but you should have told me. It's not just the bed we share Stephanie, it's our lives too.'

'Just put it down to my independent nature, but you can understand why I've been a bit edgy with you these last few weeks.'

Paul reached out and drew her to him. He kissed her and then held her close, burying his face in her red hair.

'We're both a couple of idiots,' he murmured. 'I thought you were cooling off—you started going straight to sleep at night.'

Stephanie disentangled herself from his arms. 'Well, now you know why—and before you start taking advantage of me, I'll remind you we have a dinner party invite this evening from Mike's aged aunt in Chelsea.'

* * *

Mike Reece's aunt lived alone in a roomy third floor apartment overlooking the Thames in Cheney Walk, Chelsea. The apartment block was built in the early 1900s, and had the high ceilings and antique plumbing of the period. The lift serving the block was equally old, and Stephanie crossed her fingers behind her back as Paul slammed its trellis door shut. The numbers on the lift buttons had been worn away over the years by countless tenants and visitors. Paul punched what he guessed to be the button for the third floor. The lift jerked violently into life, wheezed its way slowly upwards and stopped equally suddenly.

Paul and Stephanie were met at the apartment door by a tall grey-haired lady wearing a colourful caftan. 'Hallo, my dears, how lovely to see you both at last—do come in.'

Mike Reece's maiden aunt Muriel was in her early eighties, and by her ample girth was clearly not into dieting. She was an enthusiastic ballet and theatre goer, and a more than competent pianist. In times more favourable than the depression of the thirties, she could well have made a name for herself in the world's concert halls.

Muriel swept her visitors through into the lounge. 'Stephanie and Paul have arrived,' she announced. 'We haven't been introduced yet, but why waste time with formalities.'

Mike laughed. 'That's OK, auntie, I've told them all about you.'

Christine lifted up her daughter. 'Melanie's ready for bed, but she insisted on waiting up to say goodnight to you both.'

The sleepy blonde child solemnly accepted a kiss from Stephanie and Paul. Then, followed by an enchanted Stephanie, Christine carried her off to bed.

Mike led Paul out though the open French windows onto the balcony. They stood for a moment leaning on the wrought iron railings and gazing at the river. Beyond the lights festooning Albert bridge was the green expanse of Battersea Park, and on the far left they could just make out the four chimneys of Battersea power station outlined against the twilight sky. As they watched, an evening pleasure launch, gay with coloured lights, came into view around the bend of the river. The sounds of music and laughter drifted across the water accompanied by the occasional white flicker of a flashlight.

Paul turned his back on the river and looked at the apartment's brightly lit lounge.

'This is quite a pad for a senior citizen.'

'Yes, Muriel has been lucky in some ways. Although we've never heard more than the bare bones of the story, it seems she was engaged to a dashing young army officer during World War One. He was killed at Ypres, but his parents continued to treat Auntie as one of the family. They asked her to come here and live with them, and when eventually they both died, she found they'd left her the apartment in their will.'

'That's quite a story, and it's great she's still active enough to enjoy the London scene—which reminds me, Steffi has managed to get you two Centre Court tickets for the men's tennis final at Wimbledon Sunday week. There's speculation that Bjorn Borg may have his five-year reign as champion ended by young John McEnroe.'

'Chrissy'll go wild about the tickets—we had hoped to catch some of the matches on television over here, but there's nothing quite like being there and taking in the atmosphere.' He winked at Paul. 'It'll more than make up for her missing the Stuttgart ballet season—that's something I'm not grieving over. Opera is more my scene. I'm hoping to see the ENO's "War and Peace" at the Coliseum.'

Muriel appeared at the French windows. 'Enough gossiping you two—dinner is served.'

When the five-course meal, consumed with the help of several bottles of wine, was over, Muriel looked pointedly at the two girls. 'Although I enjoy cooking, I'm afraid I haven't got a dish washer, so I'm open to offers.' Christine pulled a face at Mike, and got up from the table, followed by Stephanie.

Muriel beamed at them. 'How very kind of you both to volunteer. For my part, I intend moving the old bones to a comfortable chair in the hope that my handsome nephew will serve us all with coffee.'

Mike grinned at Paul, and shooed the girls off into the kitchen.

Muriel accepted her coffee from Mike, and then looked across at Paul.

'Now, what's all this nonsense in the evening paper about the death of three of your company's diamond sorters?'

'Well, Auntie Muriel,' began Paul, 'It's still a bit of a mystery.'

'Yes, I thought you'd say that.' She bent down and picked up the late edition of the Evening Standard. 'If you read between the lines, the implication is that two of the young men were probably murdered. I might just believe that if it happened anywhere else—but surely not here in England.'

Mike handed Paul his coffee. 'We'll just have to see what the police uncover.' He winked at Paul and quickly switched the conversation around to the London theatre scene.

Later that evening, Muriel decided there had been enough talk. 'Now I'm going to give you all a treat,' she announced.

Mike helped her to her feet and escorted her across to the baby grand piano in the corner of the room. She waved him back to his seat, lowered herself gingerly onto the piano stool and flexed her fingers.

Muriel sat for a few seconds with her hands poised above the keyboard. Then, to her audience's surprise, she suddenly launched herself into a vigorous rendition of Chopin's Revolutionary Etude No 12 in C minor. They hardly had time to recover before she followed this with a selection from Neil Simon's 'They're Playing Our Song'.

After her impromptu recital, Muriel swung herself round on the piano stool and acknowledged her audience's applause. 'Well, children, that's my party piece over and done with, so you can all sit back again and relax.'

Paul helped her back to her chair. 'You certainly have catholic tastes in music Auntie Muriel,' he commented. 'If only I had half your talent, and a quarter of your energy...'

'It's all this clean living,' she confided. 'There has only ever been one man in my life, and he was killed in World War One—incidentally, that was the war to end wars. In the years that followed I looked around at my married friends and what did I see? Nothing but drudgery, children and more children. There were damp nappies and washing everywhere.' Muriel wrinkled her nose in distaste. 'I decided there and then that bodily urges were all very well, but the independence of a single bed suited me far better.'

The two girls glanced at each other and raised their eyebrows in wry amusement.

Muriel turned to Stephanie. 'Now you're a girl after my own heart. Although I'm no longer prepared to give up my home or my lifestyle for any man, I don't object to you young people living together when you feel the need. What I can't stand are the prissy girls who say they would never have sex before marriage—some of them might be lucky to get it afterwards! I hope your parents, Stephanie, are as broad-minded as I am.'

Stephanie grimaced. 'To tell the truth, Muriel, neither my folks nor Paul's are very pleased with our unmarried state. My own father is a retired regular army officer, and doesn't get on with Paul, partly because of his SAS background. As a result we don't see much of either set of parents.'

'That's a shame, dear. One of these days you'll have to invite all of them here to my place. On neutral ground, perhaps I could persuade them to change their minds.'

Mike caught Paul's eye and got to his feet. 'Well, auntie, we've all had an absolutely lovely evening, but I think it's high time we let our guests go home to bed—it's been a very long day for all of us.'

Muriel sniffed. 'Oh, very well, but only on condition that Stephanie and Paul visit me again—I'd like to have a real heart-to-heart with both of them.'

* * *

When Paul and Stephanie left Cheyne walk, they strolled hand-in hand to the King's Road and hailed a taxi. With little traffic about they were back at their flat in Prince Albert Road within ten minutes.

'Wow, wasn't that some performance of Muriel's,' exclaimed Stephanie.

Paul chuckled. 'Mike warned me his aunt was a little eccentric.'

'I think she's a darling,' Stephanie countered, 'and can she play the joanna—but there's one thing I've been wanting to ask you all evening.'

'What's that?'

'Muriel speaks beautifully, but I can hear a distinct trace of cockney accent in Mike's speech.'

Paul grinned. 'It's quite simple. Mike's father, Muriel's brother, was something of a rough diamond. He ran a scrap metal business in the East End of London. Before he made good and bought a place in the country, he sent Mike to school in Hackney.'

'Is the father still alive?'

'No, he died last year. Mike's mother sold their house in Kent and moved to a retirement home near Leicester. Mike had hoped she would settle down in London with Muriel, but sadly the two of them don't get on together. Incidentally, what did you think of little Melanie?'

'That child is just adorable—perhaps I'll get a chance to see her again before they return to South Africa.'

'You're not going broody on me are you?'

'No way! Auntie Muriel said it all this evening—marriage, babies and nappies are not my scene.'

'Well, you know my views on that. Now what would you say to a nightcap?'

'No thanks—I've got something far more stimulating in mind.'

When Paul walked into the bedroom he found it bathed in the light of a crescent moon. He was about to turn on his bedside lamp, but hesitated and decided to undress in the semi-dark. Stephanie was already in the en-suite bathroom humming one of the tunes from the musical that Muriel had played that evening. Paul stretched out on the large double bed and let his mind wander over the events of the day. The weather had slowly improved from the torrential rain of two days ago, and the evening was warm and calm. Looking up he could see the lace-like tracery of the Regent Park trees swaying gently in the night wind.

Stephanie tiptoed silently into the bedroom and stood naked beside the bed, the moonlight caressing her ivory breasts and throwing a halo around her mass of red hair. Paul sensed her presence and looked up.

'Aren't you going to invite me in?' she whispered.

Paul drew back the duvet and beckoned her.

'Oh, my,' she said, glancing down, 'who's the eager one then?'

'Time for actions, not words,' he murmured.

Stephanie climbed into bed and knelt over him. He reached up and pulled her down alongside him delighting in the soft pressure of her contours as their bodies met. They kissed, and then she inched her head slowly downwards, teasing his nipples with her lips and nuzzling the hair on his chest. He felt her warm breath on his stomach, and thrilled to the caress of her tongue. Suddenly her mood changed, and trembling with an urgent passion she sat up again and straddled him with her legs. He cupped her pendant breasts in his hands, delighting in their firm contours. Stephanie closed her eyes in ecstasy and dug her nails into his flesh as her nipples responded to the caress of his fingertips. Then, gripping tightly with her knees, she pushed down fiercely and took him into her. As always with Stephanie, the ride was hard and wild and swift, as if some demon was driving her to fulfilment. Then it was all over, and she lay panting beside him.

While just being near her never failed to arouse Paul, the sudden intensity of her passion had often alarmed him. Quite early on he had realised that Stephanie was only using him. There was little tenderness in their love-making, and she was equally capable of switching off and losing interest. When they first started living together, he had revelled in her aggressive sexual appetite, but now it was slowly beginning to destroy their relationship.

Long after Stephanie had fallen asleep, Paul lay awake at her side. They had not made love like that for several weeks now, and he had half hoped the lull would have brought about the flowering of a more tender bond between them.

CHAPTER 8

BANGKOK

Friday 3 July, 1981

Thailand's tropical monsoon climate ranges from a dry and just tolerable 20 to 30 degrees C during the European winter, to a humid and rainy 30 to 34 degrees during the rest of the year. The capital Bangkok sits amid a flat expanse of paddy fields on a bend of the Chao Phya river close to where it flows south into the Gulf of Thailand. Inhabitants of the city still call it by the ancient name Krungthep ('City of Angels'), although, like Los Angeles, this title could be considered an exaggeration in modern times.

The city's three principal canals, fed by the waters of the river, curve through its central and western sections, the western waterways harbouring the ever changing kaleidoscopic spectacle of the Floating Market. Smaller side canals, accessible only by shallow-draught vessels such as the 'long-tailed' tourist boats, are fronted on each side with jostling rows of crumbling stilt houses, which serve as homes for some of Bangkok's five million inhabitants. In a city of contrasts, these homes and those of the boat people lie within a few hundred yards of skyscrapers, luxurious modern hotels and the exotic golden temples of Bangkok's Grand Palace.

On this particular morning in early July, the badly drained streets in the outlying suburbs of Bangkok had been made impassable by flood waters brought on by an overnight deluge. The traffic in the centre of the city, which at best moved at a snail's pace, had been brought to a standstill amid a haze of diesel and petrol exhaust fumes.

Sergei Menakov and his assistant Andrei Bolkovski shared a house in the northern outskirts of the city, and had already spent a frustrating hour in their official car that morning attempting to find alternative routes to the Soviet Embassy. This, together with the British, American and New Zealand embassies, was located in the diplomatic enclave surrounding Wireless Road in the eastern sector of the city. The two burly Russians were officially accredited to the embassy as commercial attachés, but in reality were SMERSH agents drawn from the vast pool of operatives and enforcers under the overall command of Colonel Leo Vessovski, head of the KGB.

When the Russian agents finally arrived at the embassy and entered their office on the second floor, Sergei found a note on his desk summoning him to the Ambassador's much grander room on the ground floor.

The Russian Ambassador, Nicoli Benesh, a thick-set elderly man with greying hair and a neat goatee beard, removed his half-frame glasses as Sergei entered the room and dismissed his secretary with a curt nod.

'So you've got here at last, Sergei.'

'The roads are even worse this morning, comrade ambassador.'

Nicoli Benesh grunted and pointed at the large cardboard box sitting on a side table.

'That arrived for you in the diplomatic bag this morning.'

He flicked through the pile of correspondence on his desk, and found an envelope marked 'Strictly Confidential' and embossed with the KGB seal.

'This was also addressed to you—it arrived with the box.'

Sergei took the letter and made to open it.

The ambassador scowled at him. 'I'd rather you did that somewhere else. The less I know about your activities here, the better I'll sleep at night, so please take the box and the letter to your own office.'

'As you wish ambassador. But I hasten to assure you our services to the state are always carried out with the utmost discretion.'

Nicoli Benesh sniffed derisively and began opening his mail.

Back in his office, Sergei dumped the heavy cardboard box on the floor. Then he opened the letter and checked its contents. He turned to Andrei. 'The Moscow diamond shipment arrives in Bangkok today.'

Andrei grunted and walked across to the cardboard box. He bent down, pulled up his right trouser leg and withdrew a sheath-knife from the holster strapped to his leg. It took him several minutes to cut through the adhesive tape and plastic straps that sealed the box. When it was finally opened, Sergei joined him and inspected the contents. Inside the box were four white linen bags, each one tied with a draw string which in turn was secured with a metal seal.

Sergei pulled one of the bags out of the box. He took Andrei's knife, cut through the drawstring and tipped some of the bag's contents onto the desktop.

'If only these were the real thing...' he murmured, and prodded the pile of synthetic spinel crystals that lay glistening on the desk.

Andrei checked the labels attached to the bags. 'They're all in the one to two carat range.' He removed a small battery-powered electronic balance from the box. 'I'll start weighing them out into smaller batches.'

Sergei nodded. 'That's the one messy part of this exercise. When we substitute these for the same size stones in the Moscow shipment, it's vital we remove exactly the same weight of diamonds.'

Andrei bent down, switched on the balance and tested it with a handful of the synthetic crystals. He looked up at Sergei. 'The other thing that worries me is breaking into the Silom Road premises of ThaiExport at night.'

'Well, we could hardly walk in during office hours and demand to inspect the Russian shipment.' Sergei snapped. 'The delicate part of the operation is not the break-in itself, but having to leave a clue behind to indicate that the shipment has been interfered with. It's got to be small enough to escape detection by ThaiExport when they forward the shipment to London, but just obvious enough to register with the CMO if there's trouble.'

'Doesn't that rather defeat the whole exercise?'

Sergei looked pityingly at his assistant. 'No, you idiot. Should things go wrong, and the Diamond Syndicate in London discovers the substitute stones before they're sold at the Sights, this will serve to protect Russalmaz from any suspicion that the stones were switched in Moscow.'

He delved into the box and brought out a transparent plastic bag containing metal seals and a pair of crimping pliers.

'After we've substituted the spinels for the diamonds, we'll re-seal the cases using these. The seals that Russalmaz use are embossed with their insignia—these ones are plain. That's the insurance Kolov requested.'

The rest of the day was spent in breaking up the thousands of spinel crystals into weighed and labelled bags of five-hundred stones each. This would ease the task of blending the spinels into the Moscow shipment that night.

Over the preceding weeks Sergei had laid the foundations for the night's work by checking out each of the employees in the ThaiExport company. He discovered that one of the men had a girlfriend called Lea Kanowan who worked in the Sheherezade establishment, a popular massage parlour in Sukhumvit Soi Street. He visited the establishment several times and selected Lea on each occasion, gaining her confidence with over-generous tipping. Through the girl he managed to bribe her ThaiExport boyfriend, Cahn, to provide them with duplicates of the company's office keys and to pass on details of the company's security arrangements including the combination of the main safe.

* * *

At one o'clock the next morning, armed with a case of equipment and the bags of crystals, Sergei and Andrei drove out of the Soviet Embassy compound in their Lada, and headed south down Wireless Road. Sergei made a right turn into Rama IV Road, and then swung left into Silom Road. At this time of night the west end of Silom Road was nearly deserted, unlike the nightclub and stripshow quarter around Pat Pong street at its eastern end which was still seething with activity.

ThaiExport was on the seventh floor of the Rama Jewelry Building in Silom Road. As he approached the building, Sergei pulled up at the kerbside and checked the road on both sides for patrolling beige-uniformed police. When he was satisfied the coast was clear, he drove slowly into an alleyway at the side of the Rama block and turned off the car's lights.

Sergei motioned Andrei to stay put, and got out of the car. He strolled casually across to the building's steel sidedoor and inserted one of the duplicate keys into the lock. He turned the key and simultaneously pulled at the handle. The door creaked open. It was then he heard someone shouting and the sounds of running feet. He slipped into the darkened building and pulled the door half closed behind him. Through the open gap of the door he could see his car, but no sign of Andrei. More alarming, he could see two men running towards him. He felt in his pocket for his revolver and eased off the safety catch.

The running feet and shouting got nearer. He squinted through the door and aimed his gun at the leading figure. Just as he was about to squeeze the trigger, the man ran past the door hotly pursued by a policeman blowing his whistle. Sergei took a deep breath and put his gun away. When the sound of the whistle had died away he looked out again and checked the alleyway. A head re-appeared in the car, and Sergei beckoned his assistant to join him.

Andrei sprinted across the alleyway and dumped four bags of crystals and two torches at his boss's feet. 'That's quite enough excitement for me tonight,' he gasped.

'Save your breath and get the rest of the gear out of the car,' snapped Sergei. 'We're going in by the emergency stairs—ThaiExport are seven floors up.'

When they finally reached the top floor, Sergei shone the beam of his torch on ThaiExport's rear door. He had been warned about the company's alarm system, and had brought along a small powerful magnet. He placed the magnet on the floor and pulled a pen-sized magnetometer from his breast pocket. Andrei took the instrument from him, and moved it slowly around the edge of the door. When he reached the top right-hand corner, the instrument emitted a high pitch bleep. He moved it a few inches each way. The pitch rose and fell indicating the position and polarity of the concealed magnet holding the alarm switch closed on the far side of the door. Sergei marked the place on the door frame, picked up his own magnet and turned it to match the polarity of the concealed one. Then he positioned it over the mark and secured it to the door with adhesive tape. He inserted the second key in the lock, gingerly opened the door and listened. The building's alarm system remained silent.

Sergei picked up the bags of crystals and waved Andrei inside. He had been advised by Cahn that there was an ultrasonic movement detector protecting the safe in the inner office. The detector's control unit was hidden in a drawer of a desk near to the safe and had to be switched off within ten seconds of entering the room to prevent the alarm from operating. Sergei handed the bags to Andrei and shone his torch through the partition window. In its beam he could see the safe and the desk against the far wall. Motioning Andrei to stay put, he pushed the inner office door open and moved swiftly across to the desk. It had four drawers. He pulled out three of them before locating the control unit in the fourth. Sergei grunted with relief and flipped the unit's control switch to off. He pulled out a handkerchief and wiped the sweat from the palms of his hands.

Andrei was still hovering in the doorway holding the bags of spinel, and looking as if he was ready to make a quick exit if things went wrong. Sergei beckoned him in impatiently.

'Put the bags on the desk, but keep clear of the safe.'

Sergei had also been warned of a pressure mat located under the carpet in front of the safe. He found a wooden bench at the rear of the office, and with Andrei's help used it to straddle the carpet over the alarmed area. Andrei knelt on the bench and dialled in the sequence of numbers given them by Cahn. Then he stepped carefully to one side, swung the heavy door open and shone his torch inside. Its beam revealed a stack of thirty metal cases, each one fastened by a wire with a metal seal attached.

Sergei checked the labels on the cases and selected the six containing diamonds in the 1 to 2 carat range. Then they set to work. Taking one case at a time, Andrei scooped out a quantity of diamonds, carefully weighed them, and placed them in one of the empty linen bags. Next he emptied one of the pre-weighed bags of spinel crystals onto the balance and adjusted the quantity of crystals until they matched the weight of the removed diamonds. Finally he tipped the weight-adjusted spinels into the metal case and stirred them in with the remaining diamonds. Sergei took each case as Andrei finished with it, wired it closed again and crimped one of the plain metal seals, the tell-tale clue requested by Russalmaz, over the ends of the wire.

It was four o'clock in the morning before they completed the substitutions and returned all the metal cases to the safe. They moved the bench back where Sergei had found it, gathered up their equipment and the linen bags, now containing thousands of diamonds, and began retracing their steps. Sergei re-activated the movement detector in the inner office and swiftly exited into the outer office, taking care to close the door behind him within the ten second reset period. As they left the ThaiExport offices, Andrei carefully closed and locked the rear door, and removed his magnet.

When they reached their car, Sergei looked at his colleague and patted the heavy bags of diamonds. 'Not a bad night's work,' he grinned.

They loaded the equipment and the diamonds into the boot and locked it. Sergei started the car and drove back into the Silom Road. When they reached the Embassy, he switched off the headlights and waited while Andrei unlocked the wrought-iron security gates. After the car was safely parked inside the compound, the two men carried the bags of diamonds into the building.

Back in his office, Sergei slammed shut the door of the safe. He looked thoughtfully at Andrei, weighing up the dangers of the audacious plan that had begun to form in his mind during the drive back to the Embassy.

'Have you any idea of the value of those diamonds?'

Andrei was busy making coffee. He turned and scratched his head.

'Not really—it must be millions of roubles.'

'I prefer to think in American dollars—what would you say to a nice round figure of five million?'

Andrei handed him a mug of coffee. 'What are you getting at?'

Sergei remained silent for a few seconds, turning the plan

over in his mind. If it was to have any chance of success, he would need an accomplice. Next month, the Phase 3 interference with the shipment from Moscow would involve the substitution of twice that amount of diamonds. Finally he made up his mind—he would just have to trust his colleague.

'Comrade Andrei, let me make you a proposition.'

CHAPTER 9

LONDON

Sunday July 5, 1981

Christine and Mike left Muriel's Cheyne Walk flat at one o'clock, strolled to Sloane Square, and caught the District Line Wimbledon train. They got out at Southfields, as did the majority of their fellow passengers, and followed the crowds along Wimbledon Park and Church road to the famous grounds of the All England Lawn Tennis Club.

The Centre Court seats they had been given by Stephanie were four rows from the front on the north side of the court. Although it was a hot day, Christine, who was missing the South African temperatures, was glad to be sitting in the sun. Her slim tanned figure, enhanced by a crisp white linen blouse and a white box-pleated skirt, attracted admiring glances from several men as she and Mike squeezed past them to their seats. Mike, elegant in cream slacks and shirt, noted the interest with amusement. 'I think you've made a hit with the natives.'

Christine blushed and put on her sunglasses. She looked excitedly around the stadium, which was fast filling up. 'It looks much smaller than I imagined,' she commented.

Mike peered up at the rows of terraced seats. 'When we watch the matches on TV, it's the court that's mainly in view—sitting here surrounded by seats makes it feel almost claustrophobic.'

Christine glanced across at the stadium clock. It was only fifteen minutes to the start of the men's final, and already the buzz of conversation around the centre court was growing louder in the excitement preceding the climax to Wimbledon's prestigious two-week annual event.

'I just hope Borg wins again—I can't stand McEnroe and his tantrums.'

Mike chuckled. 'But that's all part of the entertainment. You must admit John's an inspired player.'

'Maybe, but Bjorn has won Wimbledon five years running. Last year's final against McEnroe was a real cliff-hanger. I'll always remember the picture of Bjorn going down on his knees after he'd won.'

'Sure, but don't forget the thrashing he got from McEnroe in the US Open...'

Mike broke off and stared at a man who had just sat down at the end of their row. 'Good heavens—that's Peter Caveney. I was at Imperial College with him in my student days—we shared rooms together.'

Mike stood up and waved at the man. Peter Caveney's face lit up in a broad grin of recognition. He cupped his hands to his mouth. 'See you afterwards,' he shouted.

At that moment the centre court erupted in a roar as Bjorn Borg and John McEnroe entered the arena. In keeping with tradition, the groundsman followed them carrying their bags. The Umpire then summoned the players to the net and spun a coin. Borg won the toss and elected to serve first. During the five-minute knock-up, the buzz of conversation around the court slowly swelled in volume. Just short of two o'clock, the Umpire looked at his watch and called 'Two minutes', and then, after what seemed an age, 'Time'. When both players were in position, and the crowd had quietened, he called 'Borg to serve. First set. Play', and the match began.

Borg's artistry as a top-spin server won him the first set 6-4, much to Christine's and the bulk of the crowd's relief. In the next set, McEnroe took Borg to break-point eight times in four service games, finally breaking even by winning the set 7-6 in a nail biting tie-break.

During the wild applause for both players, Mike turned to Christine. 'Tie-breaks were only introduced last year. The aim was to shorten long drawn-out sets, but they've actually made evenly-matched contests more exciting.'

McEnroe won the third set 7-6 in yet another tie-break. Although used to Borg being at a disadvantage in the early stages of a match, his supporters were now beginning to get edgy. In the fourth set, McEnroe managed to break Borg's serve once again. As he won the last point to win the match at 6-4, and gain his first Wimbledon Championship title, McEnroe threw his racket in the air and raised both arms in triumph, a gesture ecstatically copied by all of his supporters. Even Christine, in company with the majority of Bjorg's fans, found herself applauding the McEnroe triumph.

After the presentation ceremony of the Wimbledon Cup, Christine and Mike met up with Peter Caveney and moved out of the centre court. Mike introduced Christine to his friend and they chatted about the match while queuing for service in the cafeteria compound. Then they found an empty table in the sun and sat down to helpings of strawberries and cream.

Mike pointed his spoon at Peter Caveney. 'This is the character who once threw all my socks out the window of our digs.'

Peter nodded. 'We were so hard up we shared our clothes, but I drew the line at his atrocious taste in socks.'

Christine laughed. 'Things have improved a little since I took him over.'

Peter smiled at Christine. 'I had no idea Mike was married. The last time he bothered to write, he was working for the Pretoria Mining Company in South Africa.'

Mike took Christine's hand. 'I still am—that's where I met Christine, and eventually married her. Now we're on a holiday in the UK with our two-year old daughter.'

Peter sat back and looked at both of them. 'Well, I must say you're looking very well on it—congratulations.' Then he frowned. 'I seem to remember there was a bit of a rumpus some years back at the Pretoria—didn't a bunch of mercenaries try to blow up the mine?'

Christine glanced at Mike and looked embarrassed. 'As you're an old friend of Mike's, I don't mind you knowing. It's no secret there was a plot to hold the mine to ransom. After the bomb was found, it became clear my late husband was involved in the affair—in the showdown at the mine he was killed by one of the mercenaries who had been hired to plant the bomb.'

Now it was Peter's turn to be embarrassed. 'Sorry, I didn't mean to pry.' He turned to Christine. 'Anyway, I'm very glad you and Mike got together—you're obviously very happy, and I hope we can all meet up again before you go back to South Africa.'

Mike smiled at his former room mate. 'Tomorrow we're visiting my mother near Leicester. Then on Friday we're off on a three-week tour of Germany, Switzerland and Austria. Give me your phone number—I'll call you when we get back.'

As they said their farewells, Christine shook hands with Peter. 'I'm pleased we've met at last. Next time you must tell me all about Mike's shady past. Right now we're looking forward to a nice quiet few weeks away from the unrest and troubles of South Africa.'

CHAPTER 10

ANTWERP

Monday 6 July, 1981

Belgium, India, Israel, South Africa and the USA, rank as the main diamond polishing nations of the world. Among these countries, Belgium has historically been the most important, its ancient city of Antwerp, spread along the banks of the river Schelde at the start of its journey westwards to Ghent, forming Europe's largest diamond centre. In addition to its diamond polishing industry, the city has four gemstone exchanges which handle the marketing of all types of diamond, from the gem and industrial quality rough stones to the polished end product.

In Antwerp's larger diamond cutting establishments, the work of producing a polished gem from the rough stone is divided between at least six specialists. First of all, the designer inspects the stone and marks it with Indian ink to show were it can be most profitably sawn or cleaved. The stone is then given to the cleaver and the sawyer whose task it is to divide the stone up, and remove any near-surface flaws.

The results of their work are then passed to the bruter who fashions the rounded, or sometimes fancy-shaped, profile of the gem. Finally, the faceting operations are performed by two experts, the cross-worker and the brillianteerer. These are specialists who grind and polish the crown and pavilion facets on the stone to reveal the diamond's unique qualities of brilliance and fire.

Although Antwerp's main diamond polishing shops are concentrated in its outlying areas, some of the smaller ones are located within the city itself. In these more compact and often family-based firms, the cutting operations are shared between members of a smaller team, the sawyer also acting as cleaver, and just one man performing the grinding as well as the polishing operations on the diamond's facets.

One such firm had its workshop in Pelikaanstraat in a building opposite the main railway station. Jean-Paul van Rensen, the son of the owner, had spent several years learning the craft of diamond faceting as an apprentice in the polishing shops of his father's friends, and was now principal diamond cutter in the family firm.

When Jean-Paul arrived at the workshop that morning he greeted and shook hands with all the staff, a daily routine not to be missed without causing offence. Then he discarded his coat, shirt and trousers and changed into the working clothes he and his colleagues kept in the outer office—a necessary precaution against the damage done to fabrics by their exposure to the diamond dust generated in the sawing and polishing operations.

He was just about to continue blocking-in the first sequence of facets on a two-carat diamond he had begun polishing the previous day, when a shout from the firm's sawyer made him look up in surprise.

The sawyer was an old man with gaunt cheeks and a heavily furrowed forehead who had worked for Jean-Paul's father for over forty years.

'Take a look at this, Jean-Paul.' The man held up a small colourless rough crystal which was secured in a metal dop-holder. 'It's only been on the saw blade for fifteen minutes and the cut is almost completely through.'

Jean-Paul walked across to the bank of six sawing machines and took the stone and its holder from the old man.

'But that's not possible, this is a three-carater—it would take two or more days to complete the cut.'

He looked up at the sawyer. 'Are you sure you didn't start work on it last week?'

The old man snatched the stone back from him. 'I'm not getting senile if that's what you mean!'

'OK, I'm sorry I doubted you. Take the stone out of the dop and let me test it on my skaife.'

A *skaife* is a heavy cast-iron disk used for polishing the facets on a diamond. Loaded with a mixture of diamond dust and oil, it is the diamond polisher's counterpart of the smaller rotary plate used by the lapidary to polish other gemstones.

Jean Paul removed the two-carat diamond from his polishing bench and clamped the suspect stone in the holder of one of the wood and metal saddle-shaped tangs lying around the working top of the rotating skaife. Holding the tang in his hand, he gently lowered the edge of the stone onto the diamond-dust coated surface of the rotating disk. As soon as it came into contact with the disk the stone made an unusual sound. Bruters, sawyers and polishers get used to the 'note' played by the diamonds they work on. By listening to the pitch and harmonics of the sound, they can detect if the cutting operation is going smoothly, or if there is trouble.

Jean Paul snatched up the offending crystal before it could damage the surface of his skaife, and looked at it in surprise. During the few seconds the stone had been in contact with the disk, its edge had been polished away, and in its place was a large flat facet.

'One thing's for sure,' he exclaimed, 'this is far too soft to be a diamond.'

He walked across the shop and pushed open the door of his father's office. 'We've got a problem—one of the three-caraters in the Syndicate's box from the June Sight is definitely not a diamond.'

* * *

It is fairly easy to prove that a crystal is or is not a diamond. Diamond is the only natural gem material that can scratch corundum, the mineral of which ruby and sapphire are the two well-known gemstone varieties. Fortunately, synthetic corundum is plentiful and cheap, and most diamond workers and gemmologists have a scratchplate of this material in their armoury of test instruments. Because of the simplicity of the test, the scratchplate is often used in preference to the more sophisticated and expensive thermal tester employed by jewellers to distinguish polished diamonds from imitations.

That afternoon, Jean-Paul, watched by his father, used his

synthetic corundum scratchplate to carry out tests on all of the stones that had been purchased at the June Sight. All but four of the stones made a small clearly defined scratch on the plate. Of the four that made no impression, one was the three-carater that had alerted their attention, two were around three and a half carats in weight, and the largest was just under four carats.

Jean-Paul's father frowned and looked at his watch. 'I'd better contact Jim Finchley at the CMO—nothing like this has ever happened in my thirty years as Sight Holder.' He pulled the telephone towards him and began dialling a number.

* * *

In several of the larger diamond polishing companies in Antwerp, Tel Aviv and New York, and in one establishment on the South Coast of England, similar scenes were being enacted as diamond sawyers and polishers found stones in their 2 to 4 carat allocation that behaved strangely on their machines.

CHAPTER 11

LONDON

Monday 6 July, 1981

Due to renovation work, the Westminster Coroner's Court had been transferred temporarily to the magistrates court housed within Westminster Guildhall on the west side of Parliament Square. The Guildhall is an impressive edifice, and although dwarfed by its massive neighbour, Westminster Abbey, the extensive carvings which decorate its white-stone tower and frontage occasionally catch the eye of American tourists as they seek out the nearby statue of Abraham Lincoln.

Inside No 1 Criminal Court, the public gallery was crammed to capacity with a mixture of tourists and the morbidly curious. Inquests are normally dull sad affairs dealing with sudden, violent, or unnatural deaths, and are of interest only to the friends and relatives of the deceased. But today, was different. The coroner was presiding over inquests into the almost simultaneous deaths of three men, all employees of the Diamond Syndicate's Central Marketing Organisation. The inquest into Roger Black's death was under the jurisdiction of the Westminster Coroner's Court, but because of the common link, permission had been sought and granted to hold the inquests of the other two men, who had died within the City of London boundary, in the same court.

Steven Heming had been summoned as a witness in the first case, which concerned the death of Roger Black. The police sergeant who arrived at the Black's flat in response to Steven's phone call early on the morning of Friday 26 June was also present, and was the first to enter the dock and give evidence.

Reading from his notebook, the sergeant related the circumstances surrounding his visit to Black's home.

'Following Mr Heming's telephone call, Constable Powell and

I drove to Mr Roger Black's flat in Eaton Mews, Belgravia. When I arrived at nine fifteen am, I found Mr Heming standing in front of an adjoining lockup garage. The garage door had been forced open by Mr Heming. The interior of the garage was still filled with exhaust fumes, and I found Mr Black in his pyjamas lying across the back seat of a green Rover saloon. I checked the man's pulse and concluded he was dead.'

The coroner looked up from his notes. 'I take it someone had turned off the car's engine by the time you arrived?'

'Yes, sir, Mr Heming switched off the ignition immediately after he forced an entry.'

'Had an ambulance been summoned?'

'Mr Heming requested both an ambulance and the police when he made the 999 call. The ambulance arrived shortly after I had checked out the garage. When it returned to St George's hospital at Hyde Park Corner, Mr Black was logged as dead on arrival.'

It was Steven's turn then to enter the dock and give evidence.

The coroner consulted his notes again. 'I understand from your statement to the police that you were a colleague of the deceased.'

'That's right, sir, we were both employed by the same company.'

'I believe Mr Black had recently been summarily dismissed from his position with the Diamond Syndicate.'

Steven heard a murmur of subdued conversation sweep around the crowded public section of the court.

'That's correct.'

'What was the purpose of your visit that morning?'

Steven flushed. 'I wanted to make sure he and his wife were OK.'

'Was this your first visit since Black's dismissal two days earlier?'

'Yes it was.'

'So you had no idea of his state of mind—you hadn't spoken to him on the telephone for instance.'

'No, I had no suspicion, nor had his wife apparently, that he was taking his situation quite so badly.'

The coroner sniffed disapprovingly. 'Yet he was without a job, and the Diamond Syndicate had called in his company mortgage.'

Steven remained silent amid a growing swell of conversation, some of it angry, from the body of the court.

The coroner dismissed Steven, and then called on Black's widow to give evidence. Dressed in a dark grey suit, and never far from tears, she made a forlorn figure in the witness dock.

The coroner adopted a kindlier tone. 'I know this must be very distressing for you, Mrs Black, so I'll keep my questions to a minimum. Can you describe your husband's state of mind over the last two days?'

'He was naturally very upset by what had happened.'

'Did he seem noticeably depressed the evening before his death.'

'We were trying to sort out our finances..,' her voice broke, and she put her hand on the rail of the dock to steady herself.

'Take your time, my dear.'

'We were making plans to move in with his parents for a bit. Then we had a drink to cheer ourselves up. We watched some television, and then went to bed around midnight.'

'Were you aware that your husband got up early the next morning.' The woman shut her eyes and nodded. 'Yes, I vaguely remember him getting out of bed —I think he said he was going to write some letters. I must have fallen asleep again. The next thing I remember was being woken up by the door chimes.'

'Would that be when Mr Heming called?'

'That's right.'

'Your husband said he was going to write some letters—were any found?'

The woman sobbed and shook her head.

'Thank you, my dear, that will be all.'

The coroner looked up at the courtroom clock, and nodded to his clerk. 'Having heard all the evidence concerning the death of Roger Black of Eaton Mews, Belgravia in the City of Westminster, I can see no recourse but to bring in a verdict of suicide while of unsound mind.'

As Mrs Black left the witness dock, a man in the back row stood up and pointed at Steven.

'I hope the Syndicate is satisfied with their pound of flesh,' he shouted. 'I hold them directly responsible for my son's death.'

The man joined his weeping daughter-in-law and escorted her out of the courtroom amid loud cries of 'South African murderers' from a small vociferous section of the public. Two of them had smuggled in a paper banner which they now held up. It carried the message 'DIAMOND SYNDICATE—OUT'.

Two of the policemen guarding the entrance doors to the court rushed forward and began forcibly ejecting the troublemakers from the room. When order had at last been restored, the coroner started taking evidence in the case of Peter Scofield who had fallen under a train in St Pauls underground station. In both this case and that of David Crosley, who was killed only a few hundred yards away by a hit-and-run driver, he returned an open verdict and adjourned the two inquests until further police evidence was forthcoming.

When Steven emerged from the Guildhall into the bright sunshine of Parliament Square, he was startled to see a group of some fifty students milling around the pavement outside the entrance, and waving banners. One of the protesters was a young bearded man who appeared to be orchestrating the group. He carried a poster displaying the message 'BAN THE TRADE IN APARTHEID DIAMONDS'. The man recognised Steven and grabbed his arm. 'Your bosses are responsible for the deaths of three men—what are you going to do about it?'

Steven grasped the man's hand in a wrestling lock and forced him to the ground. He picked up the fallen poster and ripped it in two.

'If you lay a hand on me again buster, I'll re-arrange your face for a start.'

Steven pushed his way though the crowd and hailed a passing taxi.

'Manorhouse Street, as fast as you can.'

When the taxi turned into the road leading to the Syndicate's building, Steven could see another group of placard-waving protesters surrounding the entrance. Someone had sprayed

'South African Apartheid—Out' along the entrance's white marble facade. He paid off the taxi, jumped out and ran down the entrance ramp to the underground car park. When he finally emerged from the lift on the ground floor, the foyer appeared to be in a state of siege.

The security man at his post behind the reception desk looked up in alarm as Steven approached him.

'Thank God it's you, sir—for a moment I though they'd got in the back way.' He pointed to the glass entrance doors. 'I locked those early on.'

Steven glanced at the angry mob outside. 'Have you phoned the police?'

'Yes, they're on their way.'

'If anyone wants me, I'll be with Paul Remington.' He moved swiftly across to the main lift.

Paul was talking on the internal phone when Steven entered the office.

'Yes, Sir James, he's just walked in the office...Right, we'll come up straight away.'

Steven looked quizzically at his boss. 'I would have thought he'd got used to these protests by now.'

Paul shook his head. 'No, there's more to it than the usual anti-apartheid rentamob from outside South Africa House. We'd better move—I'll fill you in on the way.'

When they reached the third floor they caught up with Ken Burridge and Jim Finchley who had also been summoned to Sir James' office.

Paul fell into step beside Jim. 'When did the phone calls start?'

'About an hour ago. I warned Sir James, but we stalled the meeting until I was sure of the extent of the problem.'

Sir James looked up as they entered his office and waved them to the row of chairs lined up in front of his desk. 'First of all, I think we should hear from Steven on the outcome of the inquests,' he said. 'Then we can discuss this more recent development.'

Steven cleared his throat nervously. 'It certainly wasn't good publicity for the company. The court was packed, and feelings began to run high early on. By the time Mrs Black had given her evidence, and the coroner delivered his verdict of suicide, it was obvious there was a faction in the courtroom that was going to cause trouble.'

Steven gestured towards the open window through which they could hear slogans being shouted by the crowd below.

'Several people, no doubt part of that group outside, were ejected from the court before the coroner could proceed with the inquests on the deaths of Scofield and Crosley. Because of inconclusive evidence from the eyewitnesses, he entered an open verdict on both men, and then adjourned the inquest to allow the police time to complete their investigations. By the time I'd fought my way out of the court, the entrance was surrounded by groups of protesters. The ringleader gave me a mouthful, but it wasn't what he said that surprised me, it was his accent—he was a Russian.'

Sir James sat back and pressed the tips of his long elegant fingers together. 'Now that is interesting. Everything that has happened recently seems to involve our friends from the USSR.' He turned to Jim Finchley. 'Let's have your update on the phone call situation.'

Jim's hands fluttered anxiously over his sheaf of notes.

'So far I've had a total of fifteen calls from our Sight Holders,' he began. 'The first one was from Hendriks of Brighton. He complained that four of the two-caraters in his box were not diamond—he thought they might be colourless topaz crystals, but he wasn't sure. Then more calls started coming in from Sight Holders in all of the major cutting centres.'

Sir James interrupted. 'Was there any pattern to the calls?'

'Apart from the fact that they all complained of stones in their boxes that were not diamond, the one common denominator was the size of the diamonds affected. All the suspect stones were in the 2- to 4-carat range.'

Sir James turned to Paul Remington. 'I remember Ken telling me last month of something odd you had seen in the videotape recording of Roger Black.'

'That's right, the tape seemed to show him pocketing a diamond and then putting it back again.'

'He worked in the 2- to 4-carat department?'

'Yes. So did Scofield and Crosley.'

Sir James smiled frostily at the group sitting in front of him.

'Well, now we know what the three of them were doing—they were certainly stealing diamonds, but, more importantly, they were substituting them with worthless imitations.'

Paul raised his hand to attract attention.

'Their visit to the Russalmaz department in Moscow and the fifteen-thousand pounds deposited in the sorters' bank accounts—are the Russians deliberately attempting to create trouble between ourselves and the Sight Holders? Which makes the deaths of the three men begin to look more sinister. Is it possible they were only meant to salt the diamond assortment with fake stones, not to steal the diamonds? When the thefts were discovered by us, and the diamonds found in their homes, the Russians would have had good reason to want them all silenced.'

Sir James shook his head. 'I think you may be exaggerating the villainy of our Russian friends. I agree there has been a concerted attempt to upset some of our clients, perhaps with the aim of gaining their custom as direct purchasers, but to put it in perspective, the result is just an irritation—not a disaster.'

Ken Burridge spoke up for the first time.

'I'm not so sure about that, Sir James. If you remember, we used to be fed with inside information on the policy decisions of both Russalmaz and the Politburo's Trade Policy Committee. Our informant was one of the Russian team who check the Moscow diamond shipment as it goes through our sorting departments—his name was Gregoriev.'

'Didn't he meet with a fatal accident last year?'

'That's right, he fell out of an InterCity express—yet another mysterious death. Since then we've heard nothing of the Russian's plans.'

Sir James looked at his watch and sighed.

'I take your point, Ken, but to be pragmatic, now that the three sorters are sadly dead, and we are aware of a possible Russian involvement, the presence of a few hundred imitation diamonds in a single Sight of nearly a million stones is no more than an irritation. We can safely put it behind us, and concentrate on smoothing things over with our clients.'

He turned back to Jim Finchley. 'Now, what steps have you taken to put things right with the Sight Holders who rang you today?'

Jim licked his thin lips nervously. 'I've arranged for them to send the imitations back immediately. When they arrive, we'll check the weights of the stones and their categories, and send off replacements.'

Sir James nodded in agreement, then his telephone rang. He picked up the receiver.

'Good afternoon, Hank, what can I do for you?'

As he listened, Sir James' expression slowly changed to a scowl.

'I'm extremely sorry to hear that—we've had a few similar reports from our other clients, and of course we'll replace the stones immediately.'

'Yes, I realise you have still got several thousand stones to check over...'

The response to this was even audible to the listening group around the desk.

'Yes, yes. I quite understand this is a major waste of your people's time—of course I'll do anything I can to help.'

'Well, we do have two such experts on our staff—they're Fellows of the British Gemmological Association.'

'Hank, I'll get them out to you on the next flight. They can identify the problem stones, phone the details back to Jim, and he can get replacements to you within a few hours.'

'My pleasure, Hank—I assure you there will be no repeat of this unfortunate business.'

Sir James put the receiver down and turned wearily to Jim Finchley.

'I'm sure you got the gist of that. Hank Winton's sawyers have found thirty imitations in the last shipment. He's hopping mad, and he's demanding our help in checking through the rest of his goods. I want you to get your two gemmologists on the next available plane with whatever it takes in the way of equipment to sort out this mess.'

As they filed out of Sir James' office, the sound of police sirens could be heard in the street below.

* * *

Steven had been invited to Paul's flat for dinner that night. While Stephanie was preparing the meal, he and Paul sat in the lounge with their drinks, talking over the events of the day.

Steven sipped his glass of lager appreciatively. 'I still think there's something more sinister than a simple plot to win over a few of our clients to Russalmaz.'

Paul snapped open the tag on the ice cold tin and poured the beer into his glass.

'The circumstantial evidence we already have indicates a clear Russian involvement, and there's no way it can have reached even this modest level without tacit approval from the very top. I've got an uneasy feeling this is just the tip of a very nasty iceberg.'

Steven nodded in agreement. 'As soon as the imitation stones are returned, we'll get advice from our experts on what they are, and their probable source of manufacture.'

Stephanie wheeled in a hostess trolley from the kitchen.

'Time to stop the shop talk,' she announced. 'Dinner is served folks.'

Over the evening meal Stephanie seized on the opportunity to pose a few searching questions about Steven's love life.

'I'm probably well out of touch, but weren't you dating a tall brunette in Market Liaison?'

Paul grinned and nudged Steven. 'That was last month, Steffi. Our muscular Romeo here got tired of standing on a stool to kiss the girl and has moved on to more promising material.'

Stephanie fluttered her long eyelashes at him.

'Do tell, Steve. Is it Paul's giggly secretary, Debbie?'

Steven flushed darkly under his tan.

'No, her name's Kim. She's a diamond sorter on the fourth floor.'

Stephanie smiled at Paul. 'I know Kim, she's the petite blonde pin-up who's been the cause of most of the company's gossip this year. Have you been successful in dating her yet, Steve?'

'I've taken her out a couple of times, but the rumour is she's involved with one of the married men in Sales.'

Stephanie frowned. 'Yes, that's what I heard. Never mind, Steve—if you're that keen, Paul and I will just have to put our minds to the task of promoting your interests. How about us starting a few rumours about your vital statistics?'

CHAPTER 12

MOSCOW
Thursday 9 July, 1981

Moscow was sweltering in a heatwave, with temperatures soaring to the mid eighties. At lunchtime, office workers escaped from their hot airless premises to stroll across the cobbled expanse of Red Square and mingle with the camera-happy tourists. Others promenaded beneath the red-brick Kremlin walls on the shady north bank of the Moskva river, or sat astride the embankment wall to eat their sandwiches and rolls.

Inside the Kremlin, in one of the smaller offices used by the Trade Policy Committee, Oleg Aristov was having an earnest conversation with Vassily Kolov of Russalmaz.

He handed Kolov a copy of Tuesday's *Daily Telegraph* and pointed to the news item on page three. The accompanying photograph showed police confronting a group of placard-waving young men and women outside the premises of the Diamond Syndicate's building in London. Across the white marble entrance facade in the background Kolov could just make out part of a daubed slogan 'Apartheid—Out'.

Kolov grunted in admiration. 'Colonel Vessovski's men seem to have stirred up quite a hornet's nest.'

Aristov nodded. 'It started on June 26 in the *London Evening Standard* with a front page report on the deaths of the three CMO sorters. I still think Vessovski should have consulted us first before ordering their elimination.'

Kolov sighed and shrugged his shoulders. 'How else could we have prevented the Syndicate from discovering our involvement. The three men brought it on themselves by stealing the diamonds in the first place. Anyway, according to the report in the *Telegraph,* one of them appears to have taken his own life.'

'The response of the British anti-apartheid movement, encouraged no doubt by Colonel Vessovski's agents, has certainly played a useful part in your plan to discredit the Syndicate,' commented Aristov. 'By now they should be feeling the backlash from their clients as phase one starts to take effect.' He paused for a moment in thought. 'They're no fools though—if they put two and two together, they'll soon realise it was the dismissed sorters who planted the synthetic spinel crystals.'

'More to the point, with the three men out of the running, they'll also assume this was a one off ploy, and will be busy placating their Sight Holders and replacing the imitations.'

'Tell me, Kolov, now that we've abandoned the second part of phase one, which was simply going to be the introduction of a few hundred more diamond imitations at the Syndicate's London headquarters, how did the much bigger phase two operation go last week?'

'Like a dream. I have to give Vessovski's SMERSH agents in our Bangkok Embassy full credit for a smooth operation. Early last Saturday morning they managed to substitute fifty thousand carats of the spinel crystals for a similar weight of diamonds in the July shipment. They also left sufficient clues to indicate that the shipment was interfered with in Bangkok—in the event of an investigation.'

'Hopefully, that will protect us—what was the size range this time?'

Kolov consulted his notebook. 'From one to two carats. This will ensure they reach a greater number of the Syndicate's clients.'

'When will the stones be distributed?'

Kolov looked at his notes again. 'The shipment in Bangkok was flown out to the UK on Monday 6 July. The next Sights period in the Syndicate's London CMO offices is scheduled for July 13 to 17, so the stones should be going through the sorting process now.'

Oleg Aristov got up and mopped his brow. He walked to the window and opened it wider, although it was the anxiety he was feeling rather than the temperature in the room that was causing his discomfort. He paused at the window for a moment enjoying the calming influence of the view. Within the Kremlin walls, he could see the early afternoon sun glinting off the golden domes of the cathedrals. He sighed and reluctantly turned back to Kolov.

'Are you certain you'll be ready to take advantage of the chaos that will follow the final phase three introduction of diamond imitations on August 4? The timely release of press announcements and of letters to the Syndicate's principal clients is vital.'

'Relax, Aristov. Everything is in place. The letter to the CMO's Sight Holders will not of course mention the fiasco of the fake diamonds. It will simply state Russalmaz's intention to market all their diamonds direct to the trade rather than through the CMO. The letter will contain an invitation to visit our Moscow premises for the first Sight with all expenses paid.'

'Presumably we'll be undercutting the CMO prices?'

'Yes, the letter will include a summary of the price discounts we'll be offering. It may hearten you to know that some of the CMO's smaller customers have already defected to us—they were the Jewish diamantaires who were allowed to leave the USSR over the last few years and to set up again in Tel Aviv. Through their contacts in my organisation they have been allowed to buy, at an advantageous price, some of their diamond supplies. These stones are allocated from the ten percent of our diamond production we are allowed to retain for internal use in our contract with the CMO. The CMO got wind of this recently and cancelled the Sights of several of the Israeli diamantaires, who now rely entirely on us for their supplies.'

Aristov sat down again opposite Kolov. 'What are the final arrangements?'

Kolov sighed at his colleague's obvious unease. 'The last substitution in Bangkok, as you know, takes place on August 4. It involves one hundred thousand carats of imitation stones, twice the quantity of last month. These will arrive in London in time to be sorted by the Syndicate for their August Sight. Once we have confirmation of the confusion this creates in the world's diamond cutting centres, then rest assured my department will swing into action.'

Aristov wiped his brow again. 'One final question—what's

happening to the diamonds Vessovski's men remove from the Bangkok shipments?'

Kolov smiled. 'That's the same question Brezhnev's foreign trade adviser asked. He actually smiled when I informed him we'd already received payment for them from the CMO, and would shortly be able to sell them for the second time to the Syndicate's own clients. To answer your question—the diamonds, apart from the few stolen by the three CMO sorters, are quite secure. They're being stored in the embassy safe in Bangkok.'

CHAPTER 13

LONDON

Friday 31 July, 1981

Paul had arranged to be away from the office for a few hours to collect Mike, Christine and daughter Melanie from London Airport after their three-week touring holiday on the Continent. Stephanie elected to take the day off and had joined him

While they were awaiting the arrival of the Munich flight, Paul wandered over to the newsagent stand and bought a *Daily Telegraph*. In the middle of the 'Silly Season' there appeared to be little news in the paper. After the hysteria leading up to the Royal Wedding between Prince Charles and Lady Diana Spencer two days earlier, the press seemed to have run out of material. When he returned to Stephanie, a thought struck him.

'Did you remember to video the Royal Wedding programme on Wednesday evening for Christine?'

Stephanie glared at him. 'Of course I did, but no thanks to you. That was the night I let you talk me into going to bed early. Fortunately, I remembered to set the timer. Christine would have been really upset if we'd let her down.'

The clatter of the indicator flaps on the arrivals board caught their attention. The Munich flight had just landed, and some twenty minutes later, Mike, Christine and Melanie appeared through the customs exit.

Melanie ran across to Paul and took his hand. 'Look at my Aust'wian dolly,' she lisped.

Paul bent down and inspected the doll. 'She's dressed in her national costume,' he said. 'If you like, I'll get you a Welsh dolly, and you can start a collection.'

Melanie looked round at her mother, who nodded.

'Yes please, u'cle Paul—can we get it today?'

'I'm sorry, Melanie, I have to go back to work now, but tomorrow is Saturday—we can all go together to Hamleys toyshop in Regent Street and you can chose one there.'

Stephanie fell into step beside Christine. 'You've both managed to keep your sun tan—how did the tour go?'

'It was lovely. Mike took me to all his favourite places. We hired a car at Brussels airport, and made our first overnight stop at Bernkastel on the Mosel. From there we drove up to Koblenz and followed the Romantische Route down the Rhine to Heidelberg. Then we drove along the autobahn to Basle and had a few days in Switzerland. In Austria we stopped at Innsbruck, and spent several days walking in the mountains.'

'I think that's one of my favourite parts of the world—did you get to Salzburg?'

'Yes, we took in the Marionette Theatre, and a concert at the Mirabelle. We spent the last two days in Vienna and saw the Lippizaner horses. On the last evening we even managed to get tickets for Aida at the Opera House.'

'Sounds quite a marathon—how did Melanie cope with all that?'

'Well, she loved the marionettes in Salzburg, and the horses in Vienna, but she slept through the concert and the opera.'

Paul turned to Mike and laughed. 'For my money, Melanie showed great discrimination. After all that culture, she deserves her visit to Hamleys tomorrow. Right now, I'm under orders to deliver the three of you back to Auntie Muriel—she's anxious to hear all your news.'

He shepherded them out of the terminal and along the walkway to the short-stay car park.

* * *

When Paul arrived at 2 Manorhouse Street later that morning, the security officer at the desk in the foyer beckoned him.

Excuse me, sir. Mr Finchley would like to see you in his office as soon as possible.'

'Is Mr Heming in?'

'Yes, sir, he's with Mr Finchley.'

'Do me a favour—let the switchboard know where I am.'

'Of course, sir.'

Paul was surprised to find Sir James sitting behind Jim Finchley's desk when he walked into his office. At his side, Jim was perched on the edge of a chair in earnest conversation on the telephone, and Steven was checking a Thai airline timetable with Paul's secretary Debbie and the girl who ran the Syndicate's travel department.

'So, you're here at last, Paul,' snapped Sir James. 'You certainly chose a bad day to take time off.'

'What's the problem, sir?'

'For the last three hours, every one of our Sight Holders has been on the phone with complaints about the diamonds we supplied in the July Sight.'

'More imitations?'

'Yes, but this time there's been a massive substitution—around five percent. It's caused chaos among the diamond cutters, and it looks as if every stone we've supplied this month will have to be checked.'

'I take it there's no problem in replacing the imitations from the diamond stockpile?'

Sir James looked across at Jim Finchley who had just finished placating an angry client on the telephone. Jim sank wearily back in his chair.

'That's the least of our problems, Paul. Diamond stocks are high at the moment owing to a fall in demand. It's the damage being done to our image that will be more difficult to repair.'

He looked anxiously at Sir James. 'Some of our smaller clients are still upset after the relatively minor problems we had following the June Sight. Now they're threatening to return their whole allocation and buy their diamonds elsewhere. Cheaper Angolan stones available in Antwerp could easily precipitate the end of our control of the market. And certainly the end of price stability.'

Paul turned back to Sir James. 'I think the suspicions I voiced in your office earlier this month must be taken seriously now.'

Sir James sighed. 'Reluctantly, I have to admit you are right. If this is an attempt by Russalmaz to de-stabilize the market and take over our clients, their opening gambit had me completely fooled. By the way, have the police uncovered anything yet on the deaths of Scofield and Crosley?'

'Steven's contacts say they haven't been able to find any witnesses to Scofield's fall under the train—they haven't traced the hit and run driver either. They're beginning to suspect Scofield and Crosley were murdered—and it was a very professional job.'

Steven finished his discussion with Debbie and the travel department girl, and joined Paul. He handed Sir James the Thai airlines brochure.

'The first flight to Bangkok leaves this evening at six o'clock—we've booked two seats on it with open-dated returns. I've made out an expenses requisition—the extra five hundred pounds is to cover contingencies. If you sign it, Debbie can get the money organised before we leave.'

Sir James signed the requisition and handed it to Paul's secretary. Then he turned back to Paul. 'Let me put you in the picture. It'd be impossible to introduce upwards of forty thousand carats of imitation stones here in our own sorting departments. So the best guess is that the substitution is being made in the offices of our Bangkok agent, ThaiExport.'

'What about Moscow?' asked Paul.

Steven shook his head. 'If the Russians are behind this, they would make sure that any substitution was done at arms length from Russalmaz's Moscow premises.'

The door opened and one of the quality controllers walked in. He saw there was a meeting in progress and pulled up short. 'I'm sorry—I didn't realise you were here, Sir James.'

Jim frowned at him. 'Is it something important?'

'Yes, I think it is. I've just been checking over the boxes which contained the July shipment from Bangkok. Six of the seals were plain—they didn't have the Russalmaz insignia on them.' He held out the six seals.

Paul looked quizzically at Sir James. 'Well, I think that just about clinches it. The substitution must have been made in Bangkok. Have the Russians been paid yet for the July shipment?'

'Of course—we always transact our business on a cash basis.'

'What are you doing about the August shipment?'

'It's due to arrive in Bangkok on Monday 3rd August. You and Steven will arrive there tomorrow and start your undercover enquiries on site. One of our senior quality controllers is a gemmologist. He's checked out the imitations returned after the June Sight and can brief you on identification tests before you go.'

'If we find the shipment has been doctored, what action do you want us to take?'

'Do nothing that would let the Russians know we're on to them. It's clear they've got someone on the inside at ThaiExport.' Sir James smiled grimly. 'I'm relying on the two of you to penetrate the Bangkok office with your usual discretion. No-one there must know of your connection with the Diamond Syndicate, otherwise the reason for your visit will get straight back to the Russians. If you find any imitations in the shipment, phone me. But use a code phrase rather than plain language.'

He picked up the Thai airlines brochure and glanced through it. 'If you find substitutions, just phone me and say you've visited the Grand Palace. If I hear that, I'll make arrangements to delay payment. But before I blow this whole affair into the open, I want you to find out how the imitations are planted in the shipment, and, even more importantly, where they came from. If you can get me proof positive that Russalmaz are behind this, then I will lodge the strongest possible protest at diplomatic and even governmental level.'

'We'll do our best, Sir James. If we uncover anything that requires more urgent action, I'll contact you via the British Embassy—I believe the ambassador is an old friend of yours.'

Sir James' eyes glinted behind his gold framed glasses. 'I congratulate you on your information sources—yes, Sir Roland and I were at Cambridge together before the war. He looked at his watch. 'Now get moving—and good luck to both of you.'

* * *

Jeffrey Hamilton was one of two gemmologists on the Syndicate's staff. He was in his late forties, tall and angular, with a bald pate thrusting through a mop of sandy coloured hair. As a senior quality controller he was in charge of four of the CMO's diamond sorting departments.

Early in his career he had taken the British Gemmological Association's two-year course in gemstones, and qualified as a Fellow of the Association. Although his expertise as a gemmologist was seldom called upon, he had been allowed to set up a small gem test laboratory on the sixth floor alongside the acidising department. This test facility was sometimes used when a suspicious looking stone appeared in one of the sorting departments. On the rare occasions that Jeffrey was asked to check a suspect diamond, it usually turned out to be a pebble of near colourless topaz. However, in the last few weeks he had been inundated with the imitation stones returned from the Syndicate's Sight Holders.

When Paul and Steven entered the small gem laboratory, they found Jeffrey Hamilton laying out a selection of colourless diamond-like crystals on a large sheet of white sorting paper pinned to one of the work tables. Two other tables held a variety of optical and electronic test instruments, and above them on the walls several display cabinets contained a collection of rough and polished gem samples ranging from the red and purple shades of garnet, through the blues and pinks of topaz and zircon to the greens of emerald, chrysoprase and jade.

Paul picked up one of the crystals from the group Jeffrey had laid out on the sorting paper. For its size it felt heavy enough to be a diamond.

'Is this one of the fakes, Jeff?'

Jeffrey nodded, and handed Paul and Steven a hand lens each.

'Take a close look at the rest of them. I've made a selection from each of the size ranges and shapes that were returned by our clients.'

Steven picked up one of the crystals, and holding the hand lens close to his right eye, he gripped the stone between the thumb and forefinger of his left hand and rotated the crystal beneath the lens, copying the method he had seen used by the diamond sorters.

'Looks like the kosher article to me.'

Jeffrey smiled, his bald dome and circlet of hair making him look more like a monk than a diamond expert.

'That's the problem. The crystals are very good diamond look-alikes— it's not surprising they fooled the sorters.'

Paul laid his crystal back on the sorting paper. 'So what are they, if they're not diamond?'

'For a start they're rather unusual. If I tell you they are synthetic spinel crystals it won't mean much, so I'll have to bore you with a few more facts.'

Jeffrey hitched himself on to the corner of the table and motioned Paul and Steven to a chair. 'In the early days of gemstone synthesis, the first gem to be man-made was ruby because of its high value. The most successful method to mass-produce synthetic ruby was developed by a Frenchman, Auguste Verneuil in 1891. He invented a method called flame-fusion synthesis in which the powdered constituents of the ruby were dropped through an oxy-hydrogen flame, where they melted and then cooled to form a growing rod-shaped crystal called a boule. The apparatus he designed was called a Verneuil furnace, and was subsequently used to produce synthetic sapphire and synthetic spinel.'

Paul cut in. 'So these diamond imitations were grown by the Verneuil method.'

'No, that's the interesting point. As far as I know, all synthetic spinel crystals grown to date have been produced in a Verneuil furnace—they have a very recognisable round elogated shape with slightly flattened sides. They are not at all like the eight-sided octahedral crystals you've just been looking at.'

Steven stroked the lobe of his right ear pensively. 'If they're made by a new process, perhaps this'll narrow down the source of manufacture.'

Jeffrey nodded. 'It's my guess they were grown by the flux-melt technique, although that's by no means a new process. It uses a molten flux containing the necessary chemicals, and imitates the way some gemstones formed in the earth's crust. The synthetic products either grow on seed crystals in the flux or nucleate spontaneously.'

Paul held up his hands. 'Now don't let's get too technical. Who, for instance, would be using such a process?'

'There are several synthetic gem producers in Europe and the States who use the flux-melt method, but there's been no report in the technical journals of anyone synthesising spinel by this method—it wouldn't be economically worthwhile.'

Steven butted in. 'Why not?'

'The flame-fusion method is so much cheaper,' explained Jeffrey massaging his bald dome. 'The flux-melt method is a much slower and more expensive process. Because of this, it's generally reserved for those gems that can't be grown by other methods, or where the improved quality of the end product makes it a better copy of the genuine stone.'

'So if these synthetic spinels have been grown, as you suspect, by the flux-melt method, it's been done specifically to make them look like diamond crystals?'

Jeffrey nodded. 'You've got it in one. The synthetic spinels not only have the same shape as many of the rough diamonds, but they even have identical surface markings—little triangular growth features we call trigons.'

Paul leaned forward and picked up a handful of the crystals. 'So how did you prove these were synthetic spinel?'

'Well, I cheated a bit.' Jeffrey pointed to the cast iron polishing skaife mounted on one of the tables. 'I polished flats on several of the imitations, and then measured their optical properties on a refractometer. Their refractive index, among other things, identified them immediately as synthetic spinel.'

Steven frowned and stroked the lobe of his ear again.

'I hope you've got something simpler in mind for us?'

Jeffrey laughed. 'Relax, I only used the skaife because that's a convenient method for the occasional rough samples I'm given to check—it also gives me an immediate feel for the relative hardness of the material compared with diamond.'

'So how do we check out the stones in Bangkok?'

Jeffrey picked up a small metal box from one of the tables.

'This is a portable thermal conductance tester. Diamond conducts heat better than any metal, but all of the diamond imitations, including synthetic spinel, are bad conductors of heat.'

He held up the instrument's pen-like test probe.

'This contains an electrically heated metal tip. If it's held in contact with a diamond, the stone quickly conducts heat away from the tip, and the electronics in the box detect the fall in temperature and flash a green indicator lamp. If the stone is a diamond imitation, the probe tip temperature stays high and the lamp stays off.'

Paul picked up the instrument and looked at it.

'Sounds simple—so why did you go to all the trouble of polishing a facet on the imitation stones?'

'Because I wanted to know which of several possible fakes they were—this type of thermal tester only indicates whether the stone is diamond or non-diamond.'

'Are there any other tests which would tell you what the stones are if they're not diamond.'

'Several. One of them involves the use a reflectance meter—that only works with polished stones. It measures the relative lustre of the gem, but is only reliable if you've got a perfectly flat facet to test. I could also have measured the specific gravity of the crystals...'

Paul held up his hand again in protest. 'Enough—you've sold us the thermal conductance tester.'

Jeffrey walked across to a small safe set in the wall and took out several colourless crystals. Then he picked up a handful of the imitation stones and mixed them with the crystals from the safe.

'Examination time—I want both of you to take it in turns to check out this mixture of genuine and fake diamond crystals. You first, Steven.'

It took half an hour before Jeffrey Hamilton was satisfied his pupils were completely happy with the use of the instrument. Finally, he picked up the diamond crystals that had been correctly identified for the third time by both Paul and Steven, and returned them to the safe.

Paul got to his feet and stretched his lean muscular frame.

'There's just one final question that's been nagging me, Jeff.'

'I'm happy there's only one—what's on your mind?'

'We've all heard about synthetic diamonds—why weren't they used as substitutes rather than the spinels.'

Jeffrey nodded. 'That's a good point—but the synthetic diamonds you've heard about are industrial quality stones. They're poor in colour and very small. The few gem-quality synthetic diamonds that have been grown to date in the laboratories of General Electric of America, and by the Russians, would certainly have been much more difficult to detect. Fortunately, these larger synthetic diamonds cost between forty and fifty times the value of the natural stone—but in ten or twenty years time, who knows, they may even be cheaper.'

Steven turned to Paul. 'Don't forget the main purpose behind this business—the alienation of the CMO's clients. The softness of the spinels made them an ideal stone for this purpose—they were detected immediately the cutters got to work on them.'

Jeffrey picked up the thermal tester and put it in its plastic carry case. He handed the instrument to Paul. 'Good hunting and good luck—I think you're going to need it!'

Before Paul left for his flat to pack some clothes for the Bangkok visit, he returned to his office and scribbled a few lines on a piece of paper. He handed the paper to Debbie. 'Be a love and print me up half a dozen business cards—I have a feeling I'm going to need an alias on this trip.'

CHAPTER 14

BANGKOK

Saturday 1 August, 1981

It was past midnight. The Thai Airways 747 had just left Oman airspace and was cruising at 30,000 feet above the moonlit Arabian Sea. Paul and Steven had sampled the dinner and film in the first-class section, and were now enjoying a nightcap in the small lounge behind the flight deck. Their exit from London on Friday afternoon was a rushed affair. They had caught a taxi outside the CMO headquarters and stopped off briefly at their flats to pack a few clothes and other necessities. Paul managed a hurried telephone call to Stephanie before they finally departed for Heathrow. Once on the plane, they were both glad of the chance to relax and unwind.

Steven peered out of the window. Below he could just make out the rippled moonlit surface of the ocean. Even though he knew they were travelling at over 500 miles an hour, at this height the plane appeared to be moving at a snail's pace in its long haul towards India and the refuelling stop in Bombay.

He turned back from the window and yawned. 'We haven't left the UK as fast as that since our visit to Angola last November.'

Paul eased his back into the angle of the corner seat. 'Steffi wasn't well pleased when I phoned her and said we were off to Bangkok. I'd promised to take young Melanie on a shopping expedition to Hamleys this morning. To make it worse, Steffi had got tickets for 'Cats' at the New London Theatre for tonight's performance—we were making up a foursome with Mike and Christine.' He paused in thought for a moment. 'Before she slammed down the phone, she told me to bugger off and enlarge my repertoire in the Bangkok massage parlours!'

Steven chuckled. 'Well, at least you seem to be getting your oats regularity with Stephanie. I'm still trying to get to first base with Kim. She's a bit fragile at the moment—her affair with that character in Sales has broken up, and she's suffering withdrawal symptoms.'

'Not to worry—just give her some space and keep your passion on the back burner for a while. It'll come right with time.' Paul signalled to the steward to repeat their drinks. 'Strictly between you and me, I've got just the opposite problem with Steffi.'

Steven looked quizzically at Paul over his glass of whisky and water. 'I thought you two had just about reached the Darby and Joan stage.'

'Well, we've certainly been living together for over a year.' Paul hesitated. There was something about a night flight that encouraged confidences. Although he was Steven's boss, the two of them had shared enough dangerous moments together to make their working relationship more of a partnership.

Paul sipped his brandy thoughtfully. 'Sometimes I suspect Steffi is becoming a bit of a nympho. For a girl, she's got a very aggressive attitude to sex—it's more like mouth-to-mouth combat at times. Call me an old fashioned romantic, but in my book, making love is more than just having sex.'

Steven shook his head. 'Problems, problems. You and I seem to be at opposite ends of the spectrum with our women. At least with you and Stephanie there's nobody else. With Kim I get the feeling I'm a makeshift number two.'

Paul looked at his watch and sighed. 'I think it's time we got our heads down. I've an uneasy feeling that this job's going to need our undivided attention for the next few days.'

* * *

Thailand is seven time zones east of the UK, and when the 747 jumbo landed at Bangkok's Don Muang airport, the digital clock in the arrivals hall registered 14.00 hours.

Paul and Steven collected their holdalls and passed through customs. At the airport exit they had to show their baggage dockets to the police before they were allowed to leave the building.

Paul hailed a taxi. 'Last time I was here, I lost the luggage dockets, and the police hauled me into the security office to prove ownership. Although it can sometimes be a bit of a bottleneck, at least the door check has stopped the local villains' lucky-dip operation.'

The taxi that Paul flagged down, screeched to a halt in front of them. Paul checked that it displayed the official yellow plates, and then stuck his head in the cab window.

'Hotel Oriental—raka tao rai—how much?'

The young Thai driver's face lit up with an ear-to-ear grin. 'Four hundred baht, Mister Paul.'

Paul pushed his face close to the driver's and scowled. 'I know you Patana—you've driven me before. Two hundred baht, or you can sod off.'

The young Thai's grin widened. 'No problem, I give you special rate, one-eighty baht, and no-one else drive you in Bangkok.'

'It's a deal, you little ruffian. Now get us to the Oriental fast.'

They clambered aboard the taxi, and as the vehicle raced out of the airport approach road and sped south through the flat landscape of rice fields, Steven clung grimly to the door strap. 'Nice to meet up with old friends,' he commented, 'and to find they occasionally drive on the same side of the road as we do'.

Paul nodded and struggled out of his jacket. Although the temperature in August was beginning to drop from the 34 degree C highs of April, it was still a humid 32 degrees in the shade. 'Young Patana could be useful to us on this trip—he's aware what's going on in town, particularly if it's at all shady. He also knows the better-class night clubs and massage parlours.'

Steven chuckled. 'I can see you've taken Stephanie's instructions to heart.'

Paul was suddenly flung to one side as Patana took a right turn on two wheels. He prodded the young Thai in the back. 'Just get us to the hotel in one piece—forget the fast bit.'

Don Muang airport is only thirty miles north of the capital, but the journey can take up to ninety minutes due to the day-long traffic jams around the central area of the city. The hundred-year old Oriental Hotel is situated on the east bank of the Chao Phya river at the southern edge of Bangkok. For Paul and Steven's purposes, it was also conveniently within walking distance of the Silom Road premises of ThaiExport.

When they finally arrived hot and dusty at the hotel, Patana carried their holdalls into the cool marble foyer and dumped them at the reception desk. Paul extracted two one-hundred baht notes from his wallet and stuffed them in the breast pocket of Patana's denim jacket, a garment which, like his worn blue jeans, had seen better days.

'Keep the change—you can use it to have that thing you call a taxi washed.'

Patana, whose head only reached as high as Paul's chest, grinned up at him. 'You feel like little entertainment tonight, boss?'

Paul bent down and stared him in the eye. 'After thirteen hours flying, and another hour and a half in that grubby mobile sauna of yours, all I want is a shower and some sleep—just be here sharp at nine o'clock tomorrow morning.'

'Sure thing, boss. We paint the town red then, just like old times.'

After Paul and Steven had booked in, the receptionist, an attractive Thai girl dressed in a colourful sarong, beckoned one of the uniformed bell boys and handed him their room keys. They followed the young Thai through the spacious carpeted lounge to a waiting lift. Steven paused for a moment to listen to a string quartet playing Mozart.

'It's quite a classy joint,' commented Paul.

As they entered the lift, Steven grinned. 'You must tell me all about the "old times" one of these days, Paul.'

'I'll do better than that—we'll take a few hours off tomorrow and I'll show you around the town. While we're getting ourselves acclimatised, Patana can start checking out the underworld gossip, with particular reference to activities at the Soviet Embassy. In the meanwhile, I'll see you down in the bar in an hour. We can have a leisurely meal followed by an early night—and that's an order, Steve.'

Steven pulled a face. 'Stephanie will never believe me when I tell her we both went to bed with a good book on our first night in Bangkok.'

* * *

Next morning at eight o'clock, Paul and Steven met by arrangement in the hotel lounge. The Oriental Hotel occupies a prime site on the east bank of the river, its unimpressive town frontage being compensated by the lawns and flower beds that stretch from the rear of the hotel to the water's edge. For breakfast there was a choice between sitting in the air-conditioned restaurant in the hotel, or walking down to the outdoor restaurant by the river. Paul and Steven decided on the latter, but when they left the cool interior of the building and began strolling across the lawn, the intense heat of the morning sun made them change their minds and they retraced their steps to the comfort of the air-conditioned breakfast room.

While they were sipping their orange juice, Paul pulled a map from his pocket and spread it on the table. 'This morning we'll hire a long-tailed boat from the landing-stage just alongside the hotel. That'll give you an impression of the network of klongs, or canals, on the west side of the city. You'll also get a view of the way the poorer Thais live in the hundreds of old stilt houses built out over the narrow waterways. If we get away promptly, we can also catch the floating market in full swing.'

Steven spread butter on a croissant and took a bite out of it. He pointed at the 'Royal Barge Shed' marked on the map. 'I hear the royal barges are also worth seeing.'

'That's right—so here's the plan. I'll give Patana his instructions when he arrives at nine o'clock. After the long-tailed boat tour we'll take a leisurely trip up the river on a rice barge to see the royal craft. We'll have lunch on the barge, and at four o'clock rendezvous back here to see what Patana has dug up. Hopefully, with his help we'll find a way to penetrate the ThaiExport premises.'

After breakfast they strolled back to the lounge and found Patana waiting for them by the reception counter. He was resplendent in clean white trousers and a bright blue shirt.

'It was the taxi I wanted cleaned up—not you,' sighed Paul.

Patana looked crestfallen. 'You never say good things to me—always you complain.'

Steven eyed him up and down. 'You look very elegant, Patana, but Paul does have a point. You look a bit out of character for the job in hand.'

Paul beckoned Patana over to a secluded corner of the lounge. 'It's important we find out if anyone's been snooping around the ThaiExport offices in Silom Road—we may want to take a look inside the place ourselves on Monday night. Put your work clothes back on, and spend the day checking it out with your underworld friends—I also want you to find out if anything's been heard about the Soviet Embassy staff in Wireless Road. Then you can dress up again and meet us back here at four o'clock—we'll have a drink and sort out some entertainment for the evening.'

By now Patana's grin was fully restored. 'OK, boss—but it cost you. My time cheap, but information like that expensive.'

Paul sighed again. 'I've a feeling you're about to buy a new taxi—how much?'

Patana looked hurt. 'Always you have good value from me—two thousand baht.' He stepped back a pace, anticipating an outburst.

Paul took out his wallet and extracted a five-hundred baht note. 'This is an advance. If your information is good, I may give you another five hundred. If it's very good I'll double that.'

Patana took the offered note and saluted. 'You trust me—I return here at four with all you want to know. We have drinks—then we go enjoy the girls!'

After they had seen Patana off in his taxi, Paul and Steven walked down the lane alongside the hotel to the river. Lined up at a landing-stage were five long-tailed boats, their owners vying for custom. Paul selected an old man whose boat looked a shade more sound than the others.

'How much for an hour's trip around the klongs?'

The wizened old man smiled up at Paul, revealing a row of yellowing and broken teeth. 'For one hour you pay me seven hundred baht.'

Paul smiled at him sweetly and shook his head. 'I have only five hundred baht—perhaps you could recommend one of your friends.'

The old man chuckled and spat into the muddy water. 'OK—

as special favour for Englishman, I only charge you five hundred.'

The shallow-draft thirty-foot long boat was powered by an ancient diesel engine which had been ripped out of a derelict truck. The engine was mounted at the rear of the boat and connected to the propeller by a long drive shaft, giving the vessel the name 'long-tailed'. A flexible mounting allowed the craft to be steered by swivelling the drive shaft through ninety degrees in either direction. As a minor concession to comfort, a small fabric sun canopy was rigged up amidships.

Paul and Steven settled themselves gingerly one behind the other in the middle of the boat. The old man pivoted the propeller shaft into the air and started the engine, which responded with a loud explosion accompanied by a cloud of exhaust fumes. He pushed the boat away from its mooring and deftly pivoted the spinning propeller into the water. A plume of water leapt high in the air, and the boat shot out into the busy river, narrowly missing a coconut-ladened scow.

Steven gripped the sides of the boat, and cautiously turned round to face Paul. 'Am I supposed to be enjoying this?'

A few hundred yards up the river, the old man reduced speed and guided the boat into one of the main canals on the east bank side. For the next hour he took them through a labyrinth of narrow waterways. Steven was fascinated by the ramshackle old stilt houses, and by the sight of their occupants washing clothes and pots and pans in the polluted water.

He shook his head. 'I suppose they must have developed immunity several generations back—and here I am living off bottled water, and even eyeing ice cubes with suspicion.'

At the junction with another canal, they came upon a traffic jam of canoes plying fruit and vegetables to the water-front homes. After a good deal of shouting and gesturing by their ancient skipper, they managed to squeeze through. Round the next bend they surprised a half-naked young girl bathing at the bottom of a rickety wooden ladder which led down from one of the stilt houses. She shyly lowered herself into the water until all but her head was visible, and waited for them to pass out of sight.

On their return to the landing-stage, Paul paid off the old

man, and pointed to one of the crowded tourist boats making its leisurely way down the river. 'Where do we pick up the rice barge tour?'

The old man grinned and indicated another landing-stage a hundred yards down river. 'Two-hour cruise. Cost you plenty—not cheap like me.'

When they eventually boarded the rice barge, they found it was roomy and comfortably slow compared with the long-tailed boat. It took them and a dozen other sightseers slowly up-river while the boat's guide pointed out the gilded temples and ornate palaces which shared the river frontage with warehouses and large private mansions.

Steven sighed contentedly. 'You can keep your long-tailed boats—this is more my style.'

Just before they passed under the second of the two bridges that link Bangkok to the west bank towns of Nonthaburi and Pathum Thani, the barge reduced speed for the benefit of the photographers in the party, and they glided slowly by the Royal Barge Shed on the west bank. The large open-fronted building housed several of the elaborate red and gold painted vessels. The one used by the King of Thailand had an enormous five-pronged golden prow. On ceremonial occasions, their guide told them, it was propelled by fifty oarsmen.

A few hundred yards further up-river, the barge moored at a landing stage, and they enjoyed a buffet lunch of Thai spring rolls, chicken pieces fried with herbs in soya sauce and served on a leaf, platters of steamed rice, pineapple and the Thai equivalent of kiwi, all heaped on a table running down the centre of the boat. Paul and Steven rounded off the meal with several bottles of Thai Singa beer.

When they returned to the hotel, they collapsed into the yielding embrace of the lounge's comfortable leather chairs. Paul signalled to the bar waiter. 'Two BMWs, please, with plenty of ice.'

Steven looked at him in alarm. 'What the hell are BMWs?'

'Barcardi, malabu and whisky—I thought you needed a reviver.'

Shortly after four o'clock, Patana bustled through the door, his youthful face wreathed in smiles. Paul inspected his attire, and nodded approvingly. 'Apart from those grubby trainers, you look fit for polite company.'

Patana looked pained. 'You insult me again—and I work hard for you today. Just wait till you hear my news...'

Paul interrupted. 'Not here Patana—it's too public. We'll go through to the Authors Lounge, it'll be quieter there.'

The Oriental Hotel's Authors Lounge, once the haunt of Conrad, Coward and Maughan, is still a favourite meeting place for literary celebrities. Filled with elegant white bamboo chairs and tables, and brightly lit from its overhead canopy of glass, it is dominated by a magnificent twin staircase which curves up to the overhead balcony. Below in the lounge, the balcony's central support column carries framed photographs of past and present writers who have made the hotel their base. As a reminder to visitors that they are in the tropics, the all-white decor is complemented by thickets of green bamboo growing to a height of twenty foot at the sides of the staircase.

Paul chose a table under one of the yellow and white umbrellas and beckoned the Thai waitress.

'What do you recommend,' he asked the girl.

'We have six special blends of coffee.' She handed him a menu.

Paul scanned the list. 'I'll have a pot of Kilimanjaro—that sounds romantic.' The others nodded in agreement.

Patana pointed at the trolley carrying a selection of confectionery under a glass cover. He looked pleadingly at Paul. 'Can I have cake as well?'

The waitress smiled. 'I'll bring a plate of pastries with the coffee.' After they had drunk their coffee, and when only a few crumbs were left on Patana's plate to mark his rapid consumption of four cream cakes, Paul got down to business.

'OK—what have you got for us?'

Patana leaned forward, enjoying his moment of importance. 'One of my friends was having troubles with police one night in beginning of July. He runs down Silom road, and turns in street at side of Rama Jewellery Building—that is ThaiExport building.'

Paul sighed. 'Yes, we know that—what happened?'

'He got away.'

'Are you trying to make me angry?'

'No, boss, let me finish. My friend told me he saw side door of building was open. He nearly went in to escape police guy. He also saw empty car in same road. It was a Lada.'

Steven looked at Paul. 'A Russian car—and the diamond shipment was due in from Moscow on July 3.'

Patana looked pleased with himself. 'Russian car—that good, yes? I also find there is Russian guy from embassy visit Scheherazade massage parlour two-three times. Always ask for same girl. Her man work for ThaiExport.'

'Bingo!' exclaimed Paul. 'Did you get her name?'

'Of course—I not bloody fool—girls's name Lea Kanowan.'

Paul beamed at Patana. 'Well done. You've earned your extra thousand baht—have some more cake.' He passed the notes over, and beckoned the waitress for the bill.

Steven grinned at Paul. 'I think I know where we're going tonight.'

'Too right—but before that, Patana is going to show us the delights of the Patpong district, starting with the Super Star Nightclub.'

Patana wiped the crumbs from his mouth and his eyes lit up. 'Then we end night at Sheherazade—highclass girls, all clean like your Princess Diana.'

Paul raised his eyebrows at Steven. 'We'll take precautions all the same.'

* * *

Later that evening, Patana drove them to the Super Star Nightclub in Patpong at the east end of the Silom road. He parked his taxi, and then joined them at the large oval-shaped bar which enclosed a small display stage for the club's scantily clad hostesses. Some of the girls were already sitting at side tables, drinking with the regular clientele of the club. Occasionally, one of them would take her customer on to the crowded dance floor, or disappear with him in the direction of the private rooms at the rear.

Paul bought drinks for the three of them, and for a while they sat watching the girls on the miniature stage gyrating to the disco music. Patana leaned his elbows on the bar and stared up at a tall dusky hostess with short-cropped black hair. The girl was languidly moving her long shapely limbs to the rhythm of the music, but it was the girl's brief see-through body stocking, rather than her dancing, that seemed to have captured his attention,

Paul caught sight of the object of Patana's interest, and beckoned the girl to join them. She stepped gracefully onto the bar, and Steven lifted her down and gave her his seat alongside Patana.

'My name's Steven—my friends and I are celebrating a successful day's business. What can I get you to drink?'

'Thank you, Steven. My name's Karina—I'm on duty all night, so I'll have a long drink. A gin sling would be nice.'

'Let me introduce you to the gang, Karina. The tall guy on my left is Paul, and this is Patana.'

'Oh, I know Patana—he often drives me home at night in his taxi.'

Paul shook his head. 'Wouldn't you know it, he's on goodnight terms with the loveliest girl here!'

Karina laughed. 'Oh, he's not so bad. If only he was six inches taller, I might even fall for him.'

Steven grimaced. 'Well, that counts me out too.'

Patana leaned across and winked at Paul. 'It OK if you want take her back to hotel afterwards. Like me, she give good value,' he confided in a loud whisper.

Paul laughed. 'That sure is an attractive idea, but we've got some business to attend to tonight—remember.' He looked at his watch. 'We'll have another round of drinks, and then move on.'

'But we see nothing yet. Here in Patpong are live shows—make your eyes pop,' protested Patana.

'No way—we're saving all our strength for the Sheherazade tonight.'

Half an hour later, Patana picked them up in his taxi. He drove out through the eastern sector of the city into the Sukhumvit Road. They cruised along the broad thoroughfare, past brightly lit hotels and restaurants, until they reached a quieter residential section. Patana made a left turn and pulled up in front of a detached building whose discretely curtained front windows were aglow with a pale blue light. A blue neon sign spelt out the name 'Sheherazade'. Alongside it, a floodlit statue appeared to be based on an illustration from the Kama Sutra.

Steven nudged Paul, and pointed to the statue's tangle of arms and legs. 'I hope we're not expected to try that position!'

Patana ushered them through the massage parlour's ornate plate glass doors into the foyer. At the far side they could see a dimly lit glass-fronted waiting room in which several men were seated on wooden chairs.

'That is queue for low price massage,' explained Patana. 'Top class girls on next floor.'

He led them upstairs to a more sumptuously furnished waiting room with deep pile carpeting and easy chairs. At one side was another glass-fronted room in which six girls, dressed in a variety of flimsy sarongs and flowered dresses, were sitting in a row on a long settee. Concealed ultra-violet lighting helped reveal the skimpy fluorescing underwear beneath their thin outer garments. The girls were talking quietly among themselves until one of them suddenly spotted Patana. She stood up and pointed, and they all started to giggle.

'You must have a season ticket,' commented Paul.

'I take them back to their home sometime,' explained Patana, looking pleased. 'They all good girls like your Princess Di.'

Drawn by the noise, the parlour's madam, a stout middle-aged woman, appeared from behind a small reception counter at the far side of the room. She was dressed in a long black gown, its severity relieved by a pearl necklace and a diamante broach which appeared to be a miniature copy of the statue outside.

'Good evening, Patana. What can I do for your friends?' Patana pointed to Paul. 'He specially recommended for massage by Miss Lea Kanowan.'

'A good choice, but what about his friend. Would he like to select someone.' She waved at the girls who were seated on the settee.

Steven looked embarrassed. If he singled out a girl, it seemed to him he was denigrating all the others.

Madam sensed his problem and looked him over carefully. 'Yes, I think Liza will suit you.' She beckoned to a tall dusky Burmese girl wearing a yellow sarong. The girl whispered something to her companions and then came forward.

Madam beckoned a second girl whose compact but well developed figure was barely concealed by a thin floral dress. 'The tall Englishman has especially asked for you Lea.'

Lea followed Liza out of the room. When they paired off with the two men, it was a signal for renewed mirth from the remaining girls.

Paul looked at Steven and chuckled. 'I see what's amusing them—you've got the six-foot beauty, and I've got the shorty. We're beginning to look like a Whitehall farce.'

Lea Kanowan was a dark-haired Thai girl with pale flawless skin. She was verging on the plump side, but like most Thai girls had an attractive face with high cheekbones, and the dainty frame of a teenage child. She took Paul's hand and led him across to the reception counter to pay the 500 baht massage fee. At the counter, Lea was issued with two towels and a supply of soap and shampoo. Then she took Paul's hand again and led him along a corridor to her room.

As Lea opened the door, Paul noticed it was fitted with an eye-level peephole. The room itself was sparsely furnished with a bed, a chair and a dressing table. There was a wooden carving of a Thai God on the left of the curtained window, and a picture of a group of nude girls above the bed. A bath and a shower unit were tucked in a tiled alcove to the left of the door. Lying on the tiled floor by the bath was an inflated plastic airbed.

Kanowan handed him one of the towels and pointed to the chair. 'You take all clothes off and put on towel.' She kicked off her sandals, and then slipped off her dress to reveal a pair of flimsy white nylon knickers and bra. 'You had Thai massage before?'

'Yes, but I've been told yours is the best in all Bangkok.'

The girl smiled. She padded across to the chair and helped him off with his shoes and socks. 'I think you will like my massage. But first I prepare bathroom.' She left him to undress, and busied herself filling the bath. Then she made a foam of the shampoo, and spread it evenly over the airbed.

'First I give you water massage, then shampoo massage.'

Paul stood up and wound the towel round his middle. Satisfied with her preparations, Lea removed her bra and knickers and wrapped herself in the second towel. She took his hand and led him to the bath.

Paul gave her his towel, stepped into the bath and lay down in the lukewarm water. Lea took off her own towel, and to Paul's surprise joined him naked in the bath.

'This is Thai water massage,' she whispered smiling at him from the opposite end of the bath. She inched forward until she was straddling his thighs, and began kneading his stomach and chest, while her legs and feet worked on his sides and back. Just as Paul was beginning to respond to the intimacy of her wet naked body, she got out of the bath and pointed to the airbed.

'Now I give you shampoo massage.'

Following her instructions, Paul lay chest-down in the foam.

Kanowan straddled him again, and began massaging his legs, arms and back with her thighs and breasts. As he lay enjoying the soft kneading pressure of her body, he felt her small hand slip under his crutch.'

'My, you big man,' she commented. 'Now you get back in bath.'

He obeyed her, and she gently washed the foam off his body, finally handing him his towel.

'You get dry, then I give you nice massage on bed.'

Paul got up on the bed and lay face down. Kanowan climbed astride him and continued the massage, this time using her thighs and knees while pummelling him with the edge of her palms. Then she stood up on the bed, placed one foot on his left shoulder, and grasping his left hand, stretched the arm upwards until the joint cracked. She continued the treatment with his right arm, and then with his legs.

When she had finished, Paul got up and wrapped the towel round his waist again. He flexed his arms and legs. 'That was tremendous—I'm glad my friend recommended you.'

Lea wrapped her towel round her body. She sat on the end of the bed and gazed appreciatively at Paul's tanned muscular body. 'What friend told you about me?'

Paul took a chance. 'The Russian man from the Embassy.'

Her face lit up. 'You mean Sergei—he very generous man.'

'So I've heard. I can be even more generous, Lea.' Paul walked across to the chair and took the wallet out of his coat. He pulled out two 500 baht notes.

'I'd like to meet your man friend who works at ThaiExport. I've got a small job for him that will pay well.'

Lea took the notes from him and put them in her bag. 'No problem. When you like meet him?'

'Tomorrow is Monday. How about ten o'clock at the Grand Palace—let's meet just inside the Vised Chaisri Gate. Tell him my name is Paul Remington.'

'That fine—I tell him tonight.' She took off her towel again and lay back on the bed. 'Now I feel generous to you Paul Remington.' She held out her hand invitingly.

Paul smiled and discarded his towel. He removed a small packet from his wallet—it was as well he had come prepared. 'I hope Stephanie realises the sacrifices I make in the line of duty,' he murmured to himself as he walked back to the bed and took Kanowan's outstretched hand. Bending over her, he brushed his lips across her aroused nipples.

Lea sighed and closed her eyes. 'Now show me English massage.'

* * *

When Paul returned to reception he found Patana drinking coffee with madam. A few minutes later they were joined by Steven.'

Paul grinned at him. 'I see from your contented smile that the difference in height was no barrier.'

'None at all—and a Thai massage beats the public baths any day. How did things go with you?'

'Lea and I got on splendidly, and after a little persuasion I managed to fix up a meeting with her ThaiExport boyfriend for tomorrow.'

Patana finished his coffee, thanked madam, and joined the two men.

'What you think—didn't I show you best place in all Bangkok?'

Paul patted him on the back. 'You've done us proud today, and I very much like your Sheherezade. If I had the time I would certainly come here more often.'

* * *

After a leisurely breakfast on Monday morning, Paul and Steven were driven by Patana to the Grand Palace. It had been raining earlier on, and although the storm clouds were beginning to clear, the pavement alongside the Palace grounds was running with water.

On weekdays, a small charge is made to enter the grounds of the Grand Palace. On this particular day, a timeless and colourful touch was added to the splendour of the exotic edifices and golden Buddhist temples by groups of visiting saffron-robed monks, who wandered through the grounds sheltering under their umbrellas. Patana had warned Paul and Steven to wear a jacket and tie for their visit, but thinking that such formal attire would damage his own image, he opted to stay outside in his taxi.

At the entrance gate, Paul decided to separate from Steven so that he would be more easily recognised by Lea's boyfriend. After a few minutes, he was approached by a smartly dressed young Thai wearing a white suit, pink shirt and red silk tie.

'Mr Paul Remington?'

'That's right.' Paul shook hands with the young man and motioned for Steven to join them. 'This is my colleague, Steven Heming.'

'My name is Cahn. I'm assistant manager of ThaiExport. I understand you want to discuss some business with me.'

'That's right. Do you mind if we take a walk outside. I've got Patana, an old friend of Lea Kanowan's, waiting in his taxi—we can use it to talk in private.'

In the taxi, Paul told Cahn of his need to enter the ThaiExport premises. 'I simply want to inspect some goods in your safe—nothing will be disturbed, nothing will be taken.'

Cahn smiled. 'I may be able to help you, but first you must give me the reason for your interest in our business.'

Paul pulled a magazine from his pocket and showed it to

Cahn. 'My colleague and I work for the Israeli journal *Diamond World.* As you probably know, there's a lot of interest in the amount of diamonds that Russia is selling to the London Diamond Syndicate. We're preparing a survey on world diamond production, but as the Russians are very secretive about their dealings with the Syndicate, we have to find other sources of information. We know that your ThaiExport office here in Bangkok handles the five-weekly shipment of diamonds between Moscow and London. We also know you have just received this month's shipment from Moscow. If we can see how many boxes of diamonds are in your safe, from this we can make a rough estimate of their annual sales to the Syndicate.'

Cahn remained silent for a few seconds while he considered Paul's request. 'You appear to be very well informed about our operation Mr Remington. You will forgive me if I check your credentials. Do you have a business card for your magazine?'

Paul pulled out his wallet and extracted one of the cards that Debbie printed for him just before he left London.

Cahn scrutinised the card and handed it back to Paul. 'Very well, Mr Remington, it's possible I can find a way to satisfy your curiosity, but it will have to be done unofficially. I most certainly cannot myself show an interest in the amount of diamonds in our safe. I have my position to consider.'

Paul put the magazine back in his pocket. 'In that case I suggest that my colleague and I visit your premises late this evening. As you don't wish to be directly involved, I will need to know how best to enter the building. I will also require the necessary keys and precise information on your alarm system, but above all I must have the combination of the safe.'

'That's quite a tall order, Mr Remington.'

'I'm prepared to pay well for the information.'

Cahn thought for a moment. 'I can get you duplicate keys for the side entrance and the main entrance. ThaiExport are on the seventh floor. The main entrance door on the top floor is alarmed—it uses a magnetic switch. The safe is in the inner office, and this is protected by an ultrasonic movement detector. There's also a pressure pad immediately in front of the safe. All of these devices operate an alarm system which has a direct link to the police.'

Cahn glanced across at Patana and lowered his voice. 'I have to open the safe occasionally, and as I have a poor memory for numbers I have the combination written down.' He took a scrap of paper from his pocket and then put it away again. 'This, the duplicate keys, and the location of the inner office alarm switch will cost you ten thousand baht.'

Paul winced. 'That's a bit steep for a quick glance into a safe.'

'Unlike the fee for Patana's taxi, my price is not negotiable.'

'OK, Cahn. Bring the keys and the other details to the Oriental Hotel tonight. I'll have five thousand baht waiting for you—the rest you can collect from me on Tuesday evening after I've proved that the keys and the rest of your information are worth the money.'

Cahn laughed. 'I see you are a cautious man, Mr Remington. Very well I agree to your terms.' He opened the door of the taxi. 'I will be at the bar in the hotel lounge at eight o'clock tonight. But just remember this—if there is anything missing from that safe on Tuesday morning, or if you do not make the final payment, I will not hesitate to inform on you to the police.' He stepped out of the taxi and walked swiftly away.

CHAPTER 15

BANGKOK

Tuesday 4 August, 1981

The Lada coasted out through the gates of the Soviet Embassy and pulled up in Wireless Road. Andrei shut and locked the security gates and joined Sergei in the car. It was one-thirty am, and the two SMERSH agents were about to embark on Phase 3 of Kolov's plan to discredit the Diamond Syndicate. The two agents were also taking their final leave of the embassy. They had loaded the boot of the car with the one-hundred thousand carats of synthetic spinel crystals that had arrived in the diplomatic bag from Moscow the previous week. Also in the boot was their personal luggage, and a black attachécase containing the fifty-thousand carats of diamonds removed during their July infiltration of the ThaiExport premises.

When they returned from that previous visit, Sergei had sat in his office drinking coffee with Andrei. The execution of the Phase 2 substitution had demanded all his concentration that night, but during the drive back to the embassy, a breath-taking plan began to form in his mind. As he slammed shut the door of the office safe on a fortune in diamonds, he knew the success of the daring scheme would depend on his assistant's co-operation. The proposition he then outlined to an astonished Andrei, amounted to the biggest diamond theft in history.

Now, one month later, they were re-visiting the ThaiExport premises to implement the final phase of Kolov's plan, but this time they each had a one-way airline ticket to Geneva in their pockets. As they approached the Rama Jewelry Building, Sergei slowed the Lada and scanned Silom Road for signs of life. Satisfied that the area was clear, he turned into the alleyway alongside the Rama block and parked the car.

Sergei handed Andrei copies of the keys that had given them

access on the previous visit. 'Get the door open, and we'll start moving the gear across.'

This time, the transfer of the spinel crystals and equipment into the building went off without incident. Half an hour later, they were installed in the seventh floor offices of ThaiExport, and the safe was open. Halfway through the substitution of the spinel crystals for the diamonds, Andrei looked up from weighing a batch of stones.

'When we've finished tonight, we're adding another one hundred thousand carats of diamonds to the fifty thousand carats we've already got in the car.'

'That's the plan—what's on your mind?'

Andrei scratched his head. 'Why don't we go all the way, and take the lot.'

Sergei raised his eyes in despair. 'You idiot, what happens when they find a collection of empty boxes later this morning—we'll be picked up at the airport, that's what. This way the boxes will weigh the same, and even if they should be opened, they will still appear to contain the right amount of stones—now get on with your weighing.'

When all the spinels had been substituted, Andrei picked up a small grey linen bag. 'These are the original sample spinels the Chinese sent to Moscow back in February—what do you want done with them?'

Sergei paused for a moment, and then made up his mind. 'Weigh them, and I'll substitute them for the same weight of diamonds from the last box.' He grinned at Andrei. 'We might as well have the benefit of a few more carats of diamonds.'

When they had finished, Andrei shut the safe door and began packing up the equipment. Then they retraced their steps out of the building, and loaded the equipment and diamonds into the Lada.

Halfway to the airport, a thought struck Sergei.

'I don't remember seeing the small bag that contained the original spinel samples—did you pick it up with the rest of the gear?'

Andrei's face turned a shade of grey. 'No—I thought you'd taken care of that.'

Sergei hit the brake, and the Lada skidded to a halt. 'You bloody fool. If it's found it will immediately arouse suspicions. ThaiExport will then check the safe, find that some of the boxes have plain metal seals, and Cahn will be on to us.'

He swung the car round in a 'U' turn, and headed back to the city. When they reached the Rama Jewelry building he slowed the car and switched off its lights. As they coasted into the side road, he spotted a shadowy figure disappearing into the building's side entrance.

'Hell and damnation,' he cursed, 'someone's breaking in.'

'It could be Cahn,' suggested Andrei, 'he didn't know we were paying another visit.'

'Cahn wouldn't be around at this time of night—anyway he'd use the front entrance. We'll hang about for a bit and see what's going on—there's plenty of time to our flight, and it's vital we retrieve that bag before someone finds it.' Sergei's hand slipped inside his jacket and checked the reassuring bulge of his gun.

* * *

Using a small magnetic compass and a bar magnet, Paul and Steven successfully negotiated the alarmed door at the entrance to the ThaiExport office. Then, with the help of their torches, they entered the inner office and found and neutralised the ultrasonic movement detector. Steven opened his attachécase and took out the thermal conductance tester that Jeffrey Hamilton had given them in London. He placed the instrument on one of the desks, and then aimed the beam of his torch at the safe. Paul stepped to one side of the safe, carefully avoiding the area of the alarm pad under the carpet. Supporting himself with one hand on the safe, he leaned across and dialled the combination numbers from the slip of paper given him by Cahn.

Paul breathed a sigh of relief as he heard the lock tumblers drop into place. Still keeping well to the side of the safe, he grasped its handle and swung the door open. Steven joined him, and shone his flashlight into the safe's interior. 'Those boxes look familiar,' he commented.

Paul used the safe door as a support and leaned across to get a closer look at the metal boxes. 'Any one fastened with a plain seal will do.'

Steven pointed to the top box. 'That one fits the bill.'

Between them they eased the box out of the safe and placed it on the desk alongside the tester. Steven cut the wire sealing the box, and opened its lid. The diamonds filling the open-top plastic boxes reflected back multi-coloured flashes of light from the beams of their torches.

Paul inspected the stones. 'They're all in the half-carat to one-carat size range. Each of these plastic boxes holds around two hundred stones, so if we assume five to ten percent of them are fakes, there must be at least ten stones per box that are not diamonds.'

Steven nodded in agreement. 'That means we should know if the shipment's been tampered with by testing the contents of just one of them.' He carefully lifted out a plastic box, and tipped its contents on the desk alongside the thermal tester.

Paul switched on the tester and touched the tip of its pen-like probe against one of the stones. Within a second the diamond indicator lamp on the control box glowed green.

'A kosher diamond,' exclaimed Steven. 'One down, and one-hundred and ninety-nine to go.'

After ten minutes of testing, over half the stones had been returned to the plastic box as genuine diamonds, but on the desk were seven crystals that had failed the test.

Paul switched off the tester and dropped the seven fake diamonds back into the plastic box. 'That's enough proof the shipment's been interfered with. Let's close up and get out.'

Steven re-sealed the metal box, and carefully returned it to the safe. As he closed the safe door, the beam of his torch revealed a small grey bag lying on the floor.

Paul picked it up and shone his torch on its linen surface. A row of Chinese characters were stencilled across the middle of the bag. Just above them, and barely readable, the words 'Beijing University' had been scrawled with a black marker pen.

Steven gave a low whistle. 'So the spinel crystals were grown in China.'

Paul stuffed the bag in his pocket. 'We'll get the Chinese characters deciphered when we get back to London.'

They returned to street level in a jubilant mood. Paul switched off his torch, and eased open the exit door. He peered out at the dimly lit side street, and gave the thumbs up sign. Steven slipped out carrying his attachécase.

The two Russians were waiting, one on each side of the exit door.

Sergei pushed his gun into Steven's back.

'Freeze, my friend, and drop that case'.

Paul, still hidden by the door, drew back. At that moment, Andrei walked into his line of vision. Crouching low, Paul launched himself through the half-opened door in a rugger tackle, and knocked Andrei to the ground.

Sergei looked round in surprise at the two men grappling on the pavement. 'Forget it,' he snarled, 'or your colleague dies.'

Paul scrambled to his feet and raised his hands. 'OK, cool it. So what's all this about?'

Andrei got up shoved him hard against the wall. 'We saw the light of your torch from the seventh floor windows,' he hissed, 'what were you doing up there?'

Paul shrugged his shoulders. 'Bugging the telephones, if you must know. ThaiExport asked us to do an overnight job—they suspect a member of staff is selling confidential information on shipments.'

Andrei turned to Sergei. 'They must know about Cahn.'

Sergei gestured him to keep quiet. He looked the two men up and down suspiciously. 'You have just come from the seventh floor. You may have found a small bag of instruments we left there by mistake earlier this evening.'

Steven glanced at Paul and shrugged his shoulders. 'There was a small linen bag on the floor by the safe,' he volunteered, 'but it was empty—I picked it up and put it in my case.'

As Andrei bent forward to grab the case, Paul's right knee jerked up and caught him in the mouth, sending him flying across the pavement.

Steven spun round, his right arm knocking up Sergei's gun, and his left fist driving hard into his opponent's stomach.

Sergei doubled up in pain, and dropped his gun. Paul kicked it away into the gutter, and backed off warily. Andrei was sitting on the pavement spitting out blood and a broken tooth.

Steven retrieved his case and joined Paul.

'I quite enjoyed our chat. Now if you'll excuse us, we'll be on our way.' Paul saw a movement out of the corner of his eye as Andrei drew a knife from his leg holster. 'Behind you,' he shouted.

Steven half turned as Andrei sprang tiger-like across the pavement. The Russian landed off balance and fell forward, his knife slicing though Steven's right trouser leg and cutting deep into the calf muscle.

Paul dived for the gun in the gutter, rolled over and came to his feet with the gun levelled at the two Russians.

'That's enough,' he growled, 'unless you fancy a smashed kneecap apiece. Now get into your Lada and start motoring.'

Andrei got to his feet and helped Sergei back to the car. He switched its lights on, and started the engine. 'I'll run the swines down,' he muttered, dribbling blood from his torn gums.

Sergei turned on him angrily. 'Don't be a idiot—he's got my gun. If he uses it, the police will come running. They've done us a favour by picking up the bag, and they've no idea of its significance. Now get moving, we've got a plane to catch.'

Paul watched the Lada turn round and drive back into Silom road, then he walked across to his fallen companion. Steven had pulled his ripped trouser leg up over his knee and was trying to stop the flow of blood from the gash in his calf.

Paul pulled out his handkerchief and tied it tightly round the leg just below the knee. 'That'll staunch the blood until I can get a doctor to you. The Oriental is about three hundred yards away. D'you think you can make it that far?'

Steven stood up and grimaced. 'It hurts like hell, but if you can take my weight on that side, I should be OK.'

He put his right arm over Paul's shoulder. 'I just hope he didn't use that knife to clean his nails,' he grimaced, and began limping back to the hotel, supported by Paul.

It was six o'clock and dawn was breaking by the time they reached the hotel. The night manager was still on duty at the reception desk. As they approached him, his eyes opened wide at the sight of Steven's torn and bloody trousers.

Paul asked for their room keys. 'My colleague has had an accident, and needs medical help. I want you to get hold of a doctor as soon as you can and send him up to my room.'

When they reached the room, Paul helped Steven into the bathroom and sat him down alongside the bath. He removed Steven's trousers and gently lifted his gashed right leg over the edge of the bath. Then he removed the tourniquet and bathed the still bleeding wound in running water. The horizontal four-inch gash across the fleshy part of the calf looked deep, and the surrounding skin was red and angry-looking.

He soaked a clean handkerchief in antiseptic. 'This is going to hurt worse than hell,' he warned and quickly bound it around the open wound.

Steven grimaced in pain, and gripped the side of the bath with both hands as beads of sweat broke out on his forehead. Paul gave him a few minutes to recover, and then took another handkerchief and applied a fresh tourniquet.

Steven blinked the tears from his eyes. 'Thanks, pal. Where did you get your medical training, Buchenwald?'

Paul chuckled. 'I'm sure you'd do no less for me.' He glanced at his watch. 'It should be around half past midnight in the UK. I'll ring Sir James' private number, and put him in the picture.'

Steven nodded. 'Why should he sleep while we're enjoying ourselves.'

The number Paul dialled rang for several minutes before it was answered.

'Sir James here—who the blazes is that?'

'It's Paul Hamilton, sir. I thought you'd be interested to hear we had a great visit to the Grand Palace yesterday.'

The line was silent for a few seconds. 'Couldn't this have waited until the morning?'

'Hopefully I'll be halfway back to the UK by then. Steven's been hurt rather badly. Could you arrange for Stephanie to be at Heathrow with the car at 4 pm your time?'

'As you wish Paul, but make sure Steven is in good hands before you leave him.'

'No problem, I'm bringing him out with me—even if I have to carry him. I'll see you in about seventeen hours time. By the way, security will need tightening up this end—I'll fill you in later.'

The doctor Paul requested arrived at eight o'clock. He was clearly not in a good mood at being called out so early. After he had attended to the leg and dressed it, he took Paul aside.

'The gash in your friend's leg needs stitching. I've only cleaned the wound and applied a temporary dressing to hold the lips of the wound together. My advice is, get him to a hospital as soon as possible.'

After the doctor left, Paul wrote a brief note and slipped it together with some of his dwindling Thai money and the duplicate keys into an envelope addressed to Cahn.

'I've told him we had some problems with his Russian friends last night, and that I've deducted the doctor's fee and the cost of a new pair of trousers from his final payment. I'll deposit the envelope with reception as we leave.'

Steven eased his aching leg onto a stool. 'Hopefully, that should stop him contacting the police. I don't fancy a Thai jail in my condition.'

Paul picked up the telephone and dialled reception. 'I'm expecting a taxi driver—his name's Patana—send him to my room as soon as he arrives.' Then he dialled the Thai Airways number and booked them both on the 10 am flight to London.

* * *

Patana managed to break all his previous records for the 30-mile journey to the airport, and they arrived in the terminal building just as the last call was announced for the 10 am flight to London. Patana booked their luggage in, and then accompanied Paul and Steven to the passenger barrier. Dressed in his well-worn denim jacket, jeans and grubby trainers, he was on the point of tears as they thanked him for his efforts.

Paul stuffed his remaining Thai money in Patana's pocket and shook him warmly by the hand.

'We'd never have made it without you—thanks a million.'

Patana swallowed a lump in his throat. 'You good man to work for, Mr Paul. Come back soon, and we do more business together.' He patted his bulging pocket. 'Maybe I even have new taxi by then.'

Paul helped Steven up the walkway to the waiting 747. He paused at the top, and turned to wave goodbye to Patana, but the young Thai was already busy selling his services to a group of American tourists. Paul shook his head in amusement, and followed Steven into the plane.

CHAPTER 16

LONDON

Tuesday 4 August, 1981

During the thirteen hour flight from Bangkok, Steven's temperature began to rise. The 747 was only half full, and with the help of the Thai stewardess, Paul made him as comfortable as possible by converting two adjacent seats into a makeshift bed.

Eight hours into the flight, lunch was being served. Steven waved away the tray of food, and closed his eyes. The Thai stewardess glanced at Paul. 'Your friend looks unwell.'

Paul laid his hand gently on Steven's feverish brow. His colleague's shock of fair hair was wet with perspiration. 'I think you'd better get the captain to ask if there's a doctor on board.'

When the broadcast announcement brought no response, Paul decided to check the injured leg again. Blood had begun to seep through the dressing, and the leg felt hot to the touch. He looked at his watch. 'Another five hours to go,' he muttered, 'I'd better see what's in the crew's first aid box.'

Back in the first class galley, he helped the Thai stewardess check out the plane's emergency medical pack. 'I don't think we can risk taking off the dressing, but if you can find any penicillin tablets, they might just control the infection and lower his temperature.'

There were plenty of packets of Asprin and Paracetamol tablets, but nothing in the way of antibiotics. Then, at the bottom of the pack, the stewardess caught sight of a small bottle. She picked it up and handed it to Paul.

'It's labelled 'Amoxycillin 250mg tablets', but they're not on the pack list.' Paul took the bottle and peered at the label. 'Amoxycillin—sounds like a penicillin derivative. I seem to remember my girlfriend was once prescribed those for an infection. Let's try them.'

The stewardess nodded. 'I think we have to take the chance—at worst they'll have no effect. I'll give your friend one now, and one more tomorrow morning.'

A thought occurred to Paul. 'One other thing. Can you contact London Airport and have a wheelchair standing by when we arrive?'

* * *

Stephanie carefully slotted the red XJ12 into one of the few vacant spaces in the short-stay car park, and walked across to Terminal 3. The Thai Airways 747 was not due in for another thirty minutes, so she bought herself a coffee in the self-service restaurant.

When she had arrived at 2 Manorhouse Street that morning, Sir James summoned her to his office.

'I had a phone call from Paul late last night.' Sir James checked the notes he made in his desk diary. 'He and Steven are returning on the first Thai Airways flight out of Bangkok this morning—it left at 10 am local time. They're due at London Airport around 4 pm today. He wants you to meet him with the car—apparently Steven has been injured.'

On Friday, Stephanie had shown her annoyance at the suddenness of Paul's departure, but now she was concerned for his safety. 'Is Paul alright?'

Sir James smiled reassuringly. 'He certainly sounded in control when he woke me up at twelve-thirty this morning. Incidentally, he confirmed that the Russian shipment has been doctored.'

When Stephanie returned to the arrivals barrier, the Thai Airways Bangkok flight had just landed. One of the first passengers to walk through the customs exit was Paul, closely followed by a Thai stewardess pushing Steven in a wheelchair.

Stephanie hugged Paul and gave him a quick kiss. Then she turned her attention to Steven. His fever had subsided, and he had recovered sufficiently to look slightly sheepish under her gaze.

'What on earth happened to you?' Steven hung his head, so she turned back to Paul. 'Have you two been scrapping again?'

'Something of the sort—I'll fill you in while we drive. I'm booking Steven in to Bart's. He's got a nasty gash on his leg that needs stitching.'

Steven protested at this. 'It's nothing really, Paul's just being fussy.'

Paul bent down and whispered in Steven's ear. 'Shut up and enjoy the attention—if you're a good patient, I'll get Kim to visit you in hospital.'

* * *

It was nearly six o'clock before Paul and Stephanie arrived at 2 Manorhouse Street. Sir James, immaculate in his dark grey pin-stripe suit, was waiting in his office for them. Paul's secretary, Debbie, was also present and was looking distinctly uncomfortable in Sir James' company. When they were seated, he turned impatiently to Paul.

'How is Steven?'

Paul leaned back in his chair, conscious of his crumpled lightweight suit and his far from fresh sports shirt. 'He's OK—we ran into a couple of Russian heavies as we were leaving the ThaiExport premises early this morning. Steven's leg was badly slashed by one of them.' Paul ran a hand through his dark hair. 'I got a doctor to him in the hotel, but he became feverish on the plane—I think the wound must have been infected. I've booked him in a private room at Barts, and they're keeping him on antibiotics for a few days. Then they'll stitch up the gash and keep him under observation for a day or two more. Incidentally, the bad apple in the ThaiExport office is Cahn, the assistant manager—he'll have to go.'

Sir James sighed, his gaunt face showing clear signs of strain. 'I'll see to that later. Jim Finchley and I spent a gruelling ten hours yesterday trying to calm the clients' anger over the mess of the July Sight. Your news of the Russian shipment was just one more problem.' He inspected his carefully manicured nails. 'How many diamonds were substituted this time?'

'We only had time to check out one of the two-hundred carat boxes, but I estimate around ten percent.'

Sir James nodded wearily. 'This time, we'll have to test every stone in the shipment when it arrives. I've frozen payment to Russalmaz, but what I need now is proof positive of the Russians' involvement in the diamond substitution.'

Paul pulled the grey linen bag from his coat pocket, and laid it on Sir James' desk. 'I think this may be at least part of that proof. Steven found it lying beside the ThaiExport safe—the two Russians we ran into were very keen to have it back.'

Sir James picked up the bag and turned it over. 'It appears to be from Beijing University. What about the Chinese characters?'

'I've no idea what they mean, but I believe one of Roy Wakefield's hobbies is a study of Mandarin.'

'That man never ceases to amaze me.' Sir James turned to Paul's secretary. 'Debbie, ring down to personnel and ask Mr Wakefield to come to my office immediately.'

A few minutes later, the door opened, and an anxious Roy Wakefield stood hesitantly on the threshold.

'Come in, man, and take a seat,' snapped Sir James. 'I'd like your opinion on this.' He handed Roy the linen bag and pointed to the Chinese lettering.

Roy inspected the ideograms, a semblance of colour coming back to his palid cheeks. He cleared his throat nervously. 'Translated literally, the first group means imitation.' He paused in thought for a moment. 'No, I think a more accurate translation is synthetic. The rest of the ideograms, or word pictures, translate as Crystal Research Department.'

Paul looked across at Sir James. 'So, the bag came from the synthetic crystals research department of Beijing University.'

'Where does that get us?'

'Perhaps the Chinese are manufacturing the spinel crystals for the Russians.'

Sir James nodded and then remained silent for a few seconds, deep in thought. 'I was talking to the Swedish Ambassador at a Foreign Office trade reception last week. It seems their Volvo

Company has been selling a considerable number of trucks to the Chinese Government over the past two years.'

Paul looked puzzled at this turn in the conversation.

Sir James continued. 'The Chinese Government is desperately short of foreign currency, and still owes Sweden for the trucks. On Thursday of this week, Volvo are sending a trade delegation to Peking. They're hoping to reduce the debt by setting up a barter deal involving Chinese products and minerals.'

Paul caught on. 'So you want me to join the delegation as an excuse to visit Peking. Presumably I'll go as a diamond expert?'

Sir James smiled. 'I'll have a word with the Swedish Ambassador and arrange it. There's a gemmologist in the delegation, so you should be able to find an excuse to visit the University.'

Stephanie butted in. 'Excuse me, Sir James, I think I can help there.'

Sir James indicated for her to continue.

'I belong to a cultural exchange study group. Last year we visited China, and during the few days we had in Peking, one of the places we visited was Beijing University.'

Paul turned to Stephanie. 'I remember now—didn't you sign up a pen pal on the Beijing visit?'

Stephanie nodded. 'Yes, I met a nice young lab assistant who wanted to improve his English—guess which department he worked in.'

'Synthetic Crystals Research?'

'You've got it in one. His name's Lin Chung, he's married and has a five year old son. If you like I can get an express airmail letter off to him tonight to say a friend of mine is arriving in Peking and will contact him.'

Sir James stood up. 'An excellent idea. Well, that just about settles your end of it Paul.' He turned to Debbie. 'I want you to contact the Chinese Embassy first thing tomorrow and arrange a visa for Mr Remington. By then, I'll have authorization for his visit from the Swedish ambassador. Also ring Sir Edward in our embassy in Peking and let him know about Paul's visit—just in case he needs any backup.'

* * *

Stephanie and Paul had been invited to dinner at Muriel's flat in Chelsea that evening. When Paul rang the door bell, it was answered by little Melanie. She looked up at Paul. 'You not here Sat'day, U'cle Paul.'

'I had to make a very long journey—I'm sorry I couldn't keep my promise to take you to Hamleys.'

The blonde child brought a doll from behind her back. 'Aunty Steff took me—she bought me a Welsh dolly.'

'That's nice—now I've got a surprise for you.' Paul bent down and gave Melanie a gaily wrapped parcel. 'Let's go inside and you can undo it.'

Muriel greeted them in the hall. 'Hallo, children—and welcome back Paul. You must tell me all about naughty Bangkok. When I was a girl it was Brighton, or, if the man was rich, Paris!'

Paul winked at her. 'I'll tell you all about my adventures later.'

Christine and Mike were waiting for them in the lounge, and while Melanie was busy unwrapping her present, they caught up with each other's news.

Mike helped his aunt to a chair and Paul noticed that she was using a walking stick. 'How are your keeping, Muriel?' he asked.

'Oh, the old arthritis hits me now and then—I blame the dentists.'

'What on earth have dentists got to do with it?'

'Well, my dear, in medieval times, most people's teeth had rotted away or fallen out by the time they reached thirty-five. This restricted them to a diet of pap, and the majority died off by the age of forty. Nowadays, thanks to the dentists with their drills and fillings and dentures, the likes of me are kept chomping away until the rot sets in somewhere else.'

Paul chuckled. 'I just hope I have your spirit when I'm your age.'

By now Melanie had torn the wrapping paper from her present, and was excitedly showing her new doll to Christine.

'Go and say thank you to Uncle Paul.'

The child took the doll to Paul. 'Thank you—I got thwee dollies now, but I like this one best—what's her name?'

Paul bent down. 'Well, as I bought her in my hotel in Bangkok you could call her Anna. Do you know what she is?'

Melanie shook her head.

'She's a Siamese dancer—that's why she's wearing such a pretty dress and a tall golden headdress.'

While Paul was entertaining Melanie, Christine was sitting talking to Stephanie.

'So, Steven is in hospital. Do you know how he was injured?'

Stephanie grimaced. 'With the sort of capers he and Paul get up to for the company, the less I know the better. It seems they were involved in a fight with two Russians while they were checking out some shady business in Bangkok.'

'That's one thing about Britain, I feel much safer here with Melanie than in South Africa. That business three years ago at the Pretoria mine was pretty scary. I really thought Mike and I were goners.'

Stephanie nodded. 'Diamonds do seem to attract violence, and it's that side of the business Paul and Steven are mainly involved in on their overseas trips. I think we tend to forget how lucky we are in the UK. Guns aren't freely available here as they are in other parts of the world, and the streets are relatively safe to walk at night.'

'Now to more pleasant topics—is it still alright to leave Melanie with you on Monday?'

'Of course. I'm looking forward to having her. I've arranged to take the afternoon off, so you and Muriel can spend as long as you like at the National Gallery.'

* * *

Later that night, Paul lay alongside Stephanie in the large double bed listening as her breathing slowly returned to normal after another frenzied session of love-making. He raised himself on one elbow and brushed the strands of damp red hair from her face. 'Am I forgiven for my disappearing act on Friday?'

Stephanie was not in a good mood. She turned on her side and glared at him. 'I thought I'd just demonstrated that—what more do you want?'

'But that was only sex,' he protested, 'whatever happened to love?'

'You know my feelings on that subject—and not so much of the 'only', or are you telling me you prefer the services of the Bangkok massage parlours.' Stephanie's low mocking laugh ended in a yawn. 'Just be content I'm not a lesbian,' she murmured and turned her back on Paul. A few minutes later the sound of her light rhythmic breathing indicated she was asleep.

Soon, Paul told himself, I'll have to make my mind up about Stephanie. For some time, despite the occasional explosions of passion, there had been a growing coolness in their relationship. Right now he felt physically and emotionally drained, and was content to put off a showdown until after the Peking trip. Perhaps they should try living apart for a spell, and then see how they felt about each other… his thoughts drifted away as sleep overtook him.

CHAPTER 17

MOSCOW

Friday 7 August, 1981

When Oleg Aristov and Vassily Kolov entered the Kremlin office of Colonel Leo Vessovski, Head of the KGB, they knew their summons to his presence boded ill. The portly bald-headed Vessovski rose from behind his desk and welcomed them with a curt wave of his podgy hand. He was dressed as a full colonel, the ribbons on his chest proclaiming his front-line achievements during the bitter final years of World War Two.

Vessovski sat down again, and signalled for the two men to take the chairs he had placed in front of his desk. 'I've just had our ambassador in Bangkok on the line,' he grunted. 'He informs me that my two SMERSH agents have mysteriously disappeared.'

He paused and looked searchingly at the two men. 'Tell me, what arrangements, if any, did Russalmaz and the Trade Policy Committee make for the return of the diamonds that were removed from the July and August shipments?'

Kolov glanced nervously at Aristov, and licked his dry lips. 'None as yet. We thought it better to leave them in Bangkok until phase three had taken effect—after all they are perfectly secure in the Embassy safe.'

Vessovski waved a stubby finger at him. 'I've got news for you, comrade Kolov. Not only have my two men disappeared, but the diamonds have also gone missing.'

Aristov shook his head in disbelief. 'How on earth can this have happened? Vassily and I concede there were weaknesses in our plan, but we never imagined it would be put at risk by your own men. It's small comfort, but at least this latest disaster cannot be laid entirely at our door.'

Unable to contain himself any longer, and red in the face with anger, Kolov stood up and faced Vessovski across his desk. 'I've had enough of your bullying tactics—it's time you told us exactly what has been going on in Bangkok.'

Vessovski sighed. 'Sit down, comrade Kolov. You are right, we share equal responsibility for these happenings. As far as I have been able to discover, my two agents went missing sometime during Monday night. Two men fitting their description were seen at Don Muang airport next morning boarding a plane to Geneva. Their tickets were purchased several days earlier—presumably they used false passports, a commodity easily available to SMERSH agents.'

Aristov was beginning to sweat. He mopped his brow and stared wild-eyed at Vessovski. 'You know how sensitive this whole operation has become—what are you doing to recover the diamonds?'

'Calm yourself, Aristov, I also have agents in Switzerland. They have been put on full alert, and a complete dossier on the two defectors will be in their hands by tomorrow. You have my guarantee the diamonds will soon be back in our possession.'

Vessovski looked at the two worried men facing him. 'You should also know this. Our ambassador in Bangkok mentioned that two young Englishmen were seen in Bangkok last weekend. They too departed Bangkok airport on that Monday morning. By a strange coincidence, just before you arrived a telex came in from our Embassy in Peking. It seems an application has been made for an Englishman to join a Swedish trade delegation to that city.'

Volkov looked sharply at Vessovski. 'What are you trying to tell us? Have these two pieces of information anything to do with the Diamond Syndicate's Special Services operatives you mentioned at our June meeting?'

Vessovski shrugged his broad shoulders. 'Anything is possible. As a precaution. I have put my men in Peking on standby. They will shadow the trade delegation, and will also keep a special watch on the three Chinese who set up the synthesis plant in our university. The last thing we want at this stage is a connection to be made between Bangkok, Peking and your departments.'

Volkov still had his doubts. 'What happens if someone from the delegation gets close to the Beijing University people.'

Vassovski smiled coldly at the two men in front of him. 'All participants in such a contact will immediately be silenced. You already know the price we will pay if this affair degenerates into an international scandal.'

CHAPTER 18

HONG KONG—PEKING

Friday 7 August, 1981

The BA jet flew in low over the South China Sea on its approach to Hong Kong's Kai Tak airport. As the plane neared the mainland, Paul could see the airport's principal runway sticking out from Kowloon Peninsular like a beached aircraft carrier. A few minutes later, the big jet touched down gently on the seaward end of the runway. Almost immediately its cabin filled with the smell of sewage as tainted air caused by a combination of seawater pollution and oppressive weather conditions was drawn into the plane.

Paul held a handkerchief to his nose until the jet came to a halt outside the terminal buildings. When he emerged from the plane, the late afternoon humidity made him glad he was wearing an open-neck shirt and lightweight suit. Inside the terminal building the air-conditioned atmosphere helped revive him while he waited patiently by the baggage rondel for his suitcase. Fifteen minutes later, Paul's British passport gave him rapid passage through emigration control. Then, after his luggage had been scrutinised by customs, he strolled out of the airport building into the afternoon heat and joined a short queue at the taxi stand. On the advice of Lars Norstrom, head of the Volvo trade delegation, the CMO travel department had booked Paul a room at the Excelsior Hotel in the Causeway Bay area of Hong Kong Island.

When he reached the head of the queue, a Kowloon taxi with a red body and a silver-grey top pulled up. Its driver, a young cheerful Hong Kong Chinese wearing a white T-shirt and blue shorts, raised his dark glasses and peered up at him.

'Where to boss?'

'The Excelsior, Causeway Bay.'

As they sped out of the airport complex into Chatham Road, the taxi driver engaged him in conversation

'You from England?'

Paul smiled. 'Is it that obvious?'

'I tell from your suit—made in UK, not by six-hour tailor in Hong Kong.' He turned and grinned at Paul. 'I have cousin who work in London.'

They entered Hong Chong Road, skirted the railway station and paused briefly at the toll booth in the entrance to the cross-harbour tunnel.

'Tunnel toll cost ten dollar,' said the young driver, 'I add to my four dollar fare—OK?'

'You're in charge.'

The section of the tunnel under the harbour took about five minutes to navigate. On previous visits, Paul had made the trip to Hong Kong Island on one of the Star Ferry boats. Although slower, the ferry's more leisurely approach to the island allows time to enjoy the busy waterway traffic of Victoria Bay and take in the dramatic panorama of the island's skyscraper-lined fore-shore.

When they emerged into daylight at the tunnel exit, Paul caught a glimpse of Causeway Harbour and a group of what appeared to be floating covered wagons.

'Boat people,' explained the taxi driver, 'beginning to be big problem.'

The Excelsior Hotel on Gloucester Road faces out over Victoria Harbour, conveniently close to the tunnel. The taxi driver carried Paul's suitcase into the hotel and followed him to the reception desk. Paul handed the man a twenty dollar note. 'Keep the change.'

The driver bowed politely and gave Paul a card printed in Chinese and English. 'My name is Wan. Please call number on card if you want hire me again.'

Paul nodded and signed the hotel register. He picked up his room keys and turned to the receptionist. 'Has Mr Norstrom arrived yet?'

The Chinese girl checked her computer display and made a

note on Paul's hotel card. 'Mr Norstrom arrived earlier today—I've written his room number on your card.'

He thanked the girl and followed the bell boy into the lift.

Paul's room was on the eighteenth floor. It was roomy, and in addition to an inviting-looking double bed, was furnished with easy chairs, a drinks refrigerator and a writing desk. The big double-glazed window gave him a sweeping view across Victoria Harbour to Kowloon and the distant contours of the New Territories beyond.

Paul turned the room's temperature control to low. Then, feeling grubby after the long flight, he discarded his clothes and had a shower and a shave. When he returned to the bedroom wearing just a pair of briefs, a Chinese maid was turning down his bed. He smiled at the startled girl. 'Don't mind me—I'm broadminded if you are.' The girl giggled and backed out of the room.

Paul pulled on a clean blue sports shirt and white linen slacks. He helped himself to a lager from the refrigerator, sank into one of the easy chairs and dialled his Swedish contact's room number. It was answered almost immediately. 'Hello, this is Lars Norstrom.'

Paul smiled as he recognised the slightly sing-song accent.

'Hello, Lars—this is Paul Remington.'

'Welcome to Hong Kong, Paul. I hope you had a good flight?'

'No complaints. I believe your ambassador in London has already given you a rough idea why I'm here.'

'Yes, I understand it's diamond business—the gemmologist in our delegation is looking forward to meeting you. When you're ready, I suggest you join us in the Hotel lounge.'

'Give me five minutes, and I'll be with you.'

When Paul stepped from the lift onto the deep pile carpet of the Excelsior's opulent lounge, a lean fair-haired man wearing a pale blue safari suit waved to him. Lars Norstrom uncoiled his six foot length from the chair, and ambled forward to greet Paul.

'Good to see you—come along and meet the boys.'

The five male members of the Volvo trade delegation stood up and shook hands with Paul as Lars introduced them.

Lars eyes twinkled as he pointed to the last member of his

team. 'This is our gem expert. His real name is a bit of a tongue-twister, so for obvious reasons we've nicknamed him "Midnight".'

Paul gripped the big outstretched hand of a tall handsome Nigerian.

Midnight grinned at him, exposing a row of perfect white teeth. 'These Volvo people have no respect. My real name's Mogoloshanti, but you can call me Midnight if you prefer. As Lars says, my given name is a bit of a mouthful for you guys.'

Paul chuckled. 'Hi, Midnight. Thanks for the option—between us we should be able to keep these Swedes in order.'

Lars looked at his watch. 'If it's OK with you, Paul, we'd all like to eat fairly soon.'

'Fine—where did you have in mind?'

'We'll give Chinese food a miss tonight. My boys are having trouble with chopsticks—they've hardly eaten a thing since they got here earlier today. A session with knives and forks in the Hotel's Noon Gun Grill is what they'd prefer. Tomorrow we'll have a meeting after breakfast so I can put you and my team in the picture about Chinese business protocol. Then we're all catching the afternoon CAAN flight to Peking.'

* * *

After the sixteen hour flight from London, Paul had no difficulty in sleeping that night. At eight o'clock the next morning he joined Lars and the rest of the delegation for a continental breakfast in the hotel's Garden Lounge. When they had all eaten, Lars clinked a spoon against his glass for attention.

'I know some of you have been to China with me on previous trips, but I'd like to remind you of a few points before you meet our China National Arts and Crafts hosts in Peking. At our first formal meeting with them, the pecking order of our group will be assumed from the sequence in which we enter the room and are introduced. So to avoid any confusion, I'll be first in. On these occasions it's polite to stand until your host invites you to sit. It's also important to remember that theirs is a very structured organisation. You won't get a decision from the head of a department until he's cleared it with his immediate superior—and it may have to go all the way to the top and back again before you get an answer.'

Lars looked across at Paul. 'We also have to allow for the fact that each regional section of the Arts and Craft organisation is isolated, and has little knowledge of what's going on in other parts of the country. So don't ask your host questions that'll cause him to lose face by not knowing the answers.'

Lars smiled at his colleagues. 'We're here to find goods to barter against the big debt China has run up with Volvo. However, doing business with the Chinese can be a long drawn-out affair. On a first visit to China, you're regarded as a "New Friend", and you hardly ever get to first base. On the second visit they'll regard you as a "Friend", and it's possible that business will only be transacted when you've reached the status of an "Old Friend" on the third visit. We're fortunate to have gained the confidence of the Chinese government on previous visits, so, hopefully, we can get down to discussing deals immediately following the formal exchange of pleasantries.'

After breakfast, Paul returned to his room and packed his case. Then he consulted the tourist map of the island provided in the hotel folder, and decided to take a stroll along the waterfront. He left the hotel, turned right and followed the road around the green expanse of Victoria Park until he reached the promenade that ran alongside Causeway Bay.

On the far left of the bay he could see the boat people's crafts huddled together beneath the spur of land surmounted by the white-walled building of the Royal Hong Kong Yacht Club. Looking across the bay he realised why they had chosen that anchorage. This area of South East Asia was notorious for its violent hurricanes, and here their fragile vessels, together with the Club's expensive yachts, were sheltered on the seaward side by the long rock and concrete arm of a typhoon barrier.

Hurricanes were also the reason for the use of bamboo scaffold poles instead of metal ones on the building sites he had glimpsed from his bedroom window. Bamboo was far more flexible in the high winds, and if it was blown down, caused less damage.

On his way back to the Excelsior Hotel, Paul took a short-cut across the park and came upon a group of elderly Chinese going through the graceful slow-motion T'ai Chi morning exercises. He paused for a moment to watch their sculptured arm movements and gentle arabesques. 'Now that would make quite a feature in Regents Park,' he mused.

When Paul reached the Excelsior, he decided to take a look at Yee Tung Village, a shopping arcade advertised in the hotel brochure. The arcade specialised in a wide variety of Chinese artifacts, and was situated at the far end of the Hotel foyer. Inside the arcade Paul wandered along the double row of shops and stalls, inspecting jewellery, jade carvings, paintings, embroidered cotton blouses and a wide variety of other souvenirs.

At one stall he paused and bought a model of a cockerel made from yellow plastic covered wire, with red cockscomb and wattle. The wizened old Chinese in charge, grinned at him. 'You chose well—this is the Chinese Year of the Cock.' Paul was about to leave the stall when he spotted a Mandarin doll. 'Just the thing for Melanie,' he murmured, and beckoned the old man. 'I'll take the doll as well.'

On his way out of the arcade, he paused at a silk shop. A young Chinese girl was hanging out a selection of coat-length dressing gowns. A green silk one, embroidered with yellow and red dragons, caught Paul's eye. 'I can just picture Stephanie in that,' he said out loud.

'What colour your friend's hair?' asked the young girl.

'It's red,' answered Paul.

'You must buy it for her.' The girl took the gown off its hanger and held it against her slim figure'.

Paul was suddenly aware of someone standing beside him. 'You'll look real sweet in that, honey,' commented a dark brown voice.

'When I want your advice, Midnight, I'll let you know,' responded Paul, his attention divided equally between the gown and the girl's profile.

The Nigerian chuckled and nodded to the girl. 'He's just a harmless transvestite. Wrap it up—he'll buy it.'

'Hang on,' protested Paul, 'I haven't made my mind up yet.'

'I take ten percent off price.' The girl quickly folded the gown in tissue paper, slipped it in a bag and handed it to Paul.

'Remind me never to shop with you again, Midnight,' sighed Paul as he handed over the money.

They were just leaving, when the dull thud of an explosion rattled the shop's window. Midnight winked at Paul. 'That's the Noon Day Gun—time we got down to some serious drinking, my friend.'

* * *

When Paul and the Swedish trade delegation arrived at Kai Tak airport, they checked their luggage in, and then passed through immigration control. In the departure lounge they found the gate number of the CAAN 102 2.40 pm flight to Peking was already flashing on the information screens.

During the two and a half-hour China Airways flight to Peking, Lars and his Swedish companions amused themselves by photographing the stewardesses with the duty-free Polaroid cameras they purchased in Hong Kong. Paul was amused to see the girls were wearing jewellery and brightly coloured silk scarves, frivolities that would have been frowned on during the reign of the 'Gang of Four'. He was sitting alongside the Nigerian, and took the opportunity to get to know him better.

'Tell me, Midnight, how did you acquire your American accent?'

'Simple. I took the Gemological Institute of America's course in Santa Monica—the accent was just a spin-off. Now what about you? Lars tells me you're in Peking on some sort of undercover mission—sounds intriguing.'

'As far as the Chinese are concerned, I've been attached to you as a diamond expert. The real reason I'm here is to make contact with one of the laboratory technicians at Beijing University. I work for the Diamond Syndicate's Central Marketing Organisation in London, and we've been finding diamond imitations in some of our incoming shipments. All the evidence points to the university as the source of the stones.'

Midnight was clearly intrigued at this. 'What are the fakes made of?'

'Our gemmologist says they're synthetic spinels. The crystals are octahedrons—just like the diamonds.'

Midnight showed his surprise. 'They clearly weren't made by the flame-fusion method—it must be a new process for spinel.'

Paul leant closer to Midnight and lowered his voice. 'If you can spare the time, I'd appreciate your company when I visit the lab technician.'

'No sweat man, it'll make a change from checking out the gems the Chinese want to unload on us.'

* * *

The plane landed on time at Peking's Shoudu airport, but it took the courier from the China National Arts and Crafts Corporation a further hour to argue them through the bureaucratic tangle of the Chinese Immigration section. By the time the courier located the minibus that was to take them into Peking, dusk was falling. The long tree-lined avenues they drove along were crowded with evening traffic, and their driver blasted his horn at every pedestrian and sluggish vehicle in his path.

It was dark by the time they arrived at the Peking Hotel, and the courier asked them to stay in the bus while he checked their reservations. During the delay, Lars moved down the bus and sat by Paul.

'I'm hoping we're booked into the newest part—the cockroaches get more numerous as you go back in time. When I had a room in the old section last year, it even had the original iron bedstead, and after two days the beetles had set up home in my toilet bag.'

'Rather that than in the kitchens,' commented Paul wryly.

The courier re-appeared at the bus. 'Rooms ready soon. First you all come in and have evening meal.'

In the hotel lobby they were welcomed by a tall bespectacled representative of China Arts and Crafts. The meal of salt beef, sweet and sour pork followed by soup, and a desert that consisted of a Chinese version of profiteroles, proved to be yet another frustrating chopstick experience for several of the Swedes. After the meal they were allocated rooms on the fifth floor in the middle section of the hotel. They took their bags up in the ancient lift, and after arranging to meet at breakfast the following morning, they turned in for the night.

When Paul reached his room the door was open. He entered and surprised a young Chinese hotel maid who had just finished making up the bed. She smiled at him, pointed to the bathroom, and held up five fingers.

Paul grinned. 'OK, take your time.' He dumped his suitcase on the bed. 'I'm just going to unpack.'

The room was large with high ceilings. On the left of the door there was a window and to the right of this twin beds. The rest of the room was furnished with a heavy oak wardrobe, two easy chairs, and a desk. There was a fitted wall cupboard opposite the beds, and when Paul opened it he was surprised to find it contained a colour television. 'So, Chinese technology has caught up with the West—next thing they'll be opening burger bars.'

Despite the room's size it seemed stuffy to Paul and he could smell stale cigarette smoke. He strolled over to the window, unlatched it and looked out. Below he could see some taxis and blue and white buses lined up along the front of the hotel. Beyond them the wide tree-lined Chang'an thoroughfare was almost deserted.

The Chinese maid came out of the bathroom carrying her cleaning equipment. 'OK now,' she smiled.

Paul extracted a five dollar Hong Kong note from his wallet and gave it to her as she was leaving. 'I'm sure you can change this at reception'.

The maid looked at the note in surprise, her face beaming with pleasure.

'Oh—t'ank you,' she giggled and ran from the room.

Paul laughed. 'Seems I've made a friend.'

* * *

Paul woke early next morning and moved into the bathroom. He turned on the hot water tap in the bath, but nothing came out. He tried the wash basin with the same result. Then he remembered seeing a thermos flask, decorated with a flower pattern, beside his bed.

'There goes my bath,' he muttered, 'but at least they've given me some hot water for a shave.'

He shaved, dressed and then took the lift to the ground floor. In the hotel's money bureau he changed his travellers cheques for the special foreign exchange certificates. These yuan notes were issued to foreign visitors, and were only valid in designated places such as Friendship stores, and for taxi fares.

When Paul joined the Swedish group for breakfast he found the tall Arts and Crafts representative talking to them.

'First we have meeting here in hotel with my manager, then I take Mr Remington and Mr Mogoloshanti to our jewellery display premises in the Agricultural Exhibition Centre on the eastern side of the city.'

When they entered the small conference room in the old west part of the hotel, Mr Li Wang, Manager of the China National Arts and Crafts Corporation, was waiting for them with his assistant and an interpreter. They took their places around a long central table covered in a white cloth, and then at Mr Li's invitation they sat down. A teacup, complete with lid, was set at each place, and red packets of Chinese cigarettes were liberally distributed down the centre of the table. After Mr Li's formal welcoming speech, and Lars' reply on behalf of the Swedish delegation, tea was served by two young hotel waitresses. As his cup was being filled from a thermos jug, Paul recognised the floral decoration pattern on its side, and suddenly realised he must have shaved in green tea that morning.

Lars laughed when Paul whispered this revelation in his ear. 'I must tell our host—the Chinese have a sharp sense of the ridiculous. By the way, if you're not a tea addict, don't drain your cup or it'll be refilled immediately.'

* * *

Early that evening Paul and Midnight excused themselves from the evening meal, and with the help of the hotel receptionist, hired a taxi. Paul handed the driver the piece of paper on which Stephanie had written Lin Chung's address. The driver looked at the paper, shrugged his shoulders and spat out of his window.

Midnight looked at Paul. 'I think that's a qualified "yes".'

They boarded the taxi and drove out into the main thoroughfare. Paul breathed a sigh of resignation. 'I hope this isn't the start of another communication problem. Shaving in green tea is enough excitement for one day.'

Halfway down Chang'an Avenue they passed several platoons of khaki-clad soldiers. 'With a population of around a billion the army is doing its bit to reduce the unemployment problem,' commented Midnight.

At intervals during the journey the driver continued to spit out of the window. 'I don't think he likes us,' complained Paul.

Lars laughed. 'No, it's not that—he's just getting rid of the Gobi desert dust. You'll get used to the habit after a few days.'

The driver turned right and headed north out of the central area. After a further twenty minute drive, he turned left at a T-road and stopped to talk animatedly to a group of people at a bus stop.

'We're lost,' groaned Paul.

The driver turned and grinned at them, waving the scrap of paper with the address on it. He set off again, made a second left turn into an unlit side street, and came to a halt. He beckoned his passengers out of the taxi and pointed to a large grubby-looking apartment block, its tiny balconies draped with washing lines just visible through the early evening gloom.

Paul handed the driver half the fare agreed with the hotel receptionist, and pointing to his watch, indicated for him to wait.

Lin Chung's flat number was 306, so they took a chance on the Chinese numbering logic and began climbing the bare concrete stairway to the third floor. Halfway up they passed an old man sitting hunched on the stairs smoking a stained clay pipe. Paul showed him the address, and the old man grinned and pointed up the stairs with his pipe. On the third floor there were six unnumbered doors. Paul walked to the end one, crossed his fingers and knocked. The door was opened by a delicately featured young woman wearing a yellow dress and a red and black check apron. When she saw Midnight she drew back in alarm, and shut the door. They heard a brief conversation behind the door, then it opened again to reveal a man wearing a grey T-shirt and black shorts. He peered apprehensively at the Nigerian, then cocked his head sideways and looked at Paul. A smile of recognition lit up his face.

'It's Mr Paul—Miss Stephanie describe you in her letter. Welcome—you and your friend please come in.'

The small flat consisted of a combined kitchen-living room with dividing curtain, a bedroom and a toilet. Pride of place in the living room was given to a television set, and Paul glimpsed a refrigerator in the kitchen.

'Please sit,' Chung pointed to the room's two easy chairs. He and his wife drew up wooden chairs from the small dining table, and sat facing Paul and Midnight.

'My wife name is Letitia. We very honoured by your visit.'

'Thank you, Chung,' replied Paul. ' We are very pleased to meet you and your wife, and I congratulate you on your English.'

Chung's face turned pink with pleasure. He reached over and picked up an airmail envelope from the table. 'Miss Stephanie say you want talk with me.'

Paul nodded and pulled a grey linen bag from his pocket. 'I think this came from your department in the university.'

He could see from the change in his host's expression that he recognised the bag. Chung ran the tip of his tongue nervously over his lips, and then turned and whispered something to his wife. When she had disappeared in the kitchen, he turned back to Paul.

'My wife make us tea.' He lowered his voice. 'As you say in England, walls have ears. Tomorrow is Monday—I take day's holiday to show my son Forbidden City, which is now Palace Museum. I meet you ten o'clock under Gateway of Supreme Harmony—we talk more easy then.' He handed the bag back to Paul.

While they sat drinking tea, Midnight asked Chung what he thought of China's television service. Chung walked to his set and proudly switched it on. 'We have very good colour. On Sunday, much culture.'

The picture of an army choir appeared on the screen.

'This just like Red Army choir in Russia—I see them when I visit Moscow this year.'

Paul looked across at Midnight, and raised his eyebrows in surprise.

When the choir had finished their song, the camera zoomed in to centrestage. A lady announcer walked into the picture, announced the next item, and then walked off camera again.

Midnight leaned towards Paul. 'Interesting camera technique,' he murmured. Paul smiled and glanced at his watch.

'I regret we'll have to be moving, Chung. I've got a taxi waiting outside.' They shook hands with Letitia, and Chung escorted them to the door of his flat.

'I say goodbye to you here. It better we not seen together in street,' he explained. 'We meet again tomorrow, ten o'clock.'

* * *

When Paul and Midnight returned to the hotel they joined Lars and his group on a visit to the International Club in Peking's embassy enclave. At the Club, they sampled Chinese-style champagne, listened to Western pop music, and watched the younger members of the various diplomatic staffs mingle on the dance floor with the local Chinese. During a lull in the over-loud music, Paul told Lars of his meeting with Chung, and the appointment he had made with him for the following morning.

Lars picked up a bottle and poured some of its colourless liquid contents in to a small glass. 'Glad to hear you've made contact with your man.' He handed Paul the glass 'You've sampled Chinese champagne—now you must try this.'

Paul took the glass and downed its contents. The fiery liquid seared his throat and brought tears to his eyes. 'What in hell is that,' he gasped.

'It's a Chinese spirit called "Mau Tai"—you soon acquire a taste for it at Chinese business banquets. Try another one.'

Paul put a hand over his glass. 'No thanks—it might stunt my growth!'

* * *

Chung had enjoyed his meeting with Paul and Midnight, but the shock of seeing the bag that had once held the sample spinel crystals kept him awake that night. When he finally fell asleep, he once again dreamed of slogan-shouting crowds, but this time he was in Tian'anmen Square. In his dream he had mislaid his beloved bicycle, and in his frantic search for it, found himself suddenly isolated from the crowds and standing alone in front of an advancing army tank. He had woken up with the image of the confrontation engraved like a newspaper picture in his mind.

Chung did his best to shut the worrying dream out of his thoughts. The next morning, as he approached the meeting place by the Gateway of Supreme Harmony, he gripped his son's hand tightly and glanced anxiously around. Paul found himself involuntarily scanning his fellow visitors in the same manner. Neither he nor Chung saw the Russian who was parallelling Chung's path on the far side of the central courtyard. Nor did they see the man pause for a moment, plug an earpiece in his ear and remove a miniature directional microphone from his pocket.

Chung's face broke into a wide grin when he spotted Paul. 'Good morning. My son Duan would like say hello. Unfortunately he speaks no English.'

Paul shook the shy child's tiny hand. 'I'm very pleased to meet you Duan.' The boy smiled at the sound of his name, and then hid behind his father.

Chung looked anxiously around at the people criss-crossing the courtyard. 'I think it best we talk here.'

Paul nodded in agreement. 'My company in London buys rough diamonds from Moscow. Just recently the shipments from Russia have contained many fake diamonds.' He noticed Chung's expression change at these words. 'The fakes are perfect octahedral crystals—just like the diamonds they were used to replace. When we tested them, we found they were synthetic spinels.'

Chung shook his head, and looked glum.

Paul paused while a group of tourists sauntered by. 'Earlier this week I was in Bangkok—that's where the Russians send their diamonds for onwards delivery to London. When I visited the Bangkok shipping office, I found the bag I showed you last night. The printing on the bag shows it came from your Synthetic Crystal Research Department in the university.'

Chung was silent for a few seconds while he considered this information. Then, making up his mind, he drew Paul closer. 'My department develop synthetic spinel method. We give method to Russia. I visit Moscow last April to set up manufacture of spinel there.' His eyes narrowed as he recalled his own surprise at the amount of equipment. 'Big, big production.'

'Do you have any idea what they were going to use the spinels for?'

Chung nodded. 'One day, Russian in charge of Moscow University laboratory talk on telephone to someone in gem export department.'

'Did you hear what he said,' prompted Paul.

'Sure, he talk in English. He say crystals ready for London diamond sale in June.'

'Thanks, Chung—that's just what I wanted to hear.' Paul thought for a moment. 'Did Moscow send your department any letters about the spinels?'

Chung scratched his head. 'I saw Russian letter before Moscow visit. It was in office of my boss. He put it in project file.'

'Do you think you could get me that letter?'

Chung blew out his cheeks at the enormity of the suggestion.

Paul persisted. 'The Russians are doing a very bad thing to my company. They are stealing the diamonds we have paid for, and they are trying to upset our customers with the spinels you helped them produce.' He could sense that Chung was wavering. 'My company would be very generous to you in return for such information.' He looked down at little Duan who was clearly getting bored with standing still for so long. 'You could use the money to pay for extra things for your son.'

Chung screwed up his courage. 'I like you, Mr Paul—and I not happy with what Russians do. Meet me at side entrance my department at Beijing University eleven tonight. Here, I draw you plan.' He took Stephanie's airmail letter from his pocket, and sketched the position of the entrance to the Synthetic Crystal

Research Department on the envelope. 'I meet you here,' he drew a cross on the plan. 'Then I get you letter.'

At the other side of the courtyard the Russian visitor put the earpiece and microphone back in his pocket and hurried away in the direction of the exit.

* * *

Paul stopped the taxi two-hundred yards short of the grey stone edifice of Beijing University. It was twenty minutes to eleven, and the streets around the university were dark.

'We'll walk the rest of the way,' he said to Midnight, and signalled the driver to wait for them.

When they reached the far end of the building, Paul paused to peer at the sketch map Chung had drawn on Stephanie's airmail envelope. 'The entrance to the Synthetic Crystal Research Department should be down this side road.'

As they were approaching the stone steps that Chung had indicated on his sketch, Paul heard a noise behind him, and spun round. A light was weaving along the road towards them.

They watched the light draw nearer, then it suddenly flickered and went out. 'Is that you, Mr Paul?' whispered Chung, dismounting from his bicycle.

'Of course it's me,' snapped Paul, 'who else did you expect at this time of night?'

They followed Chung as he wheeled his bicycle down the steps and propped it up beside the door. Paul sensed the young laboratory technician's unease, and regretted he had spoken harshly to him. 'Would you like me to come inside with you?'

Chung took a deep breath. 'No—better you keep watch outside. If anyone come, knock on door.' He took a torch and a set of keys from his pocket and opened the side entrance.

Paul patted his shoulder. 'Take care—I'll make sure you're not disturbed.'

Chung smiled at him nervously and slipped inside the building.

While they were waiting, Paul walked back to the corner of the side road. He could just make out the taxi's parking lights some distance ahead. Beyond it he thought he could see another car with its lights out. 'I didn't notice that when we pulled up,' he muttered.

Paul retraced his steps and joined Midnight at the side entrance. 'I think we may have company—there's a car parked behind our taxi.'

Midnight drew in his breath. 'Shall I warn Chung?'

'No, just stay put.' Paul looked at him and chuckled. 'You're much less visible than me. When Chung comes out, get the letter off him, and get him away on that bike. I'll move up the road and fend off any opposition.'

Paul had just regained his vantage point at the corner of the road, when he heard the soft click of a closing door. Looking back, he could see the shadowy figure of Chung wheeling his bicycle into the road. Chung mounted the machine, switched his light on and began peddling towards Paul.

At that moment, the sound of a revving car engine shattered the silence. Paul swung round and glimpsed the dark shape of an unlit car racing towards him. 'Go back, Chung, go back,' he shouted and leaped into the middle of the road waving his arms at the car.

The car was almost on top of Paul when its driver switched on the headlights. At the last moment, Paul, half-blinded by the full beam, flung himself to one side. He heard the driver change gear as the car raced by, and saw its headlamps pick up the cyclist. Chung was pedalling straight down the middle of the road, seemingly mesmerised by the oncoming lights. The car had almost reached him, when he braked, turned his machine around and rode back down the pavement in a desperate attempt to regain the safety of the side entrance. The car swung across the road to head him off. As it gained on him, Chung looked over his shoulder and gave a thin high-pitched scream of fright. Paul saw the car mount the pavement. Over the noise of the racing engine he heard the metallic crunch of the impact followed by two sickening thuds as Chung's body bounced off the car and hit the side wall.

By the time Paul reached Chung, the car was already out of sight, and Midnight was kneeling beside the small twisted body.

Chung's eyes stared up at them sightlessly, and the spreading pool of blood from the back of his head glistened darkly on the pavement. Paul knelt down and felt for the pulse in Chung's neck. After a few seconds he straightened up.

'They've killed the poor little devil.'

Midnight pulled a crumpled letter from his pocket.

'This sure must be important—he gave it me when he came out.'

Paul took the letter from him. In the gloom he could just make out the printed Chinese characters that covered the page. He carefully folded the paper and put it in his wallet.

'I'd no idea they would go this far.'

Midnight looked at him in surprise. 'You think the Russians are behind this?'

'It's possible—they've already killed two of our people in the UK.'

'What the shit do we do now?'

'Nothing. Chung's been killed by a hit-and-run driver. We leave him and his bike exactly where they are. The Chinese police can sort it all out in the morning.'

Midnight turned on Paul, his eyes blazing. 'You cold blooded bastard —so you're simply going to walk away from all this?'

'Just think about it for a moment. If we call in the police, what the hell are we going to tell them? "Please, we were keeping a look-out for Chung in the middle of the night while he burgled his laboratory".'

Midnight took a deep breath. 'OK—I get the point. But what about Chung's wife?'

'She'll be informed soon enough by the police. When we visited their flat, it was pretty obvious Chung didn't want her to know about my business arrangements with him.' Paul paused for a moment, weighing up his options.

'Tomorrow, I'll contact the British Embassy. The ambassador is a friend of my boss, and knows I'm here. I'll arrange for his department to have the Chinese equivalent of two-thousand dollars delivered anonymously to Letitia Chung—that should keep her going for some time.'

As they walked away from Chung's body and his smashed

bicycle, Paul hesitated for a moment and looked back. 'I'd just like to get my hands on that bloody driver,' he hissed.

When they reached the taxi, they found the driver slumped across his seat. 'Jesus,' hissed Paul, 'they've chopped him too.'

At the sound of Paul's voice, the taxi driver awoke, and gazed up bleary-eyed at his two passengers.

Midnight hauled the man upright. 'Shit man, do you want to give me a heart attack?' He let go of the startled driver, and climbed angrily into the taxi.

Paul smiled reassuringly at the offended Chinese and gave him a fistful of foreign exchange notes. 'Hotel Peking—pronto.'

They drove back through the deserted streets in silence, each busy with his own thoughts. Just before they reached the hotel, Midnight sighed and looked across at Paul. 'For the sake of your conscience, I just hope that letter is worth the price it cost tonight.'

Paul shrugged his shoulders. 'Believe me, I had no idea the Russians were on to our meeting tonight—if I'd had the slightest suspicion I'd have cancelled it rather than put Chung at risk. Now it's down to me to get that letter back to London.'

After they parted company in the hotel, Paul took precautions against a possible further confrontation with the Russians. He photocopied the incriminating letter in the hotel's business section, and put the original copy and the linen bag in a padded envelope. Then he deposited both the envelope and the photocopy in the hotel manager's safe. When he returned to his room, Paul locked and bolted the door. 'If the Russian's are that desperate to cover their tracks, I must be next in the firing line.'

* * *

After a fitful sleep, Paul awoke early the next morning. He got out of bed, walked across to the window and gazed down for a few minutes at the multitude of cyclists peddling to work in Chang'an Avenue. 'The police will have discovered Chung's body by now,' he thought. 'I'll just have to find a way to put them on the track of that murdering swine in the car—I owe Chung that at least.' Then he turned and made his way to the bathroom. Something white caught his eye by the hallway door. On the floor was an envelope. He picked it up and opened it. The single sheet of folded paper contained a brief handwritten message in block capitals.

WE HAVE YOUR GIRL AND CHILD. WILL EXCHANGE THEM FOR STOLEN LETTER. IF YOU WANT TO SEE THEM ALIVE AGAIN RETURN TO LONDON IMMEDIATELY AND AWAIT INSTRUCTIONS.

CHAPTER 19

PEKING–LONDON

Tuesday 11 August, 1981

The note's stark threat jerked Paul wide awake. He grabbed the telephone and dialled the number of his Prince Albert Road flat in London, hoping that someone would still be there. Although it was midnight UK time, the phone was answered at once.

'Paul Remington's residence—who's calling?'

Even at this distance Paul could hear the strain in Mike's voice.

'It's Paul—what the hell's going on, Mike?'

'Thank God you've rung—Chrissy's been going crazy. She and Muriel were here with Melanie yesterday morning. After lunch, they left the child with Steffi while they visited the National Gallery. When they got back, the flat was empty. They thought Steffi must have taken Melanie for a walk, but two hours later it was clear something was wrong, so Chrissy rang me at Cheyne Walk...'

Paul butted in. 'OK, Mike, now listen to this. I'm still in Peking and a message has just been pushed under my bedroom door. It simply says my girl and child are being held hostage—they must think Melanie's my daughter. It also says I'm to return to London immediately and await further instructions. Has anyone been in touch with you yet?'

'Yes—after Chrissy rang, I got a taxi to your flat. I'd only just arrived when the phone rang. Chrissy took the call, and a man with a thick Russian accent told her they were holding Steffi and Melanie hostage until you got back from Peking. He said any attempt to contact the police would put both of them in danger. Then he rang off. After that, I put Christine and Muriel in a taxi and sent them back to Cheyne Walk—I figured they'd be safer there.

'Tell Christine not to worry—nothing will happen to Melanie. I've got a letter the Russians badly want, and they're willing to do an exchange. I'm catching a plane out of here in two hours, so I'll fill you in with the details when I arrive. The CAAN Peking flight is due at Heathrow 4 pm your time—can you meet me?'

'Sure—is there anything I can do before then?'

'Yes, contact Roy Wakefield at the CMO and say I want to see him urgently at my flat as soon as he's free this afternoon. If you can get in touch with Steven Heming, and he's well enough, get him along too.'

After his call to Mike, Paul went down to the foyer and retrieved the padded envelope and photocopy from the hotel manager's safe. Then he went to Lars Norstrom's room and told him of the previous night's events and the threatening note.

Lars was clearly shocked. 'That's one hell of a mess—can I do anything to help?'

'I'm catching the nine o'clock plane to London. Just in case I'm waylaid, I've put the incriminating evidence in this envelope and addressed it to Muriel Reece at her Cheyne Walk flat in London. I'd be grateful if you'd airmail it for me. A few days delay in its arrival might just prove useful. I've included a note instructing Miss Reece to leave the letter and bag in her bank's safety deposit.'

Lars considered this for a moment. 'I think the best thing is for me to follow you to the airport in a separate taxi. Then I can dispatch the envelope in person at the terminal's postal counter.'

'Agreed—I'll pack and see you in the lobby in half an hour.'

* * *

When Paul returned to his room to pack his case he found the hotel maid he had tipped three days before wheeling her trolley of cleaning equipment down the corridor. She recognised Paul and beckoned him over. 'I see man go in your room'. The girl looked concerned.

'How long ago?'

The girl held up both hands, spreading out the fingers.

'Ten minutes?'

The girl nodded. 'He big—look bad man,' she whispered.

Paul paused. 'I think it's time I persuaded one of these characters to answer a few questions,' he mused. Paul pointed to the door on the right of his room. 'Can you unlock it for me?' He mimed the action with his key.

The maid nodded and produced her master key. Paul unlocked the door and handed back the key. He slipped into the room and closed the door behind him. As he had hoped, the room was empty. He moved to the window and opened it. Looking down he could see a narrow ledge running round the outside of the building. 'I hope the masonry is sound,' he muttered and climbed onto the window sill. He turned and lowered himself gingerly on to the ledge, testing it with his weight. 'So far so good.'

Facing the wall he inched along to the right, holding on to the window frame with his left hand. The window of his own room was five yards away, and there were no obvious hand holds. Paul inspected the surface of the wall. The mortar between the blocks of masonry was missing in several places. He jammed the fingertips of his right hand into one of the crevices and let go of the window frame with his other hand, flattening himself against the wall. He found another fingertip hold for his left hand and began inching along the ledge, probing with his right hand for the next crevice. 'Piece of cake,' he re-assured himself.

When Paul reached his bedroom window he was relieved to find it still open. He peered in cautiously. The room was in a state of chaos. His belongings were scattered across the floor along with the contents of the dressing table and the wardrobe. Even the telephone and the ceiling lights had been dismantled in a thorough search. There was no sign of the intruder, so Paul climbed carefully into the room. He walked to the bathroom and cautiously opened the door.

Too late Paul sensed someone behind him. He half turned as the cord of the garotte cut into his neck.

'Got you Englishman,' snarled the intruder.

Paul dug his fingers into his neck in an attempt to loosen the cord, but it was too tight. He knew he had only seconds left before he lost consciousness. In desperation he brought his right foot up and kicked out with all his strength against the wall. The heavily built man who had moved silently across the room was caught off balance by the sudden impetus of Paul's body. He fell backwards with Paul on top of him. The garotte loosened momentarily. Paul sucked in a lungfull of air and drove his right elbow into the man's solar plexis with all his might. He rolled off his assailant as the man doubled up and gagged. Paul freed himself from the garotte and threw it across the room. The man struggled to his feet and pulled out a flick-knife. Paul side-stepped the lunge and hit the intruder squarely on the point of his chin. This time the man went down and stayed down.

'God, I must be getting careless in my old age,' wheezed Paul massaging his neck. He kicked the knife away and then knelt down and searched the man's pockets. In his wallet he found a Corps Diplomatique ID card bearing the insignia and address of the Russian Embassy in Delhi. 'They're coming out of the woodwork now,' he muttered.

Paul tied the man up and stuffed a handkerchief in his mouth. 'That should keep you quiet until I'm out of the country. Now I must move, or Lars will be getting anxious.'

* * *

During the drive to the airport, Paul kept a careful eye on the surrounding traffic. One car in particular had attracted his attention when it pulled in behind his taxi as they left the hotel. He noticed that neither the driver nor the man sitting behind him was Chinese.

At the first main intersection on the outskirts of Peking they joined a queue of vehicles and the car that had been following them pulled out and drew alongside. The driver looked across at Paul and turned to speak to the man behind him. When they moved off again the other car inched ahead. The man sitting at the rear wound down his window. Paul saw the gun in his hand and hurled himself forward from the back seat. He pulled the handbrake on hard as the man fired. The taxi stalled and lurched violently to a halt as its offside window shattered, covering Paul in fragments of glass.

The enraged taxi driver shook his fist at the other car as it moved away, released the handbrake and restarted the engine. Then, to Paul's surprise, the man swung his taxi out of the line of slowly moving vehicles, pushed the accelerator pedal to the floorboards and set off in hot pursuit of the escaping car. Soon they were speeding towards the dual carriageway approach to the airport, with fields opening out on each side. By now Paul was convinced that these new assailants were Russians too, and having killed Chung were determined to silence him. To his dismay, it was also obvious that the taxi driver was intent on catching the other car, which was now only a few yards ahead. As they overtook the Russians he could see the man in the rear angling for another shot at him. He was about to duck when the taxi driver twitched the steering wheel and they swung across the front of the other car.

There was a crunch of colliding metal and both cars rocked dangerously. The taxi driver swung his wheel again forcing the Russians' car further to the left. Too late the other driver saw the approaching central reservation where the road divided into a dual carriageway. A front wheel hit the concrete kerb and the tire exploded. Desperately the driver spun his steering wheel in an attempt to regain control. The car swerved across the road behind Paul's taxi, its wheels dropped into a deep drainage ditch and it rolled slowly over onto its roof with the engine still racing.

At that moment, a second taxi with Lars aboard overtook them and pulled up a few yards ahead. Paul signalled to his driver to stop. He slapped him on the back, thrust a wad of yuan notes into his hand and held a finger to his lips for silence. Then he grabbed his case, jumped out and ran to Lars' taxi. Together they continued the journey to the airport.

Paul grinned at Lars. 'Thanks for the back-up—I think I've given the taxi driver enough money to keep him quiet. The last thing I want now is to tangle with the police—it's bad enough I've left one Ruskie tied up in my bedroom.'

Lars shook his head. 'An attempted garotting is bad enough, but for a moment back there I thought you'd been shot, my friend.'

'Well, I certainly didn't expect my driver to go berserk like that—he was as aggressive as a London cabby. I don't envy those two Russians when he gets to them!'

Lars glanced at his watch. 'You've got another twenty minutes to your flight, so we'll separate when we get to the airport. If there's any follow up after the shooting, I'll say I was the passenger in the taxi—at least I had a grandstand view of the whole affair if they want a witness.'

'Thanks, Lars, and if you get the chance, do me one last favour. I'm pretty certain the car that ran down Chung last night is the one we've just clashed with, and probably it's the same driver. If you can get this information through to the police, I'm sure they'll find enough evidence to link the two incidents. I'd dearly like to nail the guy who killed Chung.'

'I'll do my best, Paul. The Swedish Embassy here is on good terms with the local chief of police. I'll phone them from the airport.'

* * *

When the CAAN London-bound flight lifted off from Peking's airport, Paul breathed a sigh of relief and tried to relax. In the next thirteen hours he knew he must come up with a plan to rescue Stephanie and Melanie. It was obvious now that the Russian agents who killed the two diamond sorters in London were behind the kidnapping. If Stephanie and the child had seen the men who took them, then it was possible neither of them would be allowed to live. Paul was under no illusions now about his own safety—he too would doubtless be eliminated after he had handed over the letter.

When Paul arrived at Heathrow, Mike was waiting for him in the arrivals hall. During the drive back to the centre of London, Paul related the events that had taken place in Peking. He kept back his fears for the safety of Melanie and Stephanie—there would be time enough for that when he outlined the reasoning behind his plan to snatch them from their kidnappers.

Mike parked the car outside Paul's flat and lifted his case out of the boot. He glanced at his watch—it was five-thirty. 'Roy and Steven should be arriving soon. I'll join you here later, but right now I'm going back to Cheyne Walk and bring the girls up to date. By the way, when I left your flat early this morning, I turned the answerphone on in case the Ruskies made contact again.'

When Paul got out of the lift on the third floor he found a pale and worried-looking Roy Wakefield waiting for him.

'I got your message first thing this morning—what's happened?'

'Give me a moment and I'll tell you.'

Once inside the flat, Paul checked his answerphone, but there were no further calls. He walked across to his drinks cabinet, and took out a bottle of Smirnoff vodka. 'You'll join me?'

Roy nodded and sat down nervously on the edge of a chair. Paul poured two double measures of the spirit, added some tonic and handed one of the glasses to his office colleague. Roy accepted the drink gratefully and balanced it on his knee.

'Did you get the proof you were looking for?'

Paul extracted the crumpled photocopy from his wallet. 'Yes, but at some cost—this is a copy of a letter which I believe proves the Russian's involvement in the diamond substitution. The man who gave it me has been killed, and now Stephanie and Mike's daughter Melanie are being held hostage against the return of the original letter.'

Roy was visibly shaken by the news, and he spilt some of his drink. Paul handed him the photocopy. 'It's in Chinese—can you translate it?'

Roy pulled himself together, and peered at the letter. 'The heading is in Russian—it's from Russalmaz, and it's dated 23rd March this year.'

'Yes, I've already worked that out for myself,' said Paul impatiently, 'it's also signed V. Kolov. He's head of Russalmaz and responsible for their rough diamond shipments. Now what about the Chinese?'

Roy scratched his ear. 'Give me some paper—this could take time.'

Paul handed him a writing pad. 'A rough gist of the contents will do for starters. We can get it translated professionally later.'

Roy sniffed at this affront to his ability. 'I'll do my best—just leave me alone for a while.'

At that moment the entryphone buzzed. Paul answered it and pressed the door release button. 'Steven and Mike have arrived,' he announced, but Roy was too involved with the Chinese cyphers to look up.

Paul opened the door and let the two men in. 'Come through to the dining room—Roy is in the lounge translating the Peking letter. It's better we leave him in peace.' He stood back and inspected Steven. 'How's the leg?'

'Passable—I got bored and signed myself out of Barts. Now I only limp when Kim's around—it's done wonders for my love life.'

Paul grinned and thumped his colleague on the back. 'It's good to see you back on your feet again—when your temperature began to soar on the plane from Bangkok, I thought you'd bought a one-way ticket to harpland.'

Paul indicated for them to sit round the table, and then turned to Mike.

'How's Christine bearing up?'

Mike ran a hand through his dark curly hair. 'She's taking it pretty badly. Muriel is trying to keep her spirits up, but she hasn't slept properly since the kidnapping.'

Paul shook his head. 'I'm terribly sorry to have involved you and Christine in this mess. In a way, I'm to blame. When the two diamond sorters were killed, and when we were getting close to proving the Russian involvement, I should have realised they would resort to extreme measures to silence us.'

'It's possible the Russian hierarchy is ignorant of what Russalmaz are doing,' commented Steven. 'However, the strong-arm business, in Bangkok and now in Peking, certainly links their diamond department with the KGB.'

Paul nodded. 'That could be the reason they're so desperate to recover the evidence—when it's made public, heads will roll in Moscow.'

At this point, Roy walked into the dining room. He nodded to Steven and Mike, and laid his writing pad and the Chinese letter on the table.

'You asked for the gist of the letter—here it is.'

Roy pulled a loose sheet from the pad. 'It's signed Kolov, Head of Russalmaz, and reads as follows: "Comrade Professor Liang, this is to confirm that all necessary apparatus is now assembled in the Moscow University laboratory ready for the attention of your technicians. May I stress that it is most important for this equipment to be producing several hundred carats of synthetic spinel crystals by the beginning of June. It is also essential for considerably larger quantities to be produced during subsequent months. Our Professor Balitsky is looking forward to meeting you in Moscow on April 3".'

Paul stood up and patted Roy on the back. 'Well done—this is just what we need. No wonder the Russians are keen to get the original letter back.'

Roy shook his head disparagingly. 'Some of the Chinese ideograms were badly combined. The Russian linguistic experts have obviously got rusty since the split with China. The text uses the Beijing-based standard Chinese language of *putonghua*. I've made the translation read more colloquially, but the facts are unchanged.'

Paul took Roy on one side. 'You've done a great job—I'll phone Sir James tonight and put him in the picture. Right now I'm about to discuss ways and means of freeing Stephanie and Melanie. The less you know about that the better, so this is a good moment for you to leave.'

When Roy had gone, Mike turned to Paul in despair. 'If we can't go to the police for fear of harm being done to Stephanie and the child, what the hell can we do?'

Paul sat down and spread his hands out on the table. 'Until the kidnappers make contact again, very little. The message I received in Peking told me to return here and await instructions. But that doesn't mean we can't make contingency plans. While I was on the plane today I did some hard thinking.'

Paul looked at his two colleagues. 'First of all, let's take stock of the risks. There's always the possibility with kidnappers that their victims will end up dead—even when the demands are met. We know we're dealing with very vicious people, and even if I presented them with the vital letter, I doubt if they'd allow me to walk away alive with Stephanie and Melanie.'

Mike looked disconsolate at this cheerless news. 'So what d'you suggest?'

'Simply this. If we can find out where they're being held, Steven and I will go in at night, neutralise the opposition, and move them out.'

Mike looked doubtful. 'Sounds like a very long shot, and it all depends on your "if". I'll counter that with another suggestion. If we can't locate them, we back off and hand the problem over to the police.'

'Agreed, Mike, but I think that pretty well sums up our options.'

Paul turned to Steven. 'If and when we do go in, can I count on you?'

'Have you ever known me to miss out on a good scrap?'

Mike raised his hand in protest. 'Now hold on you two, Melanie's my daughter, so if you're planning a party, you'll have to include me.'

Paul laughed grimly. 'So it's the three Musketeers versus the KGB.'

Half an hour later, the telephone rang. Paul set his answerphone to record, flipped the loudspeaker switch, and lifted the handset.

'Paul Remington speaking.'

'Ah yes, Mr Remington, I see you have followed our instructions,' said a deep heavily-accented Russian voice.

'No thanks to my last encounter with your Peking colleagues; but the police haven't been informed yet, if that's what you mean.'

'Have you got the letter you stole from Beijing University?'

'Before we discuss that, I must have proof that Stephanie and the child are unharmed.'

'I'm a reasonable man, Mr Remington. You may speak with your girl.'

There was a short pause, and then Stephanie came on the line.

'Paul—are you OK?' Her voice sounded agitated.

'Sure—what about you and Melanie?'

'We're both surviving. They say we'll be released shortly.'

'That's right—we've just got to sort out the details, then we can all get on with our lives again.'

'Paul, don't forget to pick up those tickets for the "Pearl Fishers"—that was a capital idea of yours...'

The Russian came back on the line. 'I have kept my side of the bargain, Mr Remington, now about that letter...'

'It hasn't arrived here yet—I airmailed it from Peking airport this morning.'

'It sounds as if you distrusted us, Mr Remington. You've just sentenced our two guests to a few more nights away from home. I'll contact you again on Thursday morning. For the sake of Stephanie and Melanie, I hope you will have better news for me by then. I am a patient man, but my colleague may soon wish to seek some compensation for this delay from your lovely companion.' The line went dead. Paul switched off the recorder and replaced the handset.

Steven looked at him. 'That conversation was just under a minute long—even if we'd alerted the police, there wouldn't have been time for the call to be traced.'

Paul nodded. 'They're well aware of all the tricks.' He paused in thought for a moment, and then rewound the tape. 'I think Stephanie was trying to give me a clue to her location. It's something odd she said just at the end.'

He played the recorded conversation back, and stopped it at the point where the Russian was asking about the letter. Then he wound it partly back, and replayed just his conversation with Stephanie.

'...Paul—are you OK?'

'Sure thing—what about you and Melanie?'

'We're both surviving. They say we'll be released shortly.'

'That's right—we've just got to sort out the details, then we can all get on with our lives again.'

'Paul, don't forget to pick up those tickets for the "Pearl Fishers"—that was a capital idea of yours...'

Paul switched the machine off and frowned. 'That last phrase "a capital idea" sounds a bit stilted for Stephanie, and what's all that about tickets for the "Pearl Fishers"—sounds like a pop group.'

Mike laughed. 'It's a Bizet opera set in what is now called Sri Lanka.'

'That's got to be the clue,' exclaimed Steven. '"A capital idea" coupled with Sri Lanka. The capital of Sri Lanka is Colombo—maybe she's being held in a road or street named Colombo.'

'You might just be right—let's have a look at a London street guide.' Paul hunted along the shelves of his bookcase and pulled out a copy of the Geographers' London Atlas. He turned to the index of street names at the rear. 'There's a Colombo Road in Ilford, and a Colombo Street in SE1.' He flicked over the road map pages. 'Colombo Street, SE1, is in Southwark just south of Blackfriers Bridge.'

Mike fingered his chin. 'Way back before I went to South Africa, I used to date a girl in Colombo Road. It's a quiet residential area of semis.'

'So, even if we've understood Steffi's clue correctly, we have a choice. She and Melanie could be held in Colombo Road, Ilford, or in Colombo Street, London,' added Steven, pulling his earlobe.

Paul wound the tape back again. 'I thought I could hear something in the background during the phone call. I'll play it through once more. This time, let's concentrate on the pauses in the conversation.'

They all gathered around the answerphone and listened intently as Paul replayed the tape. He held up his hand. 'There it is—and again—there.'

Paul grinned at Mike. 'You don't have quite the same sort of social event in South Africa, but I think Steve will recognise the background noise.'

Steven grinned. 'You're right, it's a pub—you can even make out the barman's voice above the general chatter. That certainly rules out Colombo Road, Ilford.'

Paul bent over the book map. 'Colombo Street is quite short, and I seem to remember there's a public house at the far end—it's mainly used by the printers from Cornwall Press.'

Mike looked over Paul's shoulder at the map. 'So what do we do now?'

'Steven and I will take a saunter around the area tonight and check it out. Tomorrow afternoon at five we'll all meet back here, and I'll brief you on my plan of attack. Right now, Mike, I suggest you return to Muriel's. Tell Christine I've spoken to Stephanie, and that she and Melanie are OK. Say we're pretty sure where they're being held, and we're going to get them out tomorrow night. Oh, and warn Muriel there'll be an airmail package arriving for her in the next day or two. The instructions inside will tell her exactly what to do with the contents.'

After Mike had left, the telephone rang again. Paul answered it.

'So you're back,' said a dry humourless voice.

'I was just about to ring you, Sir James.'

'Well, what did you find in Peking?'

'I've got a letter which clearly implicates Russalmaz in the use of a synthetic spinel manufacturing process developed in Beijing University.'

'That's excellent news. Tell me, is Stephanie with you—she didn't come in to the office today.'

'No, she's not here. The bad news is that two Russian heavies, probably the ones that killed Peter Scofield and David Crosley, have abducted both Steffi and the child she was looking after. They're being held until I return the letter.'

For several seconds there was silence. Then Sir James spoke again. 'Paul, give them back the letter—and that's an order. I don't want to risk any more lives over this affair.'

'I appreciate your concern, Sir James, but I arranged to have the letter airmailed from Peking for safety—it won't arrive here for a least another day. Meanwhile, the Russians are getting desperate—they even took a pot shot at me on the way to the airport. I'm not certain if my flat hasn't been bugged, so I don't want to say any more over the phone. If you're calling from your office, I'll be with you in fifteen minutes—we can talk there.'

'Yes, I'm still in Manorhouse Street. It's eight o'clock—I'll ring down and warn Security you're coming in.'

* * *

When Paul arrived in Sir James' office he found him talking on the telephone. 'I appreciate it's been a trying time for you,

Hank, but if you can bear with me a little longer, I promise this will be the last occasion.'

He put the receiver back on its rest, and gestured wearily for Paul to take a seat. 'I'm still trying to pacify our principal Sight Holders after the fiasco of the July Sight. Now that the Russian's August shipment has arrived, we're having to work all hours to weed out the fake stones. The next Sight is fixed for August 25 to 28, but we may have to postpone it. Now what is it you couldn't tell me over the telephone?'

'Steven and I think we've found out where the Russians are holding Steffi and the child. We can't call in the police for fear of what the Russians will do, and I can't guarantee their safety even if I do return the letter.'

'What is your solution then?'

'Steven and I will go in, SAS-style, tomorrow night. I plan to catch them off guard.'

Sir James sighed. 'I suppose I have no option but to agree. You and Steven have certainly been very successful in the past, but on this occasion I must advise extreme caution. I'll stay by my private telephone throughout tomorrow night in case you need assistance from the Yard's Anti-Terrorist Squad—the man in charge is an old friend of mine.'

Paul chuckled. 'You have a very wide circle of friends, Sir James. I'll certainly keep in touch.'

* * *

Later that night, Paul and Steven took a taxi to the north side of Blackfriers Bridge. Paul paid off the driver, and they began walking over the bridge. It was just getting dark, and they could see the street lights of Blackfriers Road stretching down as far as St George's Circus. Paul paused for a moment in the centre of the bridge to admire the view. In the half-light of dusk, London's river scene looked magical, the illuminated buildings on the river frontage and its lamp-festooned embankment vying with the floodlit dome of St Pauls Cathedral in the background. On their right they could see Somerset House and the headlights of the traffic streaming over Waterloo bridge.

When they reached the south side of Blackfriers Bridge they waited on the corner of Stamford Street for the traffic lights to change. Then, a few yards further on, they came to the junction with Colombo Street. On the corner was a church and a small graveyard surrounded by an expanse of grass. Fronting the narrow street itself was the church rectory, and on the far side of it they saw the lights of an old traditional-looking public house, the 'Eastern Star'.

'Bingo,' murmured Steven. 'I suddenly feel thirsty.'

On the opposite side of the street was a row of three small warehouses, and beyond them several cars were parked on what had once been a bomb site. Paul sauntered across the narrow street, and looked back at the pub. Like the adjoining rectory, it had three floors. The middle floor was in darkness, but he could see a faint light in two of the top floor windows. There was a short cul-de-sac separating the pub from the rectory. Halfway down it on the left Paul noticed a separate entrance at the side of the pub. He beckoned Steven, and they moved into the cul-de-sac and checked the doorway. There were two bell-pushes labelled 1a and 1b. Above the door an agent's sign advertised 'FLAT TO LET'.

'Looks promising,' commented Paul, 'I think we deserve a pint now.'

Back in Colombo Street, Steven pushed open the glass panelled door of the Eastern Star and they entered the public bar. The barman eyed them as they approached the counter.

'What can I do for you, gents?'

'Two pints of lager,' said Paul, he suddenly realised that neither of them had eaten all day, 'and two bags of crisps.'

'Who's a big spender then,' muttered Steven. He parked himself on a bar stool and peered around at the room's half-dozen occupants.

Paul picked up his glass and took a long swallow. 'Do you have any bar food?'

'Only sandwiches,' replied the man, pointing to a dog-eared menu. 'Not much call for anything else in the evenings.'

Paul ordered two rounds of ham sandwiches. 'I see you've got a 'To Let' sign at the side. Is the flat part of the pub?'

'It's on the top floor—the governor lives in the flat on the first floor.' He pushed the plate of sandwiches across the counter. 'The top flat was let about a week ago—the agents should have taken the sign down.' They finished the crisps and washed down the slightly stale sandwiches with their lager. Paul nodded his thanks to the barman, and they got up and made for the door. As they were leaving, a group of men wearing blue overalls crowded in. 'Looks like the Cornwall Press night shift,' commented Steven.

Paul nodded, and signalled for Steven to wait outside the pub. He walked down the street, following it as it turned right at the far end of the Eastern Star. In the gloom he could just make out the outline of a fire escape at the rear of the building. He walked back to Steven and pointed at the 'To Let' sign. 'Better make a note of the estate agent's name and address. You can use your charm tomorrow and get the low-down on the present tenants.'

Paul yawned and blinked his eyes.'Now I really must get my head down,' he glanced at his watch, 'quite apart from being jet-lagged, I've been up since midnight UK time—that's twenty-two hours straight off.'

* * *

Next morning, Paul, dressed in a black raincoat and wearing a peaked cap labelled 'Thames Water Authority', paid a return visit to Colombo Street. He stopped at the side entrance of the 'Eastern Star' public house, consulted the papers on his clip-board, and pressed the bell-push labelled 1b.

After a few seconds, an unshaven man in shirtsleeves and braces opened the door. 'Yes, what is it?'

Beyond the man, Paul could see a private entrance to the pub and an uncarpeted flight of stairs leading to the upper floors.

'We're replacing some pipes down the road, so your water's being turned off between 3 and 4 o'clock this afternoon.'

'Well, that's an improvement on last time—your lot turned me off right in the middle of the lunch hour.'

'You're the licensee of the Eastern Star?'

'That's right.'

Paul made a tick on his clipboard. 'Is anyone at home in the top floor flat?'

'Dunno—you'd better give them a ring. Neither of 'em will be very pleased at having to come down—one of these days the Brewery'll install doorphones.' The man shook his head in resignation, and shut the door.

Paul pressed the bell-push for flat 1a. There was no response, so he kept his finger on the button. After several minutes, he heard footsteps padding down the stairs. The door opened again, this time revealing a stocky middle-aged man smartly dressed in a dark grey suit, white shirt and silver-grey tie. He looked Paul up and down suspiciously.

'Yes, what do you want?' The man's voice was deep and sonorous, with a distinctly Russian accent. It reminded Paul of the voice he'd heard on his telephone. Below the man's left shoulder he thought he could detect the bulge of a shoulder holster under the well-cut jacket.

'No problem, sir. Just to let you know we're cutting your water off for an hour between 3 and 4 o'clock.'

The man grunted and shut the door in Paul's face.

* * *

Steven and Mike sat in the lounge of Paul's flat drinking beer. They had just helped Paul demolish a large deep-pan pizza, and were doing their best to ignore the growing pile of dirty dishes that was accumulating in the flat's small kitchen.

Paul put his glass down gingerly on the highly polished surface of the coffee table, then changed his mind and transferred it to the greasy plate at his feet. 'I'll have to straighten the place up a bit before Steffi sees it,' he sighed. 'Now, let's get down to business. This morning I confirmed there are two people in the top flat above the Eastern Star, and at least one of them is a Russian. What have you got for us Steven?'

'I told the estate agent in charge of letting the flat, that I wanted to rent it. He said the present tenants are two Russians. They claim to be Commercial attachés, and they've given the

Soviet Embassy in Kensington Palace Gardens as their main address. They've rented the flat for a month.'

Paul nodded. 'Well, that leaves us in no doubt that these are SMERSH agents.'

Steven pulled a sheet of paper from his pocket and unfolded it. 'I said I'd still consider renting the flat when it became vacant, but needed to know the layout of the accommodation. I was in luck—the agent had a floor plan of the flat. As soon as I left their office, I made a sketch from memory.'

Paul took the sketch and studied it. 'That's what I thought I saw in the dark last night—there's a fire escape at the back, and it leads to the rear balconies of the two flats. There are windows looking out over the balcony in all three of the bedrooms in the top flat, but only the principal bedroom on the left has a door giving access to the balcony and the fire escape.'

Mike was at last beginning to believe in the possibility of rescuing Stephanie and his daughter. He looked at the plan, and then turned to Paul. 'What if the Russians are armed?'

'I was about to come to that.' Paul got up and left the room. A few minutes later he returned with two cloth bundles. He unwrapped the larger one to reveal a compact short-barrelled semi-automatic pistol, complete with ammunition clip and silencer.

'It's a MAC-10,' he explained. 'It only weighs eight pounds, and with a piece of plastic behind the trigger mechanism, it converts to an automatic.'

'That's a highly illegal piece of hardware,' grunted Steven, 'Where the hell did you get it?'

'You remember the siege of the Iranian Embassy in Kensington? Before I left the Services and joined the Diamond Syndicate, I was in the SAS team that went in and freed the hostages. After it was all over, I found this lying in the rubble and liberated it.'

Paul unwrapped the smaller bundle and brought out a Colt 45. He handed it to Mike. 'This is for you. It's only for show, but its loaded, so handle it with care. I think that answers your question about the Russians being armed.'

Steven shook his head. 'So it looks as if I'm to be the unarmed decoy duck.'

Paul grinned at him. 'That's about it. Remembering your skills on the firing range, this way we'll at least avoid shooting each other. If there's a fire fight it'll be down to me—I'll be using the MAC with a silencer. They're not expecting any contact from us for at least twenty-four hours, so we'll hit them tonight after the pub closes.' He looked hard at both men. 'We've purposely not involved the authorities, so it's essential everyone comes out of this alive—including the Russians. We can't afford any messy loose ends. Now here's the plan…'

* * *

It had just gone eleven o'clock that night when the young bearded Russian agent unlocked the bedroom door and carried in two mugs of coffee on a tray. The night was warm, and he had changed into a T-shirt and jeans. Stephanie noticed he was still carrying a gun in his shoulder holster. She watched him put the tray down on a table by the door. He had done this several times previously when bringing food for her and Melanie during their two days of captivity. This time, however, the Russian made no attempt to leave, but turned around and re-locked the door.

During the daytime Stephanie's captors allowed Melanie to join her, and it had taken all of her patience to keep the child amused with stories and guessing games. At night, the older of the two Russians accompanied her while she put the child to bed in the small adjoining bedroom. Stephanie was then taken back to the bedroom at the top of the stairs and locked in again.

Melanie had been surprisingly composed during the whole affair, from their removal from the Prince Albert Road flat two days previously to their present forced imprisonment. When the younger of the two Russians blindfolded Stephanie in the car, she had pretended to Melanie it was just a game. Yesterday afternoon, while she was playing 'I spy' with the child, a scrap of paper under the bed caught her eye. She retrieved it, and to her delight discovered it was a screwed-up envelope addressed to 'The Occupier, Flat 1a, Colombo Street, London SE1.' When the older Russian called her to the telephone that evening to talk to

Paul, she had tried to pass on their location to him. As she put Melanie to bed that night, the child asked when her father and uncle Paul were coming to fetch them. Stephanie crossed her fingers and replied, 'Very soon, my darling.'

The bearded Russian picked up the two mugs of coffee from the tray, and sauntered across to where Stephanie was sitting on the bed. 'I've brought you nightcap. A little brandy in coffee—will make you relax.'

Stephanie took the mug and sipped the hot liquid. She was beginning to feel distinctly grubby, and yearned to be able to change out of her flowered nylon blouse and blue linen skirt into something fresh. When the two Russians had forced their way into the flat, she pleaded with them to leave Melanie behind, but they had laughed at her. As they bundled both of them out of the building, there had been no chance for Stephanie even to gather up her bag. Melanie, however, had refused to be parted from her Thailand doll, and it was now tucked up with her in bed.

The Russian sat down on the bed beside Stephanie and drank his coffee. 'Tomorrow, or maybe next day, you will be gone.'

Stephanie felt a shiver of apprehension run up her spine as his eyes strayed over her body. The man finished his coffee, took her half-empty mug from her, and placed both mugs on the bedside table. Then he slipped off his shoulder holster and put it, with the gun, beside him on the bed.

'You are very beautiful woman. With little time left we should be friends.' He reached out and touched her red hair.

Stephanie stood up and moved away from him. 'Right now I'm not in the mood to be friends with anyone—certainly not a Russian.'

The man got up from the bed swiftly, and grabbed her by the arm. 'You be nice to me, or maybe I teach your little Melanie new games.'

Stephanie could hear the sounds of music coming from somewhere within the flat. In desperation she broke away from the young Russian and ran across the room. She knew the bedroom door was locked, but beat on it with her fists, hoping the older man might hear and intercede. The young bearded Russian reached her and dragged her back towards the bed.

'I like woman to fight,' he hissed, and using both hands ripped her blouse open.

'Scum like you should be castrated.' Stephanie went for his eyes with her nails, but he stepped back and hit her across the face with the back of his hand, knocking her to her knees. Then he bent down and grabbed a handfull of her hair, forcing her face hard against his crotch. Although dazed from the blow, Stephanie could hear a doorbell ringing.

'Now, English bitch, I show you real man,' he snarled and dragged her towards the bed. Stephanie twisted in his grasp, struggled to her feet and brought her knee up hard into his groin. The man doubled up in pain and Stephanie broke away again, this time running to the window. She tugged open the curtains but too late remembered the window was fitted with burglar bars. She turned back, but the Russian had recovered and was facing her, his face distorted with rage.

'I too can play rough,' he hissed and moved catlike towards her.

* * *

Steven kept his finger on the bell-push for flat 1a. After what seemed an age, he heard footsteps coming down the stairs. The door was half opened by a middle-aged man. His right hand was tucked inside his jacket and rested nervously on the concealed gun in its shoulder holster. Steven groaned, sagged forward and fell at the man's feet. The surprised agent took his hand off his gun and bent over Steven.

Mike stepped into view, 'OK, Ivan, hands up.'

The Russian found himself staring up at the barrel of a Colt 45.

'Take your gun out nice and slow and lay it on the ground.'

After the Russian had obeyed, Steven scrambled to his feet and kicked the gun into the alley. He gave a silent thumbs up to Mike, and pushing past the Russian crept up the stairs. On the first floor landing he paused by the door to the publican's flat. A radio announcer could clearly be heard reading the eleven o'clock news. On the top floor he found the door to flat 1a ajar. Just inside the door he noticed a wall-mounted pay phone. The corridor beyond was only dimly lit from a single naked bulb, but light was streaming from the half-opened lounge door on the left, and he could hear music coming from inside the room.

Steven moved silently to the door and peered cautiously into the brightly lit lounge. It was empty, but he could see a half-full mug of coffee on a side table. 'Only one mug,' he murmured to himself, 'I can't believe it's going to be this easy.' He stepped back into the corridor and checked out the adjoining kitchen and bathroom. Both were empty. He tried the door of the principal bedroom opposite the bathroom. It was unlocked, and he opened it gingerly. The room was in semi-darkness but both single beds were empty. 'Looks as if the Russians are sharing,' he muttered, and then checked the door of the next bedroom. It was locked. He took a chance and tapped on the door.

'Steffi are you there?' he called, but there was no reply.

Puzzled, Steven retraced his steps along the corridor. Now his eyes were better adapted to the gloom, he could see a faint light coming from under the bedroom door nearest the stairs. He turned the door handle cautiously, but it was also locked. Then he heard Stephanie cry out. He took two paces back and threw himself at the door. As it burst open he saw Stephanie struggling in the grasp of a young bearded man as he forced her back towards the bed. Steven's impetus sent him sprawling forward. In the split second before he hit the floor, he recognised the man as the one he had wrestled to the ground outside the Syndicate's building in Manorhouse Street. The Russian threw the girl to the floor, lurched to his left and pulled a gun from the holster on the bed.

Steven saw the gun swinging towards him. As the man's finger tightened on the trigger he sat up and raised both his hands in surrender.

'Get up,' hissed the Russian, waving his gun.

Steven got slowly to his feet and placed his hands on his head. 'Take it easy my friend. We've got your colleague, so you can put the gun down.'

The man kept Steven covered and side-stepped across to Stephanie 'No way. The girl stays with me until I have letter.' He looked hard at Steven, 'I know you—we met in front of Syndicate building.'

Steven nodded. 'Where the hell is Paul,' he muttered to himself.

The Russian pulled Stephanie to her feet and held the gun to her head. 'One move from you and girl dies,' he snarled. 'Now we take our leave.' He waved Steven to one side and pushed Stephanie forward.

Behind them Steven glimpsed a movement though the half-open curtain. Before the Russian could take another step, the window exploded into shards of flying glass. The man released the girl and spun round, waving his gun uncertainly at the shattered window and fluttering curtains.

'Stephanie, get down,' Steven shouted and threw himself sideways out of the line of fire.

Invisible against the dark night sky in his black Balaclava and roll-neck sweater, Paul aimed the MAC low and fired a short burst.

Steven heard the muffled stutter of the automatic and saw the fabric rip from the Russian's jeans and the blood spurt from between his thighs. The man screamed, dropped his gun and collapsed on the floor clutching his bleeding groin.

Paul kicked in the burglar bars on the window and climbed into the room. He tore off his Balaclava, stepped over the writhing Russian, and pulled Stephanie to her feet. 'Where's Melanie?'

Stephanie choked back a sob. 'In the next bedroom—the door's locked.'

'OK, you go with Steven—he's got a way with locks. I'll get the Ruski's gun and meet you in the corridor.' Paul tucked the MAC into his black leather jacket and zipped it up. He walked back to the groaning man, retrieved the gun and followed them out of the room.

Paul watched while Steven expertly picked the bedroom lock. When the door was opened, Stephanie slipped into the room, gathered up the sleeping Melanie and wrapped her in a blanket.

At the top of the stairs Steven turned to Paul. 'What kept you back there—the bastard nearly shot me,' he whispered.

Paul grinned and slapped him on the back. 'I just about garrotted myself on a bloody clothes line—anyway I know you enjoy a little excitement. Now let's move out before the pub landlord gets nosey.'

The radio was still playing loudly as they crept past the door on the first floor landing. When they finally reached the ground floor they found the middle-aged Russian sitting at the foot of the stairs with his hands on his head while Mike covered him with the Colt 45. The man stood up and looked at Paul. 'Mr Remington I presume?'

'That's right—sorry to have kept you waiting. Please inform the Russian ambassador that your government will be hearing from us shortly.'

Mike handed his gun to Steven and gently lifted Melanie out of Stephanie's arms. The sleepy blonde child half opened her eyes. 'Daddy, it's you—look, I still got my dolly.' She tried to pull the Thai doll from the folds of the blanket, gave a big yawn and went back to sleep.

Steven looked at Stephanie's torn blouse and her bruised face. 'Sorry I didn't get to you earlier.' He took off his jacket and helped her on with it. Through the coat's material he could feel her shivering.

Paul patted Steven on the back. 'No apology needed. Your diversion was timed perfectly—we can still stage a good double act between us.' He put his arms around Stephanie, hugged her tight and kissed her. 'It's all over Steffi —let's go home.' He pointed across the road to his red XJ12. 'OK folks—everyone aboard.'

Halfway to the car Paul hesitated and turned back to the Russian. 'By the way, I suggest you phone for an ambulance—your colleague will never sing bass in the choir again!'

CHAPTER 20

MOSCOW

Thursday 13 August, 1981

The temperature in Moscow had been rising steadily all day. In the oppressive atmosphere of late afternoon, dark clouds were gathering overhead and a spattering of heavy raindrops heralded the start of a thunderstorm.

Colonel Leo Vessovski sat behind his office desk in the bleak grey stone building that housed the KGB headquarters in Leninski Prospect. He massaged his bald dome thoughtfully while he wrestled with the implications of the telephone call he had just received from the Soviet Embassy in London. Things had steadily gone from bad to worse with the plan to loosen the Diamond Syndicate's grip on the rough diamond market. Yesterday the Chinese had put his Peking agents on a plane back to Moscow. Now he had just learned that his two men in London had failed in a last ditch attempt to recover the letter in which Vassily Kolov of the Russalmaz department was revealed as the instigator of the plot.

The plan to market Russia's diamonds independently had been given the foreign trade adviser's unofficial blessing, but at the outset he had made it clear that in the event of failure, the protagonists would be regarded as having acted illegally, and would suffer the full consequences of a Soviet criminal trial.

The services of the colonel's SMERSH organisation had formed a necessary part of the plan, although early on, Leo Vessovski had expressed his criticism of the plan's inherent weaknesses. So far, the disappearance of his two SMERSH agents in Bangkok with one-hundred and fifty-thousand carats of Russian diamonds was known only to Oleg Aristov, Head of the Soviet Trade Policy Committee, and Vassily Kolov, Head of Russalmaz. Leo Vessovski was determined to keep it that way, and had already made arrangements to distance himself and his organisation from the two men. Vessovski picked up his telephone. 'Send in Comrades Aristov and Kolov.'

A few minutes later the door opened and a uniformed guard ushered the two men into the office. The colonel looked up from the papers on his desk and nodded curtly as they seated themselves in front of him. He turned and faced the gaunt bespectacled Kolov.

'I have just had confirmation from our embassy in London that my agents failed to retrieve the letter you so foolishly wrote to Professor Liang at Beijing University. By now we must assume the letter is in the hands of the Diamond Syndicate.'

Kolov flushed with anger. 'How on earth could anyone, including yourself Comrade Vessovski, have anticipated the combination of events that led to the Diamond Syndicate man's visit to Peking?'

Aristov leaned forward and wagged his finger at Vessovski. 'I must also remind you Comrade Colonel of the shortcomings of your own men in this affair. So far you have failed to recover the diamonds your two SMERSH agents stole in Bangkok.'

Vessovski smiled coldly at the two men. 'The bottom line, my friends, is that your plan has failed, and as a result we are now on the brink of a diplomatic row between our government and that of the United Kingdom.' He pressed a button beneath his desk and stood up. At this signal, the door opened and two armed guards marched into the room and positioned themselves at the side of the startled Kolov and Aristov.

Vessovski picked up a sheet of embossed paper from his desk, and waved it at the two men. 'I have instructions from Brezhnev to arrest you on the charge of illegally conspiring to market Soviet diamonds in contravention of the four-year trade agreement signed with the London Diamond Syndicate.'

The two men scrambled to their feet and looked at each other in stunned silence. Then Kolov found his voice, and turned on Vessovski. 'You will not be able to escape condemnation yourself Vessovski—there is still the matter of the stolen diamonds...'

Vessovski interrupted him. 'I have already informed Chairman Brezhnev of your lack of judgment over the security of the diamonds in our Bangkok embassy, and he has insisted on a full criminal trial for both of you. This is the only way in which our government can respond to the pressure that the British will doubtless now bring to bear.'

As the two men were being led out of the room, a lightning flash, followed immediately by the deafening crash of thunder, announced a drop in temperature as the storm broke overhead. Colonel Vessovski raised his hand, signalling for the guards to wait.

'I almost forgot—I have a message for you from Chairman Brezhnev. Should you wish to avoid the embarrassment of a trial, and the disgrace this will inevitably bring on your families, he wishes me to tell you that an alternative course of action will be provided for you in your cells. Comrades, I strongly recommend you both to take this honourable way out of your dilemma.'

CHAPTER 21

LONDON

Friday 14 August, 1981

Paul sat talking to Muriel in the oak-panelled waiting room on the ground floor of the Diamond Syndicate's Manorhouse headquarters. The security officer on the front desk had telephoned Paul when Muriel arrived, and Stephanie had arranged for coffee and biscuits to be served while they waited until Sir James was free.

Muriel had elected to wear a smart grey suit and a white lace blouse for her visit, and to set the outfit off had draped a black-and-white check scarf over her shoulders. She inspected the china cups and the coffee pot on the silver tray with approval. 'I see your company believes in looking after its visitors.'

Paul chuckled. 'Well, you are rather special, Muriel. It's not every day that Sir James has the chance to entertain someone who's been instrumental in protecting the company's interests.'

Muriel opened her document case and checked its contents. She pulled out a small revolver. 'I brought this just in case those nasty Russians tried to take the letter off me on the way here.'

Paul gasped. 'For goodness sake put it away—where on earth did you get it?'

'Oh, it's a souvenir from the last war. I always carried it around with me in those days in case I saw a German parachutist—you know, rather like Greer Garson in that Mrs Miniver wartime film. Don't fuss—it's not loaded.'

'If I'd known you had that, I might have invited you to join us on Wednesday night!'

'I was so relieved when you brought Stephanie and Melanie back. If Christine and I hadn't gone off to the National Gallery on Monday afternoon, they probably wouldn't have been kidnapped.'

Paul shook his head. 'If you'd waved that toy pistol at the Russians they might have shot you—they weren't a particularly chivalrous couple.'

The door opened and the security officer looked in. 'Sir James is free now, Miss Reece.'

Paul helped Muriel to her feet, and escorted her to the lift. He nodded to the security officer. 'That's OK, I'm going up.'

When Muriel entered Sir James' office, he rose from behind his desk and walked across the room to greet her.

'Welcome to Number Two Manorhouse Street, Miss Reece. It's very kind of you to deliver the package in person.' He pulled a chair forward and Muriel sat down.

'It was the least I could do, Sir James, after your handsome Mr Remington rescued both my nephew's daughter and your attractive secretary from those nasty people.'

Sir James waved Paul to a chair, and moved back behind his desk.

'How is the child?'

'Fine, thank you. She seems to think it was all a bit of a game.' Muriel opened her document case and pulled out a padded envelope. 'I think this is what you've been waiting for—it only arrived this morning.'

Sir James took the envelope and emptied its contents on the desk. He picked up the Chinese letter and pinned it to a copy of Roy Wakefield's translation. Then he placed the letter and the linen bag back in the envelope, and glanced across at Paul. 'I've sent Stephanie to see the estate agent who leased the Russians that flat. With any luck she should be back shortly with the final piece of the jigsaw puzzle.'

Muriel smiled at Sir James. 'I hope you won't think me a nosey old thing, but I'd love to know what you intend to do with that letter.'

Sir James removed his gold rimmed glasses and leaned back in his chair. 'To be frank with you, Miss Reece, the Diamond Syndicate has had so much bad press over the dismissal and subsequent deaths of the three diamond sorters, not to speak of the bad will created between ourselves and our Sight Holders, that I intend to use these items to put the record straight and lay the blame squarely where it belongs.'

At that moment the door opened and Stephanie walked in. She was wearing a pair of dark glasses which partially hid the bruise on her right cheekbone. Stephanie handed a photocopied document to Sir James. 'I had to give the agent the reasons for our request, but after that he was quite co-operative.'

Sir James put his glasses back on and studied the sheet of paper for a few minutes. Then he grunted with satisfaction. 'This is a copy of the lease signed by one of the two Russians who kidnapped Stephanie and Melanie. It gives the man's occupation as commercial attaché, and his address as the Soviet Embassy in London.'

Sir James turned to Muriel. 'To put you fully in the picture, Miss Reece, I have an appointment with the Foreign Secretary in an hour's time. I intend to tell him the whole story of the Russian destabilisation scheme, from the subversion and possible killing of our diamond sorters to the recent kidnapping. As proof, I will show him the Chinese letter, the bag and this copy of the Russian's lease agreement. After that I shall take part in a press conference which Rob Scot, our information officer, has arranged for midday.'

Muriel beamed at Sir James. 'Thank you for indulging my curiosity. It's not often a woman of my advanced years gets the chance to play a part in such an exciting affair—I just can't wait to see what the papers will make of it all tomorrow.'

Sir James looked at his watch. 'Now, dear Miss Reece, I must sadly take my leave of you. But before I go, would you like me to arrange for you to have a tour of our diamond departments?'

'I'd like that very much, Sir James.'

He stood up and shook Muriel's hand. 'Goodbye for now, and thank you again for coming here this morning.'

As they left the office, Paul whispered in Stephanie's ear. 'I think the old boy fancies Muriel—I've never heard him address anyone as "dear" before.'

Paul and Stephanie escorted Muriel to the Diamond Information Office on the first floor, where they handed her over to Rob Scot. When they were back in the lift, Stephanie sighed. 'It's so sad about poor little Chung—I shall miss his letters. Hopefully, his wife will get the money you arranged with the British Embassy.'

Paul nodded. 'We can rely on the British ambassador making the necessary arrangements—he's a friend of Sir James. What I'd like you to do now is write a letter to Chung's wife—Roy Wakefield can translate it into Chinese for you.'

'Good idea—I'll get on with it right away. Incidentally, I've made some enquiries and it appears that as Chung held a government job, his wife will get a widow's pension.'

* * *

At eleven o'clock that morning, Sir James visited the Foreign Office and had a meeting with the Foreign Secretary. An hour later he attended a lively confrontation with the press in the Diamond Syndicate's Information Office. When he eventually returned to his office after a late lunch, Stephanie was waiting for him. 'Could you give security desk a call. They appear to have two unscheduled visitors who insist on seeing you.'

Sir James nodded. 'It's probably the media—I'll check who they are and get Rob Scot to handle it.'

He picked up the telephone and dialled a number. 'Sir James here.'

'I'm sorry to bother you, sir,' said the worried voice of the security officer, 'but I've got two Russian gentlemen in the waiting room who insist on seeing you—they say it's of the utmost urgency.'

'Very well—I'll send my secretary down to pick them up.'

Sir James looked at Stephanie and raised his eyebrows. 'Our two visitors are Russians. Now that is intriguing.' He paused for a moment in thought. 'Before you collect them, get hold of Paul and Steven. I want them in your room listening to what's being said. If you leave your door slightly ajar, they can get a sight of the two men—I've a feeling they'll recognise them.'

A few minutes later, Stephanie ushered the two visitors into Sir James' office. She had taken the precaution of writing down their names on a memo pad, and handed this to Sir James.

'Please sit down.' He looked at the pad and then at the two Russians in front of him. 'Sergei Menakov?'

The taller of the two men inclined his head. 'Good day, Sir James. My colleague's name is Andrei Bolkovski.'

Sir James turned to Stephanie and signalled for her to stay. 'Now what can I do for you gentlemen?'

Sergei edged forward on his chair. 'We have come here to strike a deal with you, Sir James.'

'That sounds most intriguing—what sort of deal, Mr Menakov?'

'It concerns one-hundred and fifty thousand carats of diamonds.'

Sir James' eyes narrowed behind his gold-framed glasses. 'Please continue.'

'These are the diamonds that were removed from the Russian shipments in Bangkok during July and August.'

'Where are the diamonds now?'

'I have placed them in a bank safe deposit in Switzerland.'

Sir James considered this news for a few seconds. 'What are your terms for returning the stones to the Diamond Syndicate?'

Andrei turned and whispered something to his colleague. Sergei shook his head in annoyance, and turned back to Sir James. 'My friend reminds me, unnecessarily of course, that we will not be able to return the diamonds to you in England. The deal must be done in Switzerland.'

'I understand that—but first I must know your price.'

Sergei took a deep breath. 'Two million dollars, paid into a numbered Swiss account.'

Sir James shook his head. 'But we have already paid Russalmaz once for these stones.'

'I must correct you, Sir James. According to my information, your Company have only paid for the first shipment. I am happy to return the first fifty-thousand carats of diamonds for a nominal half-million dollars. The second batch of one-hundred thousand carats, however, will cost you a further one-point-five million dollars.'

'You appear to be very well informed.' Sir James picked up the pen from his blotter, and made a few calculations on his notepad. 'If I agree to your terms, how would the exchange be made?'

Sergei handed Sir James a piece of paper. 'Here are the details of my Swiss bank in Lucerne and the account number. The diamonds are in a safe deposit at the same bank. My colleague and I will meet there with the manager of your Lucerne diamond office. He can inspect the diamonds in the deposit box, and once I have verified the money is lodged in our account, I will hand your man the safe deposit keys.'

Sir James shook his head. 'I give you full marks for enterprise, but two-million dollars is still a lot of money.'

Sergei laughed. 'Of course it is—but my colleague and I have to disappear completely after this deal, or our lives will be forfeit. A new existence and identity in Brazil or Mexico does not come cheap. The price we ask is only a small fraction of the value of the diamonds.'

Sir James made up his mind. 'You have a deal. Give me your telephone number in Lucerne, and I will arrange for my manager there to contact you at the beginning of next week.'

When the two men had left, Sir James turned to Stephanie and smiled. 'I'll have to clear this at board level of course, but I don't anticipate any objection from my fellow directors when I tell them the two million dollars will be deducted from the money we owe Russalmaz for the August shipment. If we can get the stolen diamonds shipped back and sorted in the next few days, it will allow us to run the August Sight on schedule.' He walked across to his secretary's door and pushed it open. 'You can both come in now,' he called out.

Steven followed Paul into the office. Both men looked stunned at what they'd just overheard. Looking at them, Sir James had difficulty concealing a smile.

'Presumably they were the two Russians you tangled with in Bangkok?'

Paul nodded. 'They must have been on their way to the airport with the diamonds when they left us.'

Steven shook his head in disgust. 'They stand to get two million dollars, and all I collected was a stitched-up leg!'

Sir James shook his finger at the two men. 'That's their

reward for changing sides. I'm fully aware, however, that without your intervention we would be facing a very different situation—just don't forget that, and all three of you will find my appreciation of your efforts reflected in the Christmas bonus. Now I think it's time we celebrated—you'll all join me in a glass of sherry?' They murmured their agreement, and he walked across to his drinks cabinet.

When he had handed out their drinks, Sir James raised his glass. 'Here's to the conclusion of a very successful week. Stephanie and young Melanie are back safe and sound—apart from a bruise or two—and the Foreign Office is grinding into action on our behalf. Tomorrow the media will be at work restoring our image, and hopefully the missing diamonds will be back in our hands before long. When the Russian ambassador reports back to Moscow, I also have a feeling we won't be negotiating any more deals with Mr Vassily Kolov.'

Sir James refilled their glasses, his eyes twinkling under his carefully groomed white hair. 'I trust that Stephanie will show her gratitude to Paul for her timely rescue, and I understand Steven is being well looked after by one of our young lady sorters, so enjoy the weekend everyone. But do try to get in ahead of me on Monday morning for a change.'

CHAPTER 22

LONDON

Saturday 15 August, 1981

Christine, Mike and daughter Melanie spent the last day of their leave at Regents Park Zoo with Paul and Stephanie. Muriel had elected to stay behind in her Cheyne Walk flat, 'You young things go off and enjoy yourselves—I'm still recovering from yesterday's excitement.'

At Melanie's insistence they went to see the panda first. Then they visited the elephant house. By the time they reached the big cats Melanie had fallen silent. For a few minutes she stood holding Mike's hand while they watched a lion grooming itself on an elevated platform. The little girl looked up at her father. 'Why are they all in cages?' she asked.

Mike smiled at his daughter. 'It's so that people can get close to the animals and see them properly.'

'But we got close to them at home, and they weren't in cages.'

'Well there's a lot more space in South Africa. In England some of these animals wouldn't be able to live in the open because of the weather. In a zoo they can be looked after properly, and people who don't have the chance to look at them in the wild, as we do, can also enjoy seeing them.'

Melanie thought about this and then turned to the others. 'I think I like them better in the open!'

When they returned later that afternoon to the Cheyne Walk flat, Muriel had provided a cream tea for them on the balcony. She waited until they were all relaxing in garden chairs, and picked up the Saturday edition of the Daily Telegraph.

'I bought a few extra copies while you were out—I thought the main news item would make a good souvenir of your visit.' She unfolded the paper and held it up. The main headline read, 'RUSSIAN ATTEMPT AT DIAMOND TAKE-OVER FAILS'. Beneath it in smaller type was a sub heading, 'Russian Ambassador Summoned to Foreign Office. Two members of embassy staff given notice to quit'. Then followed a report on the Diamond Syndicate's press conference revelations, and the action taken by the Foreign Office.

Muriel handed the paper to Christine. 'This should provide you and Mike with some interesting reading on the plane tonight.'

Christine read the first few lines and shook her head. 'This will be quite a story to tell Melanie when she's older—it's not every child that can claim to have been the victim of a kidnapping, and then been rescued by an ex-SAS officer. I feel rather foolish now saying I felt much safer here than in South Africa.'

Stephanie looked embarrassed. 'And to think that I smugly agreed with you. I do hope it won't put you off visiting us again.'

'Don't worry—we'll be back. There are so many places I still want to see.'

At five o'clock, Paul packed their cases and holdalls in the boot of his XJ12. Then he and Stephanie got in the car while Christine, Mike and Melanie said their final goodbyes to Muriel. Melanie shed a few tears as she hugged Muriel. 'You will come to South Africa for my Bir-day,' she lisped.

'I'm afraid I won't be able to come this year, my dear, but I'll certainly wish you a happy birthday on the telephone. Mummy and Daddy have invited me to visit you next year for a holiday, so I'll see you again then.'

They squeezed into the car among the extra luggage acquired on their two-month holiday, and waited a few minutes for Muriel to return to her flat. When she finally appeared on the balcony, Christine, Melanie and Mike waved goodbye to her as Paul drove away along Cheyne Walk and headed towards the Earl's Court Road and the M4.

The Saturday night flight to Johannesburg from Terminal 1 was fully booked, and there were queues at all the SAA counters. When Christine and Mike had checked in their luggage and collected their boarding passes, there was still over half an hour to go before the flight was called.

Paul pointed to the restaurant sign. 'Let's all have drink before you go through security.'

After they were seated, he winked at Stephanie. 'I think it's time to give Melanie her birthday present.'

Stephanie pulled the package from her bag, and handed it to the wide-eyed little girl. Melanie looked up at her mother. 'Can I open now?'

'But it's not your birthday yet.'

Melanie looked pleadingly at Paul. 'I'm thwee in Sep'ember.'

'Oh, that's makes it alright then,' said Paul, 'I'll help you unwrap it.'

When she had torn off the last piece of wrapping paper, Melanie carefully lifted out the contents of the cellophane-fronted box. 'It's another dolly,' she cried and showed it to Christine.

Paul squatted down beside the child. 'It's a Mandarin doll. Do you know where he comes from?'

Melanie shook her head.

'He's from a country called China—that's a very long way from here. He's wearing those lovely clothes because he's a very important person.'

Mike smiled at Stephanie. 'That makes four in the collection now—you and Paul have certainly started something.'

At that point they heard the flight to Johannesburg being announced. Paul and Stephanie followed them to the departure barrier, and they both picked Melanie up and hugged her.

'Promise you visit me, auntie Steff and u'cle Paul,' sniffed the tearful child.

'Of course we will,' said Stephanie.

Mike shook hands with Paul. 'Take care, and thanks for everything.'

Christine kissed Stephanie. 'Thanks for taking good care of Melanie last week—I won't forget that in a hurry, and give my love to Steven. I'll write when I get back to Pretoria.'

Paul and Stephanie waved goodbye as Mike, Christine and Melanie, still clutching her new doll, disappeared from sight into the security check area.

* * *

That night, Stephanie wore the green silk dressing gown with the red and yellow embroidered dragons that Paul bought for her in Hong Kong. As they lay in bed talking over the events of the last few days, Stephanie turned on her side and looked at Paul. A full moon was shining through the trees on the opposite side of the road, the gently stirring branches making a moving pattern on the wall behind them. She traced the contours of his face with her finger, and for the first time noticed with a pang of sorrow the tiny worry lines that were evident at the corners of his eyes and mouth.

'What's the matter, Steffi,' he asked sleepily, and turned to face her.

She laid her head against his chest. 'I know I've been a cow to you these last few months—I just didn't know what I wanted. You were right about the sex—I needed you physically, but I wasn't sure I loved you enough to make a commitment and give up my freedom.'

Paul kissed her on the nose. 'You know I've always been prepared to wait for you, Steffi, and what you consider a loss of freedom can be just another aspect of love.'

She returned his kiss. 'You've been very patient with me, and I'm grateful for that. When that Russian was on the point of raping me, I suddenly realised that sex without love and affection was a pretty tawdry thing. If you still want me, I'd like to make it permanent, my darling.'

'Are you saying you're ready to throw caution to the wind and marry me?'

Stephanie laughed. 'Yes, I'm proposing to you, you idiot, and while you're getting used to the idea, let's talk about a family—that and marriage should make us acceptable to both sets of parents.'

'Hmm, I had a feeling you were getting broody over Melanie. Do you think we could manage a few girls like that between us.'

'I would even settle for a boy if he looked a little like you, but I've a feeling I'm going to be a big disappointment to Muriel.'

'Oh, I don't know—behind all that talk she's basically a romantic at heart. There's one thing these independent single ladies miss out on as they get older.'

'What's that?'

'The companionship of a husband, and seeing their children grow up. I'll make a bargain with you. If you break the news to Muriel, I'll tell Sir James. Now about this family of ours ...' He leaned over and untied the green silk belt of her dressing gown.

Stephanie sighed. 'I guess fate takes a hand sometimes—I ran out of my pills last month.'

Paul laid a finger on her lips. 'No more talk Steffi—just leave the rest to me...'